The Love we Make

HARPER BLISS

Other Harper Bliss Novels

A Family Affair
The Duet
And Then She Kissed Me
That Woman Next Door
About That Kiss
At Your Most Beautiful
A Breathless Place
If You Kiss Me Like That
Two Hearts Trilogy
Next in Line for Love
A Lesson in Love
Life in Bits (with T.B. Markinson)
A Swing at Love (with Caroline Bliss)
Once Upon a Princess (with Clare Lydon)
In the Distance There Is Light
The Road to You
Far from the World We Know
Seasons of Love
Release the Stars
At the Water's Edge
High Rise (The Complete Collection)

The Pink Bean Series
The French Kissing Series

Published by Ladylit Publishing – an imprint of First Page V.O.F., Belgium
ISBN-13 9789464339260
D/2023/15201/01
Edited by Cheyenne Blue
Proofread by Claire Jarrett
Cover design by Caroline Manchoulas

THE LOVE WE MAKE

CHAPTER 1
NORA

I've just read the final line of today's table read, but my performance—the performance of me—isn't over until I get out of here.

"Great job everyone," Jo, our showrunner, says. "Stella," she addresses my co-star. "I just want to make sure you—"

Jo's interrupted by a loud knock on the door. Before anyone can reply, the door opens. After three decades in this business, it's no surprise to me. Too many TV executives believe every closed door is always open for them—and that's hardly the worst of it.

We all look at the door, at the person so out of touch with the creative process of making television that they interrupt with no qualms.

I am surprised that the intruder is a woman. I'd say she's late fifties, but I'm fifty-one and, even though she doesn't look old, she's definitely older than me. Or maybe she hasn't had as much Botox.

She has that air of importance executives in this business like to carry around with them, as if to say: I'm here now, so you'd better stop whatever it is you're doing, even if that's the slow, difficult process of making art.

Her raven black hair is shoulder-length, her heels impressively high for a woman older than me. Her suit is high-end and stark white. Her makeup flawless. Everything about her screams money.

Jo jumps out of her chair.

"Ms. St James," she says. "You're a little early."

"Am I?" Ms. St James shrugs. "Maybe you're running late." It doesn't sound like a question. She plasters on a practiced smile.

Jo turns to us and gives an eye roll. "Everyone, please meet Michelle St James."

"Thanks, Jo." Michelle St James widens her smile. The crinkles around her eyes deepen. Definitely not a fan of Botox then —maybe to her credit. "Sorry for interrupting." If this is what sorry looks like, I might have to revise how my character acts apologetic on the show we're trying to make. "Please, continue. Pretend I'm not here."

"That's okay," Jo says. "We were as good as done." Way to stand your ground, Jo.

"Wow," Stella mutters under her breath. "Who is this woman that's got Jo all whipped?"

I lean in so that I am close to her ear. "The money," I whisper.

"I wanted to stop by while you're all gathered here to introduce myself. I'm the new CEO at Gloves Off Productions. I'm replacing Gerry, for reasons I'm sure you're all aware of." Her gaze drifts along the table, but doesn't land anywhere. "I'm a very hands-on boss, absolutely no pun intended." A touch of warmth reaches her smile. "Making television is my life, and this show is one of our company's biggest assets. This means I'll be around much more than my predecessor. I like to know what's happening on my sets." *My* sets? Also, doesn't she have better things to do with her precious time? Crunch some numbers? Analyze some data? Count her money?

"Ms. St James will be an executive producer this season," Jo chimes in. Her tone is as tense as her face. I'm guessing she didn't get a choice in the matter. But who am I to complain? This is only *Unbreak My Heart*'s third season and both Stella and I are getting producer credits already.

A couple of the actual producers—the people who put in all the grunt work—shuffle in their seats. But this is how things go. Hollywood has never been a fair town and showbiz has never been a fair business based only on merit. Still, it's odd for the CEO of the production company to demand this kind of role. I wonder if she'll become executive producer on all the shows her company produces.

"I adore this show so it's a great honor and privilege," Michelle says. Her eyebrows twitch lightly as she locks her gaze on Jo for a second.

"Oh, yes." Jo shoots Stella and me an apologetic smile before continuing. "Ms. St James would like to invite the leads to lunch."

Before we can possibly protest, Jo says, "Today."

Excuse me? Who does Michelle St James think she is to just rock up here and overhaul our schedules like this? As if there's nothing to it? As if when she says jump, our only option is to ask how high?

"Sure," Stella says, as expected. She's the kind of person who doesn't mind an impromptu change of schedule. Luckily, I've been around long enough to know that a carefully planned day is as much an illusion as the stories we tell on screen. It still irks me, though, that this woman can just waltz in here under the guise of wanting to meet us, when she's clearly looking to throw around her weight.

"Of course." I send her the fakest smile from my vast repertoire. "I'd be delighted."

"Wonderful. I look forward to it." Michelle St James turns on her stilettos and saunters out of the room.

"Way to make an entrance," Stella says, reaching for her phone.

"Don't you want to get home?" I ask.

Stella shakes her head. "One tiger mama is enough for my baby boy." She scrolls through a few pictures that her partner, Kate, has sent while her phone was on silent. "Be still my heart. Will you look at this, Nora?" She thrusts the phone in my face. To me, it doesn't look all that different from the gazillion pictures of Silas I've already had to admire.

"Adorable." Stella's son is cute, no matter how many times a picture of him is shoved into my face.

She puts her phone away. "Looks like we're having lunch together."

I can't suppress a sigh. My dogs, although always pampered in my absence, are waiting for me at home. So is the poké bowl I like to eat for lunch, prepared by Ricky exactly the way I like it. And my soft couch, where I like to unwind after emotionally exhausting meetings like this one, with three warm furry bodies on top of me. It will have to remain empty while I listen to whatever Michelle St James has to say.

CHAPTER 2
MIMI

"I'm serious, ladies," I say. "I'm not just blowing smoke up your backsides. I'm thrilled to have this job and the opportunity to work with you. *Unbreak My Heart* has been such a breath of fresh air on my TV screen." I lift my glass of cucumber water. "The three of you are a match made in heaven." I am blowing a bit of smoke up their—very shapely, but I can't say that out loud—behinds. It's what you do in this town. It's how you get overindulged people to fall in line—that and deep pockets.

"It's been a dream come true for me from day one," Stella Flack says. "All thanks to this one." She points at Nora Levine. "If it wasn't for Nora, I would never have gotten the part."

"Really?" That's the first I've heard of this. Why don't I know this?

"Oh yes!" Stella is enjoying that glass of Chablis with gusto. "Nora changed my life." She takes another sip.

"Let's not exaggerate." Nora's features have been tight since we got to the restaurant.

"It's not an exaggeration," Stella says. "I didn't get a callback until you specifically requested me, Nora."

"Stella was rejected?" I turn to Jo.

"Water under the bridge," Jo says. Apart from creative masterminds, showrunners also have to be excellent diplomats. "We're here now, on the cusp of season three, ready to make another batch of episodes of our wonderful show."

"Sorry for the delay, boss." Stella winks at Jo.

"Being a mother of four myself, I want to assure you we'll make every accommodation," I say. "I want that to be absolutely clear."

"I already made the hiatus much longer than it ought to have been." Stella flashes us a wide smile.

"You had a baby. You never have to apologize for that to anyone." I put down my fork. "Otherwise, you might as well apologize for being a woman and why on earth would you do that?"

"Hear! Hear!" Stella locks her gaze on me. "You're a woman after my own heart, Michelle St James."

"Call me Mimi, please."

"Four kids, huh, Mimi. Damn! Respect," Stella says.

"They're all grown now. My youngest is twenty-six and a huge fan of yours, Nora." I face Nora, hoping to melt some of her iciness. "He must have watched every single episode of *High Life* a dozen times by now. Even though when your show first aired, he was only seven or eight, but his sisters were so into it. In fact, my entire family is a bit nuts about you."

"Aw." Nora's not the most engaging conversationalist. In her defense, she must get this a lot. Maybe it's one of the reasons she's such a recluse.

"I'd love to bring him on set once you start shooting." Austin's already such a mama's boy. If I can arrange for him to meet Nora Levine, he may move back in with me—not that I would want him to.

"I'm sure we can make that happen," Jo says, because Nora's hardly forthcoming.

"I'd love to meet your son," Nora says eventually. "Please,

excuse me." She dons her oversized sunglasses and gets up. Even stars like Nora need to use the bathroom.

I wisely refrain from asking Stella and Jo whether Nora's always this cranky.

"Nora's a very private person," Jo offers. "It's a miracle she said yes to this project, even though I wrote the part of Jessie specifically for her. I had zero guarantees she would go for it, but once she did, by Hollywood standards, everything moved really fast."

"Some scripts are impossible to ignore." This, I mean from the bottom of my heart. "*Unbreak My Heart* is funny without being obvious. The characters are so real, they could very well be sitting in this restaurant with us."

"Nah. They don't make enough money to come here," Stella says drily. I like her. She's a lot like Megan, her character on *Unbreak My Heart*. Unlike Nora, who's nothing like sweet, caring, down-to-earth Jessie. Although Jessie's quite edgy and she's got many a flaw as well.

Nora returns to the table just as our meals are served.

"Tell me all about your little boy," I say to Stella, taking the easy route of conversation. I'll work on Nora later, when she's in a better mood.

Stella shows me pictures of her son—and her gorgeous partner, Kate, while she's at it—while regaling me with tales of all the amazing things a six-month-old can accomplish. It's been so long, I seem to have forgotten what my kids were up to in their first years of existence. As far as I can remember, all they did was cry, eat, and get their diapers changed.

From the corner of my eye, I try to keep track of Nora's reactions. She picks at her salad, not eating very much of it at all. It's obvious she'd rather be anywhere but here. I make a mental note to try and clear the air with her—if that's even possible—as quickly as I can.

After we've finished our meal, Stella says, "Let's do a thing at my house soon. I'm emerging after having created another person. I have the extreme need to be seen as something else than just my baby's mother. Did you experience this, Mimi?"

"Honestly, I don't remember. I always worked, though, bar a few months after each birth. Some women don't need to work, and no judgment on my part—every woman should do exactly as she pleases—but I needed a life outside of my family. Always have." I fix my gaze on Stella. "But I'd love to see your house. Your partner's an interior designer, isn't she?" I might have missed a few tidbits, but I've done my homework on Stella and Nora.

Stella nods. "Yep."

"Their house is absolutely gorgeous," Nora says.

"So gorgeous, in fact, Nora has actually visited it more than once," Stella quips. "How many times have you deigned to leave swanky Bel Air to come to our house, Nora?" Stella pretends to do some difficult math, counting on her fingers. "Four... five times in all the time we've been working together?"

"We hang out on set all the time," Nora says. "I fail to see why we have to hang out after hours too." The grin on her face looks genuine enough.

"If by hanging out on set you mean we're each holed up in our own trailers, then sure." There's not a hint of malice in Stella's tone, and I get the sense this is how things really are.

"We all have our own process." This is the most I've heard Nora talk since we sat down to lunch. "Mine is much more inward than yours."

Stella grins at Nora and a short silence ensues. I happily fill it.

"I'd love to visit you at home," I repeat.

"Great. I'll set it up. Kate will be thrilled to meet you. And to see you again, Nora." They're not done bantering yet. Nora doesn't seem perturbed by her co-star's teasing. Maybe it's their thing and they do this all the time as a means to defuse some of the inevitable on-set tension.

"Don't forget to invite your mother," Nora says.

"Granted, my family are a bit much." Stella shrugs. "But I didn't get to pick them."

"Maybe you and Kate can tell Mimi all about how you got together." Nora seems very pleased with herself for making that remark.

"Oh, fuck." Stella chuckles. "We've only just met. Let's have some boundaries."

I don't remember reading anything about how Stella Flack met her partner when I did my research. It must be quite the story if Nora is taking such pleasure in referencing it.

What is clear to see, however, is why Stella and Nora are such a great match on screen.

"When is this party?" I ask. "Because I can't wait."

CHAPTER 3
NORA

"Girl, please," Juan says. "Put on something else right now. You have a room full of designer dresses and this is what you're wearing?" He's sitting in a chair in my bedroom with Izzy, my pug, on his lap.

"What's wrong with this?" I look at my reflection in the mirror.

"It's jeans and a blouse," he says matter-of-factly, as though that sums up all the worst sins in fashion.

"It's just dinner at Stella's."

"Just dinner at Stella's?" Juan exclaims. "Nu-huh. It's a proper party. The first one Stella's had since she became a mama. Put in some effort. Show her you care."

"That's why I'm bringing you in all your fabulous glory."

"Tsk." He scratches Izzy behind her ear. "Do you hear that, Isabel? Your mama's using me again."

I hear shuffling downstairs. Imani must have let herself in. My posse is complete.

"Up here, girl," Juan shouts, and puts Izzy on the floor. She scampers into the corner to wait until she can get his full attention again.

We both wait with bated breath for Imani to make her, no doubt, impressive entrance into my bedroom.

"This is how you dress for a par-tay!" Juan says, holding up his hand for a high-five with Imani.

I hug my best friend, careful not to ruffle her stunningly colorful silk dress.

"I get what you're saying, Jay." I address him. "Imani looks magnificent, but in the end, it's just a dress. So what's the big difference?"

"I'm not gonna tell you again, sister," Juan says, all theatrics. When I see them next to each other, they must have coordinated their outfits. Juan and Imani will, as usual, be the belles of the ball, which is exactly how I like it.

They're the front I hide behind when I go out, according to an unspoken pact we made decades ago. When they walk in anywhere, all eyes are on them, even if I'm right behind. Compared to their vibrant colors, I'm inconspicuously beige. In their bubble of extroverted fabulousness, I feel safe and secure. They're my connection to the outside world. My lifeline. They're all the things I'm not but need to be to survive in this town. Sometimes, only Juan accompanies me and other times only Imani, but most of the time, it's the three of us together.

"Leave her alone, Jay," Imani says. She gives me a once-over. "You look absolutely fine." She puts her hands on my shoulders. "Do you feel comfortable?"

I nod.

"Perfect." She kisses my cheek. "Then let's go. I can't wait to dress down this bossy executive you told me about."

I railed about the impromptu lunch Michelle St James invited me to, as I always do. Venting is how I process a lot of the tension in my life. That, and long, exhausting sessions with Marcy, my personal trainer.

"Is Chad staying with the babies?" Juan crouches next to Izzy. If it were possible, he'd be more obsessed with my dogs than I am. Izzy turns onto her back for him and presents her belly for a rub. Juan happily obliges.

"Yes," I confirm.

"Who's your daddy, girl?" he whispers to Izzy, who wiggles her tiny body around in response.

I say goodbye to Izzy as well, and pet Rogue and Princess profusely on my way to the door. Before I head out, Juan rolls a lint brush over my clothes.

"Nora and her girls are ready to crush this party," Juan says, as we step into the car.

"Who is that absolutely gorgeous drink of water?" Through the doorway, Juan eyes the young man Michelle St James brought to Stella's party. "I highly doubt they're dating. His queer vibes are through the roof."

"Even from here, I can see he's too young for you, Jay," Imani says. "Have some self-respect."

"I have no shortage in that department, darling." Juan drapes his arm around Imani's shoulders. "Let's work the room and make stuff happen."

We walk in and Juan and Imani do a great job of deflecting initial attention, but it's only a matter of minutes before all eyes are on me.

I introduce them to Michelle, whose plus-one's mouth falls open when I stand in front of him. A reaction I'm all too familiar with.

"This is Austin," Michelle says. "My son."

Ah, the huge *High Life* fan.

"Oh, my god," Austin squeals. "Nora Levine! No fucking way."

"Language, dear," Michelle says, but she doesn't sound scolding. If anything, she looks amused. She leans into my ear.

"I knew it was going to be like this." She rolls her eyes. "Don't feel as though you need to indulge him. He's a big boy."

"Mom. You're embarrassing me," Austin says.

"I think you're doing a pretty good job of that yourself, darling."

"You must have known I was coming," I say to Austin.

"Of course, that's why I'm here. I'm sorry. I don't really know how to behave."

This is where Juan usually comes to my verbal rescue, but he seems entranced with Austin beyond the point of speech. *Great.*

"It's lovely to see you again, Nora," Mimi says, filling the awkward silence. "You look amazing." She sounds like she really means it. "I was hoping that after my son is done fawning over you, we could have a private chat. There are a few things I'd like to discuss."

"Oh. Okay."

"Not business, I hope." Juan has gathered himself. "You look fab as well, darling, by the way." Only Juan can get away with calling my new boss 'darling' mere minutes after meeting her.

Austin bursts into a chuckle, then looks at his mother expectantly.

"All pleasure, and ditto," Michelle says.

Is that a flash of awe crossing Austin's face? Maybe he hasn't met a lot of people who speak to his mother without much deference.

"Seriously, though, Nora." Austin's focus is back on me. "I watched *High Life* so much in my teens, it kind of felt like you were a friend. You were always there. And always hilarious, but sexy at the same time. Like this absolutely perfect human."

That was my character, I'd like to say, but don't. There's no point in bursting Austin's bubble and I'm sure he knows the difference by now. It's just one of those things people say.

"Imani!" Stella shouts behind us. "You don't call. You don't text." Stella throws her arms around my friend. When Imani comes with me to the set, she and Stella are thick as thieves.

Stella greets us all, then immediately falls into a deep conversation with Imani—the way two people sometimes do but has, in all my fifty-one years, never happened to me.

Juan is already relentless with Austin, and Mimi's son enjoys his attention to such an extent that he seems to have forgotten why he came to this party in the first place.

This leaves Mimi and me standing next to each other in silence.

"How about that chat now?" Mimi asks.

"Sure."

I nod hello to a few people but don't stop for chitchat as we make our way to the backyard. Juan was right. This is a proper party. It wouldn't be the first time Stella has lured me to her and Kate's house under the guise of a small dinner party, only to spring more than a dozen people on me.

"Your friend seems to have taken a shine to my son," Mimi says as she finds a chair.

"Looks like it." I can hardly apologize for Juan. As Mimi said earlier, Austin's a big boy. "Handsome men in their twenties always have that effect on Juan."

"How old is he?" Mimi sounds trepidatious.

"Forty-four."

She scrunches up her lips and nods. "Austin's last boyfriend was in his late fifties, so… Anyway, I've been told too many times to stay out of it, so that's what I will wisely do." Her smile isn't brimming with confidence.

I don't tell her that Juan isn't the type of man to want a long-term boyfriend. I've known him since the last year of my *High Life* days—for almost two full decades—and I can still count his relationships that lasted longer than a few months on the fingers of one hand.

I sit next to Mimi. A waiter stops by to offer us a cocktail. I happily accept one while Mimi asks for water with a slice of lime.

"Juan's a good guy," I say, whatever that might mean in this context. He's definitely an excellent friend to me, but I'm not a gay man in my twenties.

"I'm sure he is. You brought two plus-ones." Mimi's smile widens.

"I usually do." I don't explain myself further. I stopped doing that a long time ago.

"I wanted to make sure we didn't get off on the wrong foot the other day," Mimi says. "When I barged into your table read and demanded you and Stella have lunch with me, I got the distinct impression that didn't go down too well with you." She puts a hand to her chest. "I apologize if that's the case."

The waiter has returned with Mimi's water. She takes a few sips.

"It's okay. I'm used to that kind of alpha behavior from people like you."

"That hardly makes it okay." She sets down her glass. "But I appreciated how you didn't even try to hide how you felt about that."

"How do you mean?"

"You might have physically been there, but…" Mimi chuckles. "Well, your ass was in the chair and that's about it."

"There was a time when I might have made more effort, when I cared about how my behavior made me look, but I had to let that go, for the sake of my own sanity." I pause for effect. "Turns out not caring what others think of you is very liberating. You have so much more energy left for things that actually matter."

"Such as?" Michelle fixes her dark-eyed gaze on me.

She's caught me off guard. Usually, recipients of my little speech either take it as a personal affront or are too stumped to inquire further.

"Personal things," I manage to say.

"Okay." She leans back and slings one leg over the other. "So, no hard feelings?"

"None whatsoever."

"Good." Mimi takes her glass and tilts it in my direction. "How about we have dinner just the two of us some time?"

The sip of cocktail I just took catches in my throat. "What?"

"Oh." Mimi gives a hearty chuckle. "Just dinner. Definitely not a date or anything like that. After what happened with Gerry, I won't be asking anyone who works with me on any sort of date." She grins at me. "I meant like a working dinner. Just to get to know you as a co-worker. I get the feeling a more private setting works better for you." She gazes into the house. "Or is that unthinkable without your entourage?"

"I'd have to think about that." I quickly regroup. "And just for the record, I didn't for a second consider you were asking me on a date."

"Good. Because I most certainly wasn't." Another grin. "Imagine Austin's reaction if I did."

"Do you, um, date women?" It's a bit forward, but she invited me to dinner and I hardly saw that coming either.

"Yeah." She nods wistfully. "I'm quite gay, actually." She locks her gaze on mine again. "And by 'quite' I mean 'extremely.'"

"Okay." This raises quite a few questions, but I'm sure I can find the answer to most on the internet. Hot shots like Michelle St James always have a Wikipedia page with some details of their personal life recorded for all the world to read.

"How about I tell you all about it over dinner soon? I'm a decent enough cook so if you'd prefer not to go to a restaurant, you're very welcome to come to my house."

At the very least, I'm intrigued. "Sure. I'll have dinner with you."

"Just out of curiosity and since we're asking personal questions." Mimi tilts her head. "Are you and Imani together?"

I can't help but chuckle. "Me and Imani?" I knit my eyebrows together. "No." Where did she even get that idea?

"Just wondering."

"Now you know." It dawns on me she might be asking for

different reasons than wanting to know about *my* relationship status. "She's single, for your information." I'm fairly certain Mimi's not Imani's type, but who am I to decide these things?

"Oh, God. I keep giving you the wrong idea, Nora. That's really not why I asked. How old is she? She's gorgeous, but no."

"You can't tell by looking at her, but Imani's almost fifty."

"Fuck me." Mimi's eyes go wide. "The wonders of this town never cease to amaze me."

CHAPTER 4
MIMI

It's hard to get a read on Nora, but she's charming in her own way—even with the camera off.

"That's where you've been hiding." Stella's partner, Kate, walks up to us.

Nora gets up and gives Kate a hug. "Good to see you." After they break from their embrace, Nora holds her at arm's length. "Look at you. You're beaming."

"You mean you can't tell I was up half the night with Silas? And the night before that? And all the ones before that as well?"

"Absolutely not."

"You're too kind." Kate looks at me. "Michelle, right? Stella's new boss?"

"I wouldn't say boss." I plaster on my widest smile.

Nora clears her throat.

Kate sinks into a chair. "I'm glad you're all here, and I get that Stella wanted to have a party, but fuck, I'm so tired." She turns her head to me. "You have four children, don't you? Any tips are welcome."

I send Kate a soft smile. "The first few years, when they're entirely reliant on you, are always hard. And the first child is a massive shock to your system, because it's so much more challenging than you could ever have imagined. Try to get as much sleep as possible. You can deal better with everything if you manage to get some sleep."

"Yeah." Kate just nods wistfully.

"Are you back at work as well?" Nora asks.

"Only part-time," Kate says. "I want to be there for Silas as much as I can, especially now that Stella's back to it." She expels a deep sigh. "He's with his granny tonight, so we can at least sleep in tomorrow."

"Raising a child will be the hardest thing you'll ever do, but also the best. Take it from a woman who has brought up four. There's simply nothing else like it." I give her my most encouraging smile.

"Kate!" someone yells. "Can you come over here, please?"

"Duty calls." She pushes herself out of the chair. "Thanks for the advice, Michelle."

After Kate has left, Nora peers at me through narrowed eyes.

"You look like you have a burning question on your mind?" I hold up my palms. "Shoot. I don't have many secrets."

"Did you raise your kids alone?"

"Good heavens, no. Their father's still around, but we divorced when Austin was ten."

It's almost as if I can see her doing the math in her head.

"But you consider yourself 'extremely gay.'" Nora's directness doesn't offend me—it's quite refreshing, actually.

"I am and I've always known. But I wanted a family, so I married a man. It seemed by far the easiest way to go about it." I scan Nora's face for a reaction, but it's quite expressionless. "Things were very different when I was in my twenties."

Nora nods pensively. "Did your husband know?"

Austin interrupts me before I can reply.

"Mom!" he says. "You're hogging Nora." He flashes Nora a big smile.

"I was under the distinct impression you'd lost all interest in your big idol," I say.

Austin brings a dramatic hand to his chest. "How dare you even insinuate such a thing. Please don't listen to my mother, Nora."

"I'll do my best not to." Nora grins at Austin. "I hope Juan is behaving himself."

Austin's face goes soft. But he's my youngest, and I've learned to go with the flow—with the many ups and downs—of my children's love life and dating shenanigans. He will always be my baby and I can't bear for him to have his heart broken, but it's a long way from flirtation to heartbreak—most of the time.

"Juan's amazing." Austin slants himself toward Nora and half-whispers, so I can still hear him say, "We're going on a date next week."

"Jesus," Nora mutters. "You're certainly not wasting any time."

"Why would we?" Austin pretends to flick hair he doesn't have behind his shoulder. This boy. He's delighted me from the second he was born. Because he was my fourth, everything was just so much easier with him. I could actually enjoy being the mother of a toddler instead of being run ragged all the time—and I could also afford to hire a lot of help by then.

Imani and Juan approach, circling around Nora. Austin is easily absorbed into their little bubble. I observe them for a while, unable to suppress a smile. My biggest job of the day is done: I made my son happy. I've always been a working mother, but nevertheless, my family has always come firmly first. I can't wait until tomorrow when they all descend onto my home, all flocking around me like Nora's entourage is doing around her now.

———

Despite not needing a ride home last night, Austin's the first to arrive for brunch the next day. Before I can quiz him on what happened after I left, Heather gets there with her husband, Bobby, and her two young boys.

The minute she walks in, Austin hooks his arm through his sister's and walks her into the backyard. I can clearly hear the words 'Nora' and 'Levine' being mentioned over and over again.

The boys have run outside, and I pour my son-in-law a cup of coffee, enjoying the relative quiet for a few seconds.

"Mom," Heather appears in the door frame. "Why didn't you tell me you were working with Nora Levine?"

"I'm pretty sure I did, darling." When you have a three and a five-year-old, things tend to get lost in conversation.

"No way. I would have remembered."

"Well, now you know."

"And you took Austin to meet her!" It's as though Heather has time-traveled back to her teens.

"I could hardly take all four of you," I say matter-of-factly.

"Austin always gets everything in this family, just 'cause he's the youngest." She play-punches her brother in the biceps.

"You don't know the half of it," Austin replies.

"What do you mean?" Heather narrows her eyes.

"Meeting Nora was out of this world, but…" Austin pauses for effect. "Meeting her best friend Juan was something else entirely."

Before Heather can question her brother further—and I hear something I'd rather not—Lauren and Jennifer arrive in quick succession.

Heather immediately whisks Jennifer, her twin, away and they disappear into their twin bubble.

Lauren kisses me on the cheek, expels a deep sigh, and hands me her one-year-old baby girl. "Guess who refused to sleep more than two hours last night?"

"Where's Gus?" I cradle my granddaughter in my arms, melting at the sight of her.

"He's taking a much-needed power nap. He'll be here in an hour or so." Lauren sinks into a chair.

Austin walks over to her and puts his hands on her shoulders. "Do you need some little brother magic?" he asks.

Lauren lets her head fall back and looks up at him. "Depends where those hands have been lately." She bursts into a grin.

"Don't ask me something you don't want the answer to." Austin grins back before massaging his sister's shoulders.

I exchange a glance with my son-in-law while my children are busy with each other. Depending on how long it's been since Heather and Jennifer spoke, we might not see them for a while.

I remember what Nora asked me last night about my family. I might have sacrificed certain parts of myself for the sake of them, but it was only for a while, and I never regretted it for one single second, because I've always been abundantly rewarded.

"Is there anything—" Bobby's interrupted by the twins bounding into the kitchen.

"It's been decided, Mom," Heather says. "You need to invite Nora Levine to brunch with all of us sooner rather than later. How about next weekend?"

I burst into a chuckle. "Yeah, right." I've worked in TV all my life and my kids are not easily impressed by fame—but I guess any *High Life* cast member is an exception. I'd best not share Nora Levine is coming to dinner here sometime soon. "I don't think that would be Nora's jam."

"Why not?" Lauren asks.

"That's the impression I get."

Jennifer reaches for her niece, and I pass her my granddaughter so I can get on with preparing brunch.

"Is she nice?" Jennifer asks.

"Very nice," Austin says. "And gorgeous and fabulous and

to top it all off, she has the most amazing friends." He gives Lauren's shoulders one last squeeze. "One of whom yours truly is going on a date with tomorrow night."

"No way." Lauren's eyes go wide. "Wait. How old is he?"

Austin puts his hands back on her shoulders and gives her a light shake. "Old enough," is all he says.

Just as I've learned to not express my opinion on my son's dating life, I also know when to stay out of a conversation between my kids.

"In his sixties?" Lauren asks.

Austin rolls his eyes, although Lauren can't see. "His name's Juan and he's forty-four," he says, after a beat.

"Only forty-four?" Jennifer says. "Are you okay, bro? Do we need to take you in for an emergency check-up?"

"Ha ha. Very funny." Austin's used to digs from all his sisters about this topic. "Wait until you meet Juan. He's just so charming. Don't you think, Mom?"

"Very," I concur. I hold my tongue and don't add that they haven't even been on a date yet, and speculation about Juan meeting his siblings is a lot of wishful thinking on his part.

I only catch snatches of their conversation as Bobby and I lay the table. From what I gather, the girls appear more interested in Nora Levine than in Austin's possible new love interest.

"Seriously, though, Mom," Jennifer says after we've all sat and my granddaughter is dozing in her crib. "Are you going to be working closely with Nora?"

"That's the idea. But she's not the only one working on that show. How about Stella Flack?"

"Stella Flack wasn't on TV all the time when we were growing up," Heather says while cutting up some eggs for her youngest boy. "Nora Levine is this huge icon from our youth."

"But you do like *Unbreak My Heart*?"

"Honestly, Mom," Lauren says, "I haven't had time to watch."

"There are two seasons for you to stream whenever you

want." I glance at Lauren and am taken aback by the dark circles underneath her eyes. Maybe she should have taken that power nap instead of her husband.

"I love it," Austin says. "Nora and Stella are great together on screen." He bats his lashes. "And in real life, of course."

"God," Heather says on an exaggerated sigh. "How are you not some gossip journalist, sordidly detailing the intimate lives of Hollywood stars?"

"My mother would never have allowed it," Austin deadpans. He's a civil engineer, just like his father—albeit a bit more camp.

Even though they grew up in Los Angeles with a TV exec as their mother, none of my children have gone into showbiz. Jennifer invented an app for menstrual health. Lauren co-owns a boutique on Rodeo Drive. And Heather's currently a stay-at-home mom—by far the hardest thing for me to accept about any of my children.

"I always said you could and should become anything you wanted," I play along.

"Even a paparazzo?" Heather asks. "Or a die-hard lover of sugar daddies?"

"Jesus," Austin hisses. "That spiraled out of control quickly."

"I'm still processing that you spent time with Nora Levine," Heather says on a sigh. "I told Bobby on our very first date that she's my free pass and always will be."

Bobby nods in that laconic way he has—this particular son-in-law is not easily perturbed by anything. "She's mine as well, so maybe you shouldn't invite her over after all, Mimi."

"What's a free pass?" Heather's oldest, Wyatt, asks.

"It's a grown-up thing, baby," Heather says.

"Can I have a sugar daddy?" Wyatt's on a roll.

We all burst out laughing.

"Maybe when you're older," Austin says.

"Honestly, guys," Jennifer, always the more serious of my

kids, says. "This conversation is not suitable for children. Would you quit already?"

"Oh, come on, Jen." Austin's the polar opposite of his oldest sister. "Don't be so buttoned up. Or is the self-partnership no longer working out for you?"

"I don't want Wyatt and Lucas to hear any more of your inappropriate chatter, that's all."

"*My* inappropriate chatter? Heather started it, for your information."

"Uncle Austin's right," Wyatt says, defusing the situation instantly with his remark.

"Thanks, buddy." Austin holds up his hand for a high-five.

With a smile on my face, I lean back in my chair. This has always been what having four kids has been like. At each other's throat one second, ready to forget all about it the next. I wouldn't want it any other way.

CHAPTER 5
NORA

"Why am I going to dinner at this woman's house?" I'm talking to Izzy, who can't bear to be in another room when I'm home. "How did this happen?" I pace through my walk-in wardrobe. "Here I was, convinced I had perfected the art of saying no." I crouch and pick up my dog. "What the hell am I going to wear? And does it even matter?" Izzy quirks up one eyebrow. "You're right. It doesn't." I pick out a colorful blouse Juan would approve of and one of many pairs of jeans.

Izzy briefly whimpers when I put her down, but I need to get dressed. For some reason I can no longer recall, I'm having dinner with Michelle St James at her house, while I'd much rather spend my Saturday night at home with my dogs in my lap—there truly is no other place I'd rather be.

It's been a long week of rehearsals. We're starting to shoot soon, which is always exhausting. I need some extra me-time to adjust to the change in my schedule. Instead, I'm having dinner with a woman I barely know and, as time ticks away, I find myself more and more inclined to cancel. But I've waited too long. Chad, who babysits my dogs, informs me that my car has arrived.

On the way over, I call Juan for some words of social-interaction wisdom and encouragement.

"It's never a bad thing to spend time with an exec, darling," he says. "Or with the son of an exec. Trust me when I tell you I'm working that as hard as I can."

I already know his and Austin's first date was a dream date worthy of the most romantic movie.

"We're seeing each other again tonight." Juan's voice softens. "Apparently, all his sisters are hella jealous."

"Of him dating you?"

"Of the connection with Nora Levine, who is universally adored among the St James siblings."

"You really like this guy, huh?" I can tell that he does, which is why I'm asking.

"He's just so dreamy, Nora. And I'm not sick of him yet."

"Wow. And that after one date," I joke.

"This might be a thing. I don't know. It's making me a little nervous."

"Juan Diaz, say it ain't so. Are you experiencing that most elusive of things? Romantic feelings for another human being?"

"Now you make me sound like a monster."

"Just like someone with pretty obvious commitment issues, darling." I could do this with Juan for hours. He has that effect on me. We'd only be rehashing a version of the conversation we've been having for years. But my car is slowing down already. Traffic is light and it's not a long drive from Bel Air to Beverly Hills.

"We're here, Miss Levine," the driver says.

"My carriage has arrived, Jay. You be good tonight. Don't break my new boss's son's fragile little heart."

"His heart? What about my own?" Juan smooches into the phone. "Have fun. I'll call you tomorrow."

The front door swings open before I can take a good look at Michelle's house. Despite the fancy zip code, it's modest, although that could just be to my standards.

Michelle ushers me in and invites me into her backyard.

"I'm so glad you came." She pulls a bottle of wine from an ice bucket. "I have a lovely cold Meursault here, if you like."

Meursault is one of my favorite Burgundy wines. Maybe she had a minion scour every interview I've ever done for a mention of my preferred foods and beverages.

"Sure. I'll have a glass of that."

She pours us each a glass. I remember previously she only drank water, but she seems to be indulging tonight.

I cast my gaze over her garden. The trees in the distance are backlit with the orange glow of the setting sun.

"Lovely place," I say.

"Thanks." She has barely sipped from her glass before she puts it down.

"You don't have to drink wine because I am," I blurt, probably because this is making me a little nervous—because I don't really know what this is.

"Don't worry. I'm not. Just a few sips. I'm not much of a booze aficionado."

"All the rage in LA these days. You're very much on trend." I'm not, I think, as I swallow a generous gulp.

"Am I?" She grins. "Alcohol's just never been my thing, despite its non-stop glorification on screen." She leans toward the table and pushes the tray with nibbles in my direction. I spot olives, crackers, and hummus—nothing too fancy.

"I forgot to ask if you're gluten-free. Austin is, so I made what I would make for him."

"Gluten and carb-free all the way." I spear an olive onto a cocktail stick. "Have been ever since my first days on *High Life*."

"Are you serious?"

"I know things are changing for the better, but surely you know that when we were making *High Life*, me and the other female leads being as thin as possible was the one and only gold standard. It's a hard thing to shake."

"I'm sorry about that," Michelle says.

"It's hardly your fault."

"I've been part of Hollywood and the system for a long time, so I am guilty. We're all guilty of promoting unrealistic standards." Michelle shakes her head. "The male leads' weight clearly went up and down all the time, which makes it an unrealistic as well as a double standard."

"You're very woke for a TV exec."

"Most of us are. Now."

"Because you have to be."

"I'm the mother of three girls. I've witnessed first-hand what unrealistic standards can do to an impressionable teenage brain. If I'm woke, it's not because I have to be. It's because I love my kids and I care about people in general."

"Are your daughters okay?" It wouldn't be the first time I hurt an unsuspecting stranger's feelings by blurting something out inadvertently.

"They're absolutely fine. So is my son, by the way." It's hard to gauge whether her smile is genuine or a little forced. "I hear he's on a hot date tonight."

"You and Austin must be very close." I can't imagine sharing that kind of intimate detail with my own mother.

"We are. He's much younger than the girls and after the divorce, we spent a lot of time just the two of us."

"I think Juan really likes Austin." I don't think I'm speaking out of turn—Jay just told me.

"From what I gather, that feeling is mutual, although to be honest, I'm not entirely sure that doesn't have something to do with Juan's proximity to you. In my family, you're as close to TV royalty as it gets. All my kids still revere you."

"Aw." I never really know what to say to that. It's easy enough to brush off in a furtive social situation, but face-to-face with Michelle, it's a little awkward. "I know *High Life* meant a lot to many people." Platitudes have saved the day many a time for me. "You work in TV. You know what we sell is illusions most of all."

Michelle arches up her eyebrows. "I couldn't disagree more with you on that. We don't sell illusions. We tell stories. We delight viewers with characters they can't help but fall utterly in love with, like Emily on *High Life*. We make people's lives better by giving them something to unwind to at the end of a long day, and by giving them characters to laugh and bond with when they feel lonely."

"Damn. You really believe in what you do."

"I'm truly obsessed with television," Michelle says. "I'm utterly thrilled we're now in the golden age of TV. The content that gets made these days is unbelievable. The level of entertainment we bring is off the charts. It's a privilege to be a part of that."

Michelle St James is a true television believer. I've met a few in my career, but not as many as I would have liked to. Now, in my fifties, it's hard not to take it all with a very large pinch of salt. Decades in this business don't seem to have had the same effect on Michelle.

"If you put it like that." I drink some more wine.

"How would you put it?"

"It's very different for me. I'm an actor. I'm just a tiny cog in the wheel."

"Again, I must disagree." She sounds adamant. "Casting is one of the most important aspects of any project. The right actor for a role can make or break a show. You're the perfect example of that. No one else could have made the part of Emily in *High Life* as iconic as you. It's not just the part that sprouted in the writers' mind, and it's not just you either, it's the special alchemy of the two together. You brought Emily to life in your own unique way. You made her loved by billions of viewers and had them return to the show in droves every week."

I stopped thinking about what made the part of Emily larger than life a long time ago—because that stuff will drive you crazy.

When I don't respond, Michelle continues. "Why did you

specifically request Stella get a callback for the part of Megan?" She regards me intently.

"Because I didn't get the right vibe off any of the other actors they'd selected for the chemistry test and I'd just seen Stella in *Like No One Else*."

"My point exactly." Michelle's gaze on me doesn't waver. "You were looking for the spark, that thing between certain people that causes magic on screen."

"Maybe, but coincidence and timing had a lot to do with it as well. If I hadn't just been bowled over by that Lana Lynch movie, I would never have heard of Stella, and the part of Megan would have gone to someone else."

"What you call coincidence, I call the stars of TV history aligning."

I can't help but scoff. "So much in our business is down to sheer coincidence."

"So is a lot that happens in life. If Gerry hadn't sent those pictures, you and I wouldn't be sitting here tonight."

I'm vaguely aware the former CEO of Gloves Off Productions sent inappropriate pictures to female members of staff, but I prefer not to remember the details.

I take a sip of wine. Michelle doesn't touch hers. "I love TV too. I love that this is my job. I love acting more than anything else." I put up with a lot in order to be able to do it, I think, but don't say out loud to someone like Mimi—I reserve those conversations for my two best friends. "I love that you're so passionate about it."

"Maybe a bit too much." Mimi spears an olive onto a toothpick. "I've spent the best part of my working life on TV sets, getting things done, and I've always preferred it to the endless meetings and yammering on about the non-creative stuff."

"Really?" And this from a top executive.

"Yes, but the creative doesn't exist without the non-creative and vice versa." Her features soften. "Honestly, my big teenage dream was always to become a director. But… well, I wanted a lot of things, and I realized pretty quickly you risk getting nothing if you don't learn to compromise."

"Like you did when you married your husband?" Oops. There I go again. And I've only had half a glass of wine. "Sorry." I shoot Michelle my most apologetic smile. "I shouldn't have said that."

"It's okay. Really." Michelle leans forward and taps her fingertips to my knee. "I appreciate your directness." She has a very active way of showing it.

"But still."

"No, seriously, Nora. It's refreshing."

"People usually call it obnoxious and annoying, so I'll take refreshing." The smile I give her now originates somewhere deep in my core.

"You're right. Marrying Eric was a compromise. Just as deciding to focus on the business side of things instead of trying to become something unattainable when I was in my twenties, thirties, and forties, for that matter: a female director." Michelle shakes her head. "Life's much easier once you accept you can't have everything you want." Michelle takes her wine glass in her hands and twirls it around. "Better as well. I have so much. Four wonderful children. Three adorable grandkids. A great career in a business I love."

Michelle doesn't look as though she wants for anything in life. She has that calm, content glow about her of a woman without regrets. It's easy enough to warm to. She exudes the kind of confidence I enjoy basking in.

"I hear you," I say. "To the outside world, it must look as though I'm the luckiest woman alive. I get to do what I love and am paid an obscene amount of money to do so. But there's a flip side to everything. The side people prefer to look away from."

"Fame," Michelle says matter-of-factly. "I've seen it destroy good people time and time again." She finds my gaze. "It takes a lot to survive your level of fame, Nora. Most people don't. I have a lot of respect for that—for you."

"Wow." It's rare that someone expresses the very thing I've found so hard to express—that I've had to squash because of expectations and conditioning—for such a long time, just like that. As if it's a given. "Thank you for saying that."

"For telling the truth? You never have to thank me for that."

CHAPTER 6
MIMI

I've served Nora my son's favorite dish of oven-baked salmon and asparagus. Although she said earlier it was delicious, she eats with the restraint of someone's who's been told off about her food choices too many times. A bit like Jen does sometimes, despite my best efforts.

Nora doesn't hold back when it comes to wine, however. She's downed most of the Meursault, making it a good time to ask her a more personal question. There's a lot of speculation on celebrity gossip websites, but as far as the outside world is concerned, Nora Levine has been single most of her life.

"That picture over there." I point to a frame boasting a snap of my three girls. "The middle one. The tall one with the short hair. That's Jennifer. My oldest, although only by thirty minutes." My lips curl into an inadvertent smile every time I mention the twins. "She's what she likes to call 'self-partnered.'" Not everyone in the family managed to keep a straight face when Jennifer used that particular term to tell us not to expect her to introduce a romantic partner any time soon. That she's perfectly happy on her own, so happy in fact, that she can't imagine ever sharing her life with anyone else—that would only be giving in to the patriarchal and, when you really think about it, nonsensical notion that any person can only ever be completed by another person.

"You mean single?" There's not a hint of sarcasm in Nora's tone. I suppress my glee at her straightforwardness.

"Yeah. Single. But I'm not allowed to call her single because of how 'less-than' it makes her sound according to society's ridiculous standards."

"Take it from someone whose had half the world obsessed with her relationship status for a long time: being single is totally underrated. I daresay it's the single—no pun intended—most underrated state of being. The way people carry on trying to find a partner has always astounded me. So yeah, I'm Team Jennifer all the way. No disrespect to your other kids, but so far, she sounds like the smartest one to me."

"She sure would love to hear you say that. Can I record this, please?" I joke. "I'd be mother of the year to at least one of my kids for the rest of my life, although the other three wouldn't be able to cope." Imagine the mayhem at our next family meal.

Nora puts her fork down. She only finished half of her plate. But I guess she did pretty much answer my question with what she just said.

"Tell me more about your kids," she says.

This might be Nora's way of dodging a question that she has been asked too many times in her life, but like most mothers, you don't have to ask me twice.

"Jennifer and Heather are twins. They're almost forty." I refuse to be bashful about my age. Why would I be? "Jennifer's in tech. Heather's a stay-at-home mom. She has two young boys. Lauren's thirty-five and co-owns Silk on Rodeo Drive. She and her husband, Gus, have a one-year-old daughter, Lily. And you've met Austin. I'm sure you've heard many more sordid details about his date with Juan than I have."

Nora purses her lips and nods. "Quite a few things no mother should ever hear about her child." She holds up her hand. "Just kidding. Juan was surprisingly restrained when describing their date. Maybe because you're my boss."

"Just for the record, I don't see myself as your boss."

"Oh," is all she says—as though that's so hard to believe.

"Jo runs the show. She's the boss," I add.

"But you're *her* boss."

"Technically, I guess I am, but things don't really work that way."

"Could have fooled me."

"What do you mean?"

"The number of times I've had to do reshoots because some studio suit believed a scene didn't test well with a sample audience..."

"Well, yes, of course. These things happen."

"But, anyway, you're not like that." Nora pins her gaze on me.

"I can be if I have to. There's nothing wrong with protecting your company's investment. Since the earliest days of commercializing art, there's always been friction between the creative and the business side. But I truly believe the best executives can create the perfect balance required to let everyone thrive."

"Sure. TV's a money game, just like any other business. That's never going to change. Thank god a lot of other things have changed."

I nod. "Anyway, I don't feel as though I'm your boss, Nora. That's all I was trying to say."

"It's just how you walked into the room the other day, as though you had a big point to prove, and invited Stella and me to lunch, summoned us, really, just because you could... After that, it's hard to shake the idea that you're the big boss."

"That's why I invited you here. To undo that first impression of me."

"It's a bit funny to undo one invitation to a meal with another." Nora reaches for her empty wine glass. When I try to refill it, she stops me. She pours herself some water instead.

"I hadn't thought about it that way." I rise. "Dessert?"

"Sure." Nora stands as well. "Let me help you with these."

Telling my kids Nora Levine helped me clear the table will be the highlight of my week—unless I decide not to tell them Nora was here at all.

Before grabbing dessert from the fridge, I take a moment to watch Nora stack plates in the sink. She's been surprisingly open to me tonight—at least compared to our first lunch—but she remains the same enigma. An image she has cultivated to a T since she first shot to fame thirty years ago.

She's dressed casually in a pair of jeans and the kind of blouse that Lauren would put front and center in the window display of her shop.

"Anything else I can do for you?" She wipes her hands on a towel.

"Would you like some coffee? Tea?"

"No, thanks."

"Night cap?" Even though I'm not much of a drinker, I keep a well-stocked liquor cabinet. I open the door so Nora can see. "Whatever tickles your fancy."

"You know what? You're a good influence on me. If you're not drinking, I'm not drinking either." She huffs out some air. "If only Juan and Imani weren't so fond of Dom Pérignon. I'd drink a whole lot less myself."

My kitchen is hardly tiny, but Nora and I find ourselves in close proximity regardless. It's hard to tell how much makeup she's wearing, if any at all. Her skin is surprisingly smooth for a woman in her early fifties. I do recognize the tell-tale curve of the upper lip post filler.

"If you're sure." I ask.

"Do you have another drug of choice? Some Mary-Jane? Funny gummies?"

I shake my head. "No. A clear head has always been my most preferred state."

"Unlike most humans. Fascinating."

"I'm afraid I don't have anything else to offer other than what you just saw."

"Oh." Nora chuckles. "That's not what I meant. I was trying to say that alcohol is actually my drug of choice. I've tried a thing or two in my life—as you may have heard, a few of my *High Life* cast mates had a steady supply of whatever was the rage back then—but nothing does the trick for me better than a nice glass of wine. Of which you provided plenty. So, thank you." Nora heads back to the dining table. I follow with dessert.

"Did you make this?" Nora asks when I present her with dessert.

"God, no. Some things are better left to professionals."

"I agree." Nora smiles at me and she looks genuinely relaxed. Not that she gave the impression that she didn't want to be here, but it has taken her a while to thaw, to let some warmth radiate from her gaze. "For your information, I don't cook, so I wouldn't sit around waiting for a reciprocal invitation."

"I won't hold my breath." She really does blurt out the bluntest phrases.

"God, I'm sorry. Again. This is why I don't have many friends." Nora says it as though she just told me the weather forecast for tomorrow.

"What do you mean?"

"The minefield that is social interaction." She gazes at the chocolate ganache on her fork. "When you're famous for playing America's favorite bubbly TV character, people can't help but have certain expectations of you in real life. I'm so unlike Emily, yet people often confuse me with that character. Don't get me wrong, it was a true joy for me to play that kind of person for such a long time. Like, fundamentally, in here." She taps her fingers briefly to her chest. "It taught me so much to be able to find that in myself somewhere, and so easily. To embody this human, who looked exactly like me but acted nothing like me. To do that for ten years—that will do something to you. But I'm not Emily and I will never be Emily."

There's a lot to unpack in Nora's sudden unburdening. "For the record, you're excellent company, Nora. I'd much rather have dinner with you than with Emily."

"Thank you. Seriously. Ninety percent of the people I meet either expect to see Emily or only want to see Emily. It's always Nora-Levine-this and Nora-Levine-that, but most people don't want anything to do with Nora. They want the character they think they know and love."

"Like Austin."

"Yeah. I mean, I don't blame him. Television truly is powerful that way, but, um, yeah…" Nora runs out of steam.

"Hey." Her sudden vulnerability moves me. It's unexpected as well as beautiful. "I get it. I totally do." I may say that, but of course I don't really know what it's like to be Nora Levine, to have that kind of expectation precede you everywhere you go.

"It's okay. I chose this job. I wanted to do this. Ever since grown-ups started asking me that annoying question of what I wanted to be when I grew up, I've always replied with 'an actor'." She takes the kind of subtle but deep breath that must be practiced. "What did your kids want to be when they were little?"

"Nora," I say softly. "You don't have to bring the conversation back to my kids when you don't want to talk about something anymore. You can just say so."

"Oh, sorry. I should have asked what you wanted to be when you were little. Or no, you already told me. The female Martin Scorsese."

"That was much later. I'm a little older than you."

"So? What did you want to be?"

"No one has asked me that in such a long time. I don't remember. All I know is that my answer can't possibly have been a television producer."

"Or CEO of Gloves Off Productions."

"Exactly."

"Are your parents still, um, with us?"

I shake my head. "Sadly, no. They both died well before their time."

"I'm sorry," Nora says.

"Yours?"

"Still alive and kicking, but, um, we're not exactly close."

I can't help it, but as a mother, it always sends a chill up my spine when someone confesses to not being close to their parents. Apart from one of my kids dying, having them become distant is my biggest nightmare. But I also know there are all sorts of parents and a million different circumstances that can drive a wedge between a mother and her child.

"I'm not going to get into that," Nora says with the same deadpan intonation she used to claim not to have many friends earlier. She pushes her dessert plate a few inches away from her. She's left half the portion. "In fact, I think I might let you go off to bed."

"I'm not tired yet." I'd very much like Nora to stay a little longer, but I don't want her here against her will, of course.

"Thank you so much for a lovely dinner, Michelle."

"Mimi, please. And you're very welcome."

"Oh, right. You are very kind, Mimi, and your kids and grandkids are very lucky to have you."

"I hope the *Unbreak My Heart* cast and crew will feel the same way."

Nora gets up. I have to do the same to escort her out.

"I won't hold my breath for dinner at yours, then," I joke.

"I'll see you on set," Nora says.

"You will." I don't know what I was expecting from this evening. Although I get the feeling Nora has shown much more of herself than she perhaps wanted, I get the impression I've barely scratched the surface of who she really is. "It was a real joy to welcome you into my home, Nora. Maybe we can do it again some time."

"Maybe," she says, and never has a 'maybe' sounded more like a clear no. "Thanks again." She leans toward me and brushes her lips against my cheek so softly, I hardly feel them.

I take a deep breath and inhale her scent. As I open the door to Nora and watch her walk to the car, something niggles at me —a stubbornness I won't be able to ignore and that will make it an important mission to, despite her reluctance, have Nora Levine be excited about having dinner with me again.

CHAPTER 7
NORA

"I don't know what's happening to me." Juan's up to his usual over-the-top theatrics. "Imani, check my temperature, please. I'm sure I have a fever."

Imani and I exchange a look. We all but roll our eyes. Juan may, for some inexplicable reason, think this is the first time in his life he's felt this way, but Imani and I know better.

"This boy. This *man*." Juan stares intensely into the pool. "He's too good for me. I can't be with a wholesome man like Austin, yet it's all I want."

"Darling." Imani shuffles around until she's sitting right in front of him, her legs dangling in the pool. "Listen to me." She snaps her fingers in front of Juan a couple of times. "You're smitten. It happens once in a while. You'll feel discombobulated for a few weeks, but then it will pass." She doesn't add that, if he follows his usual routine, Juan will probably dump Austin once this intoxicating cocktail of hormones has left his blood. "Pull yourself together, please. Just a touch. Just so we can have a pleasant Sunday together."

"Neither one of you understands romance the way I do," Juan says on a dramatic sigh. "When were you last in love?"

Oh, so now he's in love. I wonder if Austin has said

anything to his mother about Juan. I'm in two minds to text her, to get Austin's perspective—and find out how much Juan is exaggerating.

"Not all that long ago." Imani's voice is low, almost threatening.

"I'm sorry." Juan scoots over to her and puts his hands on her knees. "In all my excitement, I forgot about The Bitch for a second."

"At Stella's party, Mimi asked if you and I were a couple, Imani."

"Mimi?" Imani narrows her eyes.

"Michelle St James," Juan says. "Austin's mama."

"You and I would make a stunning pair." Imani flutters her long lashes "So, no offense taken." She grins at me. "You've been awfully quiet about your dinner at *Mimi*'s house last night, by the way. Care to share with your friends?"

"It was just a producer making dinner for a cast member," I respond.

"You're Nora Levine, darling," Juan says. "You're never just a cast member."

"Which is probably why Mimi was so keen to invite me to her house."

"What was she like? Bitchy? Demonstrative of... I don't know, her wealth? Her influence? The fact that she had you there, right where she wanted you?" Imani's sounding more than a touch jaded today.

"Are you okay?" I ask.

"It's Jay with all this Austin stuff, and you having dinner with Mimi while I was on my own last night eating ice cream straight out of the container."

"Just to be clear," I'm quick to say, "me having dinner at Mimi's is totally different than Juan going on a date with Austin."

"I'd say," Juan says. "I had my lips all over—"

"No!" Imani holds up her hands. "We're not doing that today."

"How dare you cramp my sexually liberated style, sister." Juan splashes water on Imani, who tickles him with her feet. A short bout of swimming pool antics later, they've calmed down.

"Okay." Juan heaves himself out and sits next to Imani. "We need to get you some loving. What can we do?"

"I just never thought I would be this incredibly single at nearly fifty, you know?" Imani sighs. "I feel like I've failed at something."

"What if instead of calling it single, you call it self-partnered," I offer, earning me a well-deserved eye roll from Juan. He's got this. I should know to let them do their thing by now.

"We're all single here," Juan says.

"Oh, really? You haven't been giving off a lot of single vibes since you met Austin," Imani says. "He's fabulous, don't get me wrong, but it's just so easy for you. It's like you just turn up somewhere, and bam! A gorgeous guy flutters to you."

I block out their conversation for a few minutes. I don't have much to contribute and I've heard it countless times before. Besides, no one cheers up Imani like Juan does.

I recline on my lounge chair, gazing up at the blue LA sky. Inadvertently, some of the things I said last night pop up in my head—as they always do. Things I perhaps shouldn't have said. But with age has come the ability to let go. To no longer rehash a conversation until I've sucked all the lingering joy out of it. To twist it this way and that in my head, scrutinizing it for every possible mistake I might have made and every time I broke the conventional rules of conversation.

It *was* just dinner at a TV producer's house. And I made it abundantly clear that there wouldn't be a follow-up. Even though Mimi was none of the things Imani summed up earlier. On the contrary. She was lovely and warm and welcoming. Kind and a surprisingly good listener. She gave the impression of not jumping to any conclusions or being judgmental, even after the things I blurted out. Come to think of it, I quite liked her. I won't mind bumping into her on set. In that respect, it was an excellent move on her part to invite me to her house and clear the air of whatever it needed clearing of. Unlike my own, her people skills are on point.

My phone chimes with a message. Only a select group of people can reach me directly, so I always check when I get a notification.

"Who's that?" Juan asks from the side of the pool.

I haven't had a chance to redirect Mimi's number to my assistant—my tried-and-tested modus operandi after politely exchanging phone numbers with anyone.

"Austin's mom." I shoot him a grin. I wonder what Mimi has to say.

"Don't forget to thank her for dinner, darling." Juan likes to remind me of these things, although he's right to do so in this instance. "Also, what is she saying?"

Austin can't stop talking about Juan. Help! ;-) Mimi

A mere half hour ago, I wanted to send Mimi a message just like this one.

Same here, I reply. *Juan's insufferable, but also kind of cute.*

"Nora?" Juan stands next to me, dripping onto my legs.

"Are we back in high school, or what?" I ask.

My phone chimes again.

According to Austin, they're totally in love already. Should a mother worry about scenarios that involve eloping to Vegas?

My chuckle drives Juan crazy.

"Mimi wants to know if you and Austin have any plans for a shotgun wedding in Las Vegas." I smirk up at him.

"I doubt either one of us will find themselves unexpectedly with child, so no," Juan says drily, before perching on the edge of my chair. "Is it some sort of weird sign that I've met his mother already? Does it mean that this is different?"

"Different from what, darling?"

"From all the other ones?" Juan purses his lips. "What if we do end up getting married?" His teeth flash brightly as he grins at me. "How will you look back on this moment then?"

"I'm not letting you marry a man twenty years your junior," I say. "So don't worry about that."

"Correction," Juan says. "Eighteen years is not the same as twenty."

"What's that thing again with the seven years?" Imani looks up at us from the pool. "When the age gap becomes almost acceptable?"

Juan heaves a big sigh.

"Half Juan's age, plus seven. Twenty-two plus seven equals twenty-nine. That makes it totally unacceptable, Jay."

"Big surprise," Imani adds.

"Don't you have to text my future mother-in-law back?" Juan quips. "I take it you're aware she's into women?" Juan looks at me as though he knows something I don't.

"So?" I stare at my phone screen, thinking of something witty to write back.

"Maybe she had an ulterior motive for inviting you to dinner and you were too naive to notice." Juan cocks his head.

"Did Austin say something about that?" If so, I'll stop texting Mimi immediately. I don't want her to get the wrong idea.

Juan shakes his head. "Nah. Honestly, not a word. He loves his mother, though. Total mama's boy. He'd love for her to meet someone."

I scoff. "You've known me long enough to know that someone's not going to be me."

"I know." Juan pats my knee.

I text back, safe in the knowledge there's no subtext I'm missing.

Juan assures me that no engagement rings have been procured.

I glance over at Imani. "Are you ready to get back into the game, girl?"

"I don't know. Maybe just for a fling. A bit of fun and attention. Have someone coo over me for a night."

Juan shoots up and jumps into the pool, emerging next to Imani. "That's what you have me for."

"That's very sweet of you, darling, but there are certain itches I have that you simply can't scratch."

Juan drapes his arm over Imani's shoulders. These two. I don't know what I'd do without them.

"Maybe Austin knows an eligible woman to cheer Imani up," I offer.

Juan's eyes go wide, as though he's just had the most brilliant brainwave. "How about Mimi?" He fixes his gaze on Imani.

"Are you crazy?" Imani playfully pushes him away. "I'm not going on a date with your new plaything's mother. What do you take me for?"

Juan holds up a finger. "Firstly, Austin's not just my plaything." He pauses. "But yeah, that would be weird. Let's not do that. I got a little carried away. Sorry, darling."

"Why don't the four of us have dinner soon?" I ask. "If you're going to marry this guy, I need to spend some time with him first."

"That would be so nice, Nora, although he might want to marry you instead." He turns to Imani. "Meanwhile, I will scour his friends for a suitable match for you, darling."

I'm still holding my phone, which is remaining silent. No more messages from Mimi. She's probably busy with all her children and grandchildren. But I have my chosen family here with me, and my three dogs lurking in the shade. I have everything I could possibly wish for.

CHAPTER 8
MIMI

Although there's nothing for me to actually do here, I love being on set. Especially the set of my favorite show, *Unbreak My Heart*. I marked the first day of shooting for the new season in my calendar weeks ago. The buzz is electrifying. There's a nervous tension in the air that excites me. This is when the magic actually happens. All the work that has come before has led to this moment and what gets shot today will be the raw material for post-production. This is where our show gets made. This is the very essence of it.

Stella emerges from her trailer with her partner Kate in tow. Kate has their son strapped to her chest. It makes me think of my own son. Although Austin's twenty-six years older than Stella and Kate's, I sometimes still consider him my baby—and my baby is dating a man almost twenty years his senior. I wonder if I'll run into Juan today. If not, Austin's bringing him to Sunday brunch next weekend. Things are moving fast—I've even heard rumors of Austin having dinner with Nora Levine one of these days.

The intercom is calling Nora to the sound stage. Stella and Kate have joined me and we all watch, as though our gaze is pulled to her through sheer force of magic, as Nora rounds the corner and walks toward us. She's dressed as her character, who is in business attire for the first scene. Nora looks smashing in Jessie's navy pants suit. Her gaze halts on me for a moment as she spots me. She gives me the smallest of nods. I know better than to chitchat with an actor before they're about to shoot a scene. I send her a warm smile. The director calls Stella and Nora over to discuss the upcoming scene.

"I had to be here today," Kate says. "I wanted Silas to be here too, even though he won't remember." She fishes her phone out of her pocket. "Would you mind snapping a quick pic of me with Stella in the background? Just so that I have something to show my son when he questions whether he really was here." Kate flashes me a dazzling smile. That reminds me that I still don't know how she and Stella met. Maybe I should ask Nora—she seemed to find a lot of glee in referencing it that time we went to lunch.

"Sure." Or maybe I can just ask Kate. I take a picture of her and Silas with Stella and Nora in the background.

"Thank you so much."

"Don't mention it." I flash Kate my brightest smile. She really is a stunning woman. Maybe it's only fair that I invite her and Stella to dinner at my house as well, but somehow, it feels less necessary than inviting Nora. For starters, there isn't any air to clear between us. Although I could just do it for the sheer fun of it. For the vibe of having two lovely women come to my house with the singular purpose of having a good time. Kate could give me her professional opinion on how my house is decorated. If she can ever tear her gaze away from her son. In that respect, she reminds me of Heather, who had a successful career as a lawyer, but whose focus shifted entirely to her child months before Wyatt was even born. Wyatt is five now and Heather hasn't once mentioned going back to work.

My knees go a little weak at the sight of Kate and Silas. At the way she looks at him as though, despite standing in the middle of a tv set with a million things going on around her, and her partner about to shoot her first scene of the season, her son is the only person that exists in the whole wide world. Even though my youngest is in his twenties now, I can still so easily tap into that intoxicating feeling, even just for a few moments.

"If only he would sleep like this at night," Kate says. "I told him that his mama needed her beauty sleep, that she had a big day today, but this guy doesn't care about any of that."

I send her a knowing smile. "Would you and Stella like to come to dinner at my house some time? You can bring Silas, of course."

"Oh." Kate looks at me as though I just asked her to marry me instead of inviting her and Stella to dinner. "Yeah. Sure. Why not?"

"No pressure. I know it's hard to get away when you have a little one." I rest my gaze on her. "I like to get to know the people I'm working with and I had Nora over, so."

"You had Nora over?" This seems to pique Kate's interest.

I nod.

"How did you swing that?"

"I invited her, and she said yes."

Kate pulls a face I can't decipher. "Wow. She must like you, then." She gives me a once-over.

"She did say not to expect a return invitation."

"That sounds more like Nora."

"Do you know her well?" *My* interest is definitely piqued now.

"I wish I did, but… I mean, we try. The number of times Stella has tried to get together, or even just have Nora come over for coffee or a cocktail. Sometimes, she says yes, because I do think Nora likes Stella. They get along fine, but there's this thing… I don't know how to describe it. This wall. This—"

"Silence, please," The assistant director says. "Places."

I've only had one dinner with Nora, but I know what Kate means. It's not an unwillingness on Nora's part, I believe.

Maybe more of a means of self-preservation. Or just, very simply, how she is.

Kate and I watch Stella and Nora play their scene. It's striking how differently they approach it. Stella's character seems to be almost a continuation of herself. But Jessie, Nora's character, is totally different to her own, and it's almost shocking to see Nora change, seemingly just like that, although there's so much more to it than meets the eye. If some people are put on this earth with the purpose of playing other people, Nora is one of them. Once she's in character, it's impossible to look away.

Even someone like me, who has worked in television for most of her life, can't understand why Nora doesn't have shelves full of Emmys. Although it's not that hard to work out —she hasn't taken on any significant parts since *High Life* ended twenty years ago. As though it took her two decades to recover from everything that playing Emily Brooks, easily one of the most-beloved characters in the history of television, put her through. She alluded to it during our dinner. It takes a lot to carry the burden of that kind of fame and some actors naturally know how to handle it better than others.

In between takes, Nora hardly moves. Stella chats with the people around her, but Nora is all focus. Kate and I remain silent, both of us transfixed in our own way, as we watch Stella and Nora play Megan and Jessie.

"I'll be in touch about dinner," Kate says after the director has called the scene. "I'm sure Stella will be up for it." Stella's walking toward us.

"What did the little man make of that?" She heaves a fake sigh. "Don't tell me he slept right through it."

"Sorry, babe." Kate softly caresses Stella's shoulder. "But Michelle and I loved it. Great job."

"Amazing," I say, resorting to typical hyperbolic TV exec speak.

Kate leaves her hand on Stella's shoulder, as though she

simply has to be in physical contact with the woman she loves, and a pang of something travels through me. Maybe I've been single for too long. Maybe it's time I put myself out there and found myself someone who can't help but touch me like that whenever she clasps eyes on me. Cathy and I broke up almost two years ago.

From the corner of my eye, I see Nora approach. At first, it looks as though she might walk right past us, but then she seems to change her mind.

"Hey." She gives me the tightest of nods. As though we are nothing more than distant acquaintances. I hardly think we're friends, but we did spend, in my opinion, a lovely evening together.

For a few seconds, her face melts as she looks at Silas.

"Forty-five minutes until the next scene," someone says.

"Can we go over that scene again, Stella?" Nora asks, barely acknowledging Kate and me. But she's working, and Kate and I are only visitors. I'd be a fool to hold this against her, yet it stings a little that, to Nora Levine, I might as well not be here. I might as well not exist.

"Sure. I'll be there in a sec." Stella and Kate disappear into their family-of-three bubble.

Before Nora has a chance to walk off, I remind her that I'm here. That I'm a person, too.

"You're probably, like, in the zone, but, um, great job." What the hell was that? It's as though I, too, have forgotten who I am. Nora has that kind of disorienting effect on me.

"Hm," is all she says, before she disappears around the corner.

"Don't take it personally," Kate says after Stella has gone after Nora to rehearse their next scene. "Nora's like that with everyone. Well, except her holy gay twosome, Juan and Imani. They're the only two people who are special to her."

As though he senses that his other mother has left, Silas starts fussing.

"Someone's hungry," Kate says. "I'd better take care of this. See you later, Michelle."

I look over the set, pondering Nora Levine a few minutes longer. The previous weekend, when Austin just kept going on and on about how absolutely out-of-this-world amazing Juan was, I went out on a limb and texted Nora. I hadn't expected her to text me back, but she did, and we had a short but fun exchange. But Kate's right. I shouldn't take any of this personally. Besides, it's about time to stop thinking about Nora Levine altogether—and, perhaps, focus my attention on finding someone who delights in seeing me.

CHAPTER 9
NORA

Austin must really take after his father, because he doesn't look like Mimi at all. He's all curly blond locks and piercing blue eyes. His cheeks are the kind you'd want to pinch, if you were so inclined, whereas Mimi's cheekbones are sharp and defined. He does have the same warm, enthusiastic way his mother has. It's easy enough to see why anyone would fall for him, although I still have my doubts about Juan. Sure, he's smitten now, but how long will it last?

"My mom says hi," Austin says. "While my sisters are the greenest of green with envy." He looks at Imani's dress. "Come to think of it, about as green as that lovely shade of emerald you have on, darling." He speaks to Imani as though he has known her forever.

"Are you sure you don't want to join me for brunch at the St James' tomorrow, Nora?" Juan asks. "You'd make their day."

"I'm sure," I say drily. "You can always take Imani if you need a wingwoman."

"No more wing persons required." Austin drapes his arm over Juan's shoulders and smooches him on the cheek. "It's all in the bag already."

Granted, they are cute together, but someone has to keep a shred of realism about them—it's usually me.

"Is your self-partnered sister into men or women?" Juan leans into Austin's embrace. "'Cause this gorgeous lady's on the prowl." He points at Imani.

"Jen's not looking," Austin says matter-of-factly.

"A bit like Nora then. I get it and I respect it," Juan says.

"You must have so many suitors though, Nora." Austin hasn't been around me long enough to know not to say silly things like that. Juan leaves me to fend for myself. His boyfriend and I are getting to know each other so I'll let him off the hook. Austin slants his head. "I totally respect my sister's decision to be single, although I'm not allowed to call it single when I'm around her. I'd never dream of pushing her into doing something she doesn't want to. But boy, is it wonderful to be in love."

"Aw," Imani says.

"Does that mean you are also self-partnered?" Austin asks me. His sister has him drilled pretty good.

I scoff. "I'm just—yeah. I guess I am. If that means I'm perfectly happy by myself and prefer to be single, then yes. I declare myself successfully self-partnered."

"Jennifer's going to love you," Austin says, as though it's a foregone conclusion that I'm going to meet his sister just because he's dating my best friend. At least he doesn't ask me what most people would: but for heaven's sake, Nora, why? Maybe Juan did warn him about that.

"What about your mom?" Juan asks.

"What about her?" There's something instantly defensive about Austin at the mention of his mother.

"She's single and looking," Juan says.

"Jay," Imani says, using her stern voice. "Please."

"Oh, I'm just playing. I can't wait to get to know your family better, babe—especially your mom."

"You'll have to get past my sisters first." Austin grins at

Juan. "They're going to be all over you. Prepare for twenty-thousand questions about Nora."

"Story of my life." Juan shrugs. "But if it weren't for Nora, I might never have met you." The smile on his face as he leans into Austin is so sweet, I barely recognize my best friend.

"So." Austin fixes his gaze on Imani. "What's your story, girl? Why is a delightful, charming, intelligent, and gorgeous woman like yourself single?"

"Because The Bitch left her and broke her heart into a million pieces," Juan says.

"She must really be quite the bitch if she left the likes of you." Austin shakes his head.

"Darling," Imani says, "What you see here, is not all you get." She laughs her devilish laugh—the one she only belts out occasionally.

"I didn't for one second think it was," Austin replies. He's not intimidated by my friends in the least—maybe he also gets that from his mother.

I tune out their banter and wonder what Mimi is doing tonight. Working? Babysitting one of her grandkids? Or maybe she's on a date. Did Juan just imply she was looking? When we had dinner, Mimi asked about my relationship status, but I never asked about hers, although I know she's single. Why would I need to know more than that? I only have to look at my own life to realize that the ways of the world can be strange and unpredictable, and maybe Mimi and Imani will somehow end up together—who knows?—but until then, I don't need to worry about Austin's mother's dating life for one single second. Nor about my own.

"I would like for my mom to find someone again," Austin says.

My ears perk up and I focus on the conversation again.

"We all say this about our own mothers, no doubt, but she truly is the best mom in the world."

All three of us scoff in our own way. "Yeah, right," Juan says. "You're just lucky."

"I know. I'm sorry, babe. I wasn't thinking." Austin briefly rests his head on Juan's shoulder. Juan's family broke ties with him when he came out of the closet.

"What about your dad?" I'm curious to find out about this man who married Mimi knowing that she could never love him in the way that he might need her to.

"My dad's great. I mean, it's been complicated at times, and I've always sort of known that they didn't really belong together. You know, in their heart of hearts. But I honestly couldn't have wished for a better set of parents." He pauses. "It's almost as if because they knew that they didn't have this textbook marriage, they tried extra hard for us kids. Or maybe that's just because I'm the youngest."

"Did you know, growing up, that—" For once, I'm aware that I'm about to be very impertinent.

"That my mom was a big old lesbo?" Austin's so disarming. He doesn't seem to have many hang-ups talking about this.

I nod and gaze into his bright blue eyes. I'm beginning to really like this man as well.

"They divorced when I was ten and they told me why, so yes, I've pretty much always known."

"What did they tell you?" I ask.

"Nora," Imani whispers.

I look at her and she gives me a slight shake of the head. I've asked one question too many. I guess I'll have to ask Mimi herself if I want to know the answer.

"It's okay," Austin says. "Because my parents have always been so open with me, I don't have any issues talking about this. I know it was an unusual situation, but not in the way you might expect. It was unusual because my mom has always been honest about who she was but also about what she wanted. With most couples, that's not the case." From the solemn expression on his face, I can tell he has nothing but respect for his parents and the choices they made. "Communication and compromise," Austin says. "That's what they taught me are the most important things in life and I haven't come across anyone who could prove them wrong."

"Is your dad single?" Imani asks.

"He remarried a long time ago." He smiles as he says it. "Abby is lovely. She and my mom get along eerily well, but then again, why wouldn't they?"

"Wow." Imani genuinely looks stunned at this tale of familial bliss.

"Can you imagine me at the same table as that family?" Juan grins.

"Don't worry, babe," Austin says. "After the last man I brought home, my family will welcome you with open arms."

Mimi did say something about Austin's penchant for older men.

"We," Imani says, "as Juan's chosen family, do the same to you, darling."

"Thank you so much." Austin has a twinkle in his eyes. "I love my family very much, but I'd happily swap one of my sisters for you, Nora." He holds up his hands. "Just joking, although, come to think of it, any one of them would swap me to have you as a sister. No doubt."

"And here I was thinking you were dating me for me," Juan says. "While all you really want is to be closer to Nora."

"I can have both." Austin plants a kiss on Juan's cheek.

Just because we're sitting at the same table, I think, doesn't mean we're close. But when I look at Austin, I think again. I don't meet many people who give me the kind of vibe that makes me want to spend more time with them but, by the end of this evening, I might be rooting for this thing between Austin and Juan to last. One thing is extremely obvious: no matter their situation, his parents raised a mighty fine son.

CHAPTER 10
MIMI

I've set an extra place at the table for Austin's new boyfriend —Juan's title in our family now.

"We tried and tried," Austin says to his sisters. "But Nora could not be swayed to join us for brunch. Maybe next time." He glances at Juan with a lot of hope in his eyes.

"I don't want to break your tender, Nora-Levine-loving St James' hearts," Juan says, "but I wouldn't hold my breath. Nora's simply not like that."

So many times I've heard something similar said about Nora since I met her. Not a word of it a lie, either. I already know that from experience.

"But this little bastard got to spend yesterday evening with her," Heather says. Bobby and the boys are at home nursing colds, so she's more liberal with calling her brother names.

"Not so little anymore." Austin makes sure he towers over his sister.

I glance at the elaborate bouquet of flowers Juan brought me.

"Is it exhausting?" I ask him. "Everywhere you go, everyone's always talking about Nora."

"It's not like this everywhere I go," Juan says. "Your kids are just extra ferocious when it comes to Nora."

"How is she?" I coax him into the kitchen with me while the kids banter.

"Fine. She said to say hello." He rests his dark-brown eyes on me.

"Did she?"

"Yeah. I think you swayed her with that dinner. She quite likes you now."

"You mean she puts up with me more willingly." I hand him a mimosa.

Juan chuckles. "Nora's Nora. She is who she is and she isn't going to change anymore now." He glances around the kitchen. "This is a gorgeous kitchen in a lovely home, Mimi." He leans toward me. "And for your information, I've never met a man who has so many nice things to say about his own mother. It's a real credit to you that Austin speaks about you the way he does."

"Oh, you know, a gay son and his mother. It's a special bond."

"Trust me," Juan says, sounding suddenly wistful, "it's really not."

"Juan!" Lauren shouts. They're all a bit more rowdy than usual. "Tell us, in your own words, how you met Nora."

"I did my best with them," I say loud enough for everyone to hear. "But when it comes to certain celebrities, they have no manners whatsoever."

I join Juan at the table because I'm interested in this story as well.

"Listen carefully, kids." Juan clearly enjoys being the center of attention—and has zero qualms talking about Nora. "I was volunteering at the LGBT Center, just going about my day, being my normal fabulous self, when all of a sudden, everyone starts acting bat-shit crazy. Surely, I was aware of Nora Levine. I may have spent a large part of my teens in not-so-nice places, but even so, it was hard not to know about *High Life*." He rests his chin on an upturned finger. "I knew who she was when she walked in, but it wasn't that big a deal to me as it was to the others. Let's just say I had other fish to fry, and more important things to do than fawn over some overpaid actor. Like make rent and keep my head above water."

Austin's told me some things about Juan's past, but I don't know all the details.

"And staying alive with a few shreds of dignity intact," Juan continues.

The girls are hanging on his every word.

"Anyway, I kid you not when I say it was like something out of a movie. In walks the biggest TV star the world has ever known at the absolute peak of her fame. Our eyes meet. She looks at me; I look at her. And boom, it's like something magical happens between us. There's no other way to describe it. Like love at first sight. Purely platonic, obviously." Eyebrows arched all the way up, he nods. "Nora did her thing at the Center. Dropping off a fat check, thank you very much. And all the time, I felt completely drawn to her. I wasn't the only one, of course. Every last one of us was losing our shit over Nora. She has always given generously to the Center, but it was hardly just that. I didn't know what she was really like at the time, and she has changed so much since, but back then, when Nora walked in, it was like the air changed. Like all the atoms in the atmosphere rearranged themselves just to please her, to accommodate her very existence."

Juan should have gone into theater with the way he can enthrall the people around him.

"I wasn't nearly as fabulous back then as I am now, but I must have had something, because Nora was drawn to me like a moth to a flame. We hit it off, and my life has never been the same since. She took me under her wing and we've been best friends ever since."

"If you can get Nora Levine to fall for you like that, our little bro never stood a chance," Jennifer says.

"I never stopped volunteering at the LGBT Center," Juan says. "I still work there most days. I basically owe my life to that place and Nora has been more than generous."

"Is she queer?" Heather asks.

"Who knows what Nora is?" Juan does his best to keep Nora's cloak of secrecy intact.

"She pretty much told me last night," Austin says. "She's like you, Jen."

"Single?" Heather asks.

"*Self-partnered,*" Jennifer and Lauren say in unison.

"She hasn't been with anyone since you met her? When was this?" Heather asks.

"Twenty years ago. During the last season of *High Life*." Juan expels some air. "Anything else you want to know is not for me to say. Sorry, darlings."

Lauren and Gus have left early with Lily and Jennifer and Heather are chattering away. Austin is looking for an old lamp in the garage, leaving me alone with Juan.

"Please, Mimi, sit. I'll take care of the dishes. Lord knows I've done enough of them in my time." He moves graciously behind the kitchen island. "Do you have a particular system of dishwasher stacking I need to adhere to?"

I shake my head. "Do as you please, Juan. Thank you." This man does not look as though he cares one iota about the position of crockery in a dishwasher, but looks can be deceiving.

"As I please? Are you sure about that?" He flashes me one of his smiles. It's hard to say who was luckier when Juan met Nora. Maybe they both got lucky that day. But I mustn't get too attached to him. He might be out of all of our lives sooner rather than later, and it's completely out of my control.

What I can do is luxuriate in the sensation of liking my son's new boyfriend—it hasn't always been an easy feat. But Juan makes it incredibly easy.

"That was quite the story you told earlier. About meeting Nora." Surely, some of it was dramatized, fictionalized even, for effect.

"Every word of it true," Juan says, as though he can read my mind. "The other day, we were talking about chosen family versus blood family. I might no longer exist for my blood family, but I sure got lucky with my chosen family. Nora has been so amazing. In the beginning, it was almost like she wanted to mother me. Like she saw that need in me that I didn't even know I had, or didn't want to believe I had, after my own mother kicked me out of her house." He stops what he's doing and plants his hands on the kitchen counter. "You have no idea what it means to me for you to welcome me into your home like this, Mimi." Did his voice just break a little? "Your family… it's like this perfect fantasy family."

Maybe Austin hasn't given his boyfriend all the particulars of his parents' marriage.

"No family's perfect."

"True. Perfect's not the right word for it. But there's an abundance of love and acceptance and warmth here. That's all you need, really." He inhales sharply. "Nora, Imani, and I are all such misfits when it comes to our own families. We never really fitted anywhere, except with each other." I wonder how Imani became part of their gang of three, but that's a question for another day. "But hey, it just goes to show that you don't need a dream childhood to have a fabulous life when you're older." He clears his throat. "I mean, adult. Not *old*, obviously." He shoots me a wink.

"Obviously." At least Juan's a good deal younger than me and Austin's father. Would I prefer my son to bring home a man in his twenties once in a while? Sure. But again, it's not up to me. And who am I to have any say about my children's—or anyone else's, for that matter—love life? We all have our own reasons for making the choices we make. "I'm sorry about your family." That reminds me Nora said she's not close to her parents either.

"Not everyone can handle this level of fab." Juan sounds as though he means every word of it. As though, over the years, he has steeled himself against any mention of his family.

"I assure you that I can." I have to smile when I look at him. "And you're always welcome here."

"I'll wait a little while before I start calling you mom." Juan's chuckle is infectious and when Austin walks back into the kitchen, his boyfriend and I are both giggling like schoolgirls.

CHAPTER 11
NORA

When my phone rings, I scold myself for the inexplicable oversight of not having diverted Michelle St James' calls yet. Does she really think she has a direct line to me for the rest of her life? I'm in two minds about picking up. On set, I like to keep my focus as much as possible, and I haven't really spoken to Mimi. I remind myself that I like her, and that Juan now, apparently, is as crazy about her as he is about his new boyfriend. Fuck it. I pick up.

"Hi, Nora. I'm so glad I caught you," Mimi says. "It's rare to be able to call someone like you directly. I usually have to go through a plethora of agents and managers and assistants."

"Yeah." It's been a few weeks since we had dinner. How did I miss diverting her number? It's unlike me. Maybe it's a subconscious thing.

"I'm having Stella and Kate over for dinner on Saturday and I was wondering if you'd like to join us."

As usual, as soon as I get an invitation for a social event, everything inside me screams no, no, no. I don't want to go. But my more rational side knows I need to have some interaction with the people I work with outside of work. I can't shut myself off completely. Sometimes, I even have fun. I would even catalogue my dinner at Mimi's under the fun events.

"Feel free to bring your posse," Mimi says when I don't immediately reply.

"Juan's no longer free on Saturdays."

"He and Austin are going away this weekend. Stella's family has this cabin in Topanga."

"I know," I say matter-of-factly. "Can you imagine Juan and Austin hiking through the canyon together?"

"It's what I prefer to imagine when I think of the two of them on a weekend away."

I chuckle. "Right. I get it." I pause. "I need to check with Imani." Maybe it will save her from another lonely night on her couch with a tub of ice cream, although that was probably greatly exaggerated. Imani's not the type to stay in and sulk like that.

"I'll take that as a yes. Great."

Did I just say yes? "Um, yeah. Okay," I stammer. "It's a small thing, right?" I ask, to be absolutely sure.

"Just the people I mentioned. You have my word." There's not a hint of irony in Mimi's tone, which I appreciate.

"Okay. I'll let you know about Imani soon."

"I look forward to seeing you again, Nora." There's so much warmth in Mimi's voice. It makes me want to hear it again. That's probably why I said yes before I even thought I might.

"I don't mean to be indiscreet," Mimi says, while she pours wine for everyone but herself. "But it's been weeks since I was promised the story of how you two met." She pins her gaze on Stella, then on Kate. "It's about time someone told me."

"Is that why you invited us?" Stella says. "To find that out?"

Kate shifts her weight in her chair. This all happened years ago, before we started making *Unbreak My Heart*, but it's the sort of thing, I suspect, that will always make her uncomfortable.

"Of course not." Mimi sits and expertly folds one leg over the other. I would never wear a tight skirt like that of my own volition, but for some reason, the characters I play tend to dress in them. "I just wanted the pleasure of your company."

"Kate used to be married to my brother," Stella says.

Imani and I know what the deal is, of course, but it's always fun to watch someone's first reaction to this juicy nugget of information.

"Excuse me?" Mimi's head bobs forward a bit, as though she didn't quite catch that.

"It's not as salacious as it sounds," Kate says. "My marriage to Kevin was basically over, but yeah. There's no two ways about it. We fell in love while I was still married to Stella's brother."

For the first time since I met her, Mimi seems stumped for words. Maybe she's trying to imagine what something like that would do to her own brood of children.

"Wow." This kind of thing will test the limits of anyone's open-mindedness.

"You asked, Mimi," I say, just to take the heat off Stella for a bit. Although Kate and Stella can take it. They're like this perfect dream couple—like an ad for falling in love, if that's what you're into.

"I know. My curiosity got the better of me. I just, um, wasn't expecting that for an answer. I won't pry any further, but, if you don't mind me asking, how are things in your family? How did your parents take this news?"

I've met Stella's mother, acclaimed architect Mary Flack, a few times. She doesn't seem to adore her daughter any less for running off with her son's wife.

"It's only my mom and my brother, who has a new wife and a bunch of kids now as well," Stella says. "Kevin lives in Washington DC. And my mom…" Stella swallows. "My mom is like the superstar of moms."

"Mary Flack. Of course." Mimi seems genuinely discombobulated. "I love her work."

"Stella used to be Mary Flack's daughter, but now Mary's known more as Stella's mother," Kate says proudly.

Imani and I exchange a glance. I'm not sure what she's thinking, but I don't spend a lot of time thinking about my own mother, even though she is, by far, a much better person than Imani's mother ever was.

"To family then." Mimi raises her glass of water.

I glance at Imani again, to see what she'll do. I would never in a million years ask my friends to toast to their families, but that's the thing about spending time with people you don't know very well. It's an emotional and psychological minefield. But if anyone can take it, it's my beautiful friend Imani. She half-raises her glass and pretends. Either way, a toast to Mary Flack is never a wasted one. I enjoy Mary's company whenever I see her.

"Mom has Nathan now, so." Stella grins. "When they first started dating, I thought he was just a gold-digging toyboy, but people really can surprise you. He's a bit too young for me to call him stepdad, but he's my go-to guy for anything I can't talk to my mom about."

"How much younger is he?" Mimi asks.

"He's barely a year older than me," Stella says. "I used to be such a brat about that. I couldn't cope with Mom bringing this much younger guy into our house. But then I got to know him, and he was really there for everyone when the shit hit the fan. He's just a good, stand-up guy. I should have trusted Mom to make the right choice. But it's all good now. Surprisingly, we're just one big happy family. And Nathan loves babysitting, so."

"Huge plus." Kate drapes an arm over Stella.

"You might have noticed at your party that my son can't resist the odd silver fox," Mimi says.

Silver fox? If Juan were here, this house would be too small to contain his outrage.

Imani bursts out laughing. "Please, let me be in the room when you call Juan a silver fox."

"Oh, I know he's only in his forties. But Austin..." Mimi shakes her head. "It's not like he had an absent father. I made absolutely sure of that. I can't explain why he likes older guys so much."

"With Juan" Imani says, as though it's the one and only conclusion possible, "it's probably not just an age thing. He's just such a beautiful human being."

Mimi nods, as though she agrees. In my biased opinion, it's impossible to dislike Juan. Clearly, he's got Mimi under his spell also.

"The girls really took to him as well," Mimi says, confirming my suspicion.

It's funny to me how, even when he's not here, Juan's such a big topic of conversation.

"Trust me," Stella says. "An age gap is one of the easiest things to accept in a family context."

"You would say that." Kate grins at her partner. "Now that you adore Nathan."

"He's Silas' godfather," Stella says.

"We could hardly ask Kevin." Kate tries to keep a straight face.

"I guess, with time, most things can be accepted," Mimi says. "I'm the oldest one here, so I should know."

Imani scoffs. Sometimes, it gets the better of her—especially when there's lots of talk of the unbreakable bonds of family, not something she has to worry about when she's with Juan and me.

"Maybe in a perfect world." Stella looks at Imani. They're friends. She knows Imani's story. "Sorry, darling."

"It's okay. I've made my peace now. My parents were of a different time."

But still, I think, although I get it. Generational differences are only one of the issues I have with my own parents.

"How old are they?" Mimi asks.

"They're dead," Imani says. "Although they were no longer in my life decades before they passed away."

"I'm so sorry. I really am," Mimi says.

"They had me late. My mother was forty-one. My father almost fifty. He was pushing seventy when I told him I was a girl, and not the boy he thought I was. This was more than thirty years ago. Thank goodness times have changed."

Mimi hides her double-take well, but I've got my eye on her, and I've noticed. Imani's used to this reaction by now, and either way, it wouldn't bother her to shock someone with this.

"Their loss for not knowing their magnificent daughter," Mimi says. "Their huge loss."

Imani lifts a perfectly sculpted eyebrow. "Maybe we can talk about something other than family now."

CHAPTER 12
MIMI

By the time we sit down to dinner, I'm a bit dizzy with all the revelations. And all I've drunk is water. I keep trying to imagine Heather running off with Lauren's husband or the other way around. Or even more dramatic, one of my sons-in-law falling for my son. It makes my head spin so badly, I need to take a deep breath before I serve the food.

"I've gone back to apps now," I hear Imani say as I sit. "But I haven't had much luck so far."

While they all coo over the meal I've prepared, I sneak a quick peek at Nora. She seems to be having fun. I wonder what went wrong in her family for her to be so drawn to people who got rejected by theirs just for being who they are—for being what their parents made them and still not living up to their expectations.

"What about you, Mimi?" Imani asks.

"What about me?" I've lost track of the conversation.

"Are you into any of the dating apps? I can recommend a couple where a woman like you would score highly."

"Score highly?" I scoff. "Is that what the kids are calling it these days?"

"I'm hardly a child." Imani's gaze on me lingers. "You're

successful, beautiful, obviously kind, and you know how to cook a great meal."

"Stop it already." I fan my hand next to my cheek. "You're making me blush." Did she just hit on me? Or was she simply being a complementary guest?

"Jay's been raving about you non-stop since he came to brunch last weekend."

"That's very sweet of him."

"I can see why." Imani looks into my eyes. "Anyway, just let me know if you need any help with those apps."

"Austin said you were 'looking.'" Nora curls her fingers into air quotes—and greatly surprises me in the process.

"Looking's a big word for it." I examine Nora's face. "I haven't actually taken any steps, but I'm not going to lie. It would be nice to meet someone. I'm ready for it and I don't feel as though I've reached my sell-by date just yet."

All four of them break out into loud protests simultaneously, tripping over themselves calling out the patriarchy and capitalism for writing off women once they're above a certain age—Nora the loudest of all. Her wine glass is empty again already.

"What's your type?" Imani asks when the hubbub has died down. I'm so out of practice, I don't know if she's asking for herself or just out of general curiosity. "I may know someone."

I can play this game. Although, admittedly, it's a bit disconcerting to do so with three pairs of eyes on me.

"Hot," I say, rather facetiously, while gazing back into her eyes.

She slants her head slightly. "Ever since I walked in here, I've been picturing you with my friend, Simone." Imani smiles at me.

"Oh, come on," Nora interjects. "Not Sad Simi."

"She's not sad." Imani's tone is suddenly sharp.

"She is a bit." Nora pipes down instantly. "Sorry. Personally, I can't really see it."

"Let's talk in private some time, Mimi." Imani sends me another smile. "Away from prying ears."

"I'm not prying." Nora holds up her hands. "Anyway, you can all date who you want to. I'm staying out of it."

I'm not sure what it is I'm witnessing here.

"Mom met Nathan on an app, so it can work," Stella says.

If it was Nora's intention to instantly put me off Simone, it worked. But why would Nora even bother? I lean back in my chair and turn to her. I catch her staring at me. Maybe she's had a few too many.

Stella and Kate left an hour ago—new mothers don't tend to stay out too late. Imani just got into a taxi after fruitlessly trying to get Nora to join her. Apparently, Nora doesn't feel like going home just yet—and she's very adamant about it. Whereas last time she was here, all of a sudden, it felt as though she couldn't get out of my house fast enough. She didn't drink as much wine then.

Imani could only be persuaded to leave after I promised, on all my children and grandchildren's lives, that I would safely put Nora up in my guest room.

"It's my job to take care of her when she's like this," Imani said. "It's rare that she gets this wasted."

"I've got this," I assured her, secretly relishing the prospect of an intoxicated Nora Levine in my house. "Take the rest of the evening off."

"Call me if you need anything. Anything at all." The reluctance with which Imani left made me think she might come back later to check on Nora.

"Imani, please go. I'm a big girl. I can take care of myself," Nora slurred.

"It'll be a while before she changes her mind," Imani said as she called for a car. "She's unbelievably stubborn like that."

"I'll make her down a few liters of water and everything will be okay. I promise."

"Here we are," Nora says, after Imani has left. "My chaperone's finally left me alone."

I pour us both a large glass of water and then lead by example by knocking most of it back.

Nora takes a few sips from hers, then asks, "Don't you have anything stronger?" She looks around the kitchen. "Which one's your booze cabinet again? I can serve myself. You put your feet up. You've been such a wonderful host. You must be exhausted." She covers her mouth with her hands. "Oh, no. I'm being one of those cliché celebs who's too self-absorbed to read the room and rudely overstays her welcome, aren't I?"

"You are very welcome here. Although I will draw the line at another drink. I can make you some tea or coffee, if you like."

She waves off my offer and takes another sip of water. "I know I've had enough. Sometimes, I can't stop myself. Imani's been giving me the evil eye for the past two hours, but when you know someone for as long as I've known her, you become very adept at ignoring what you don't want to see."

"It's okay. I'm not judging you. It's quite amusing, actually." I've certainly never seen her this relaxed.

"I know you won't take advantage of me by asking indiscreet questions." She's not that drunk that she forgets who she is—a woman with a secret or two.

"I'll do my best."

"I like you, Mimi. You… make me feel safe, somehow. Apart from that first day we met, when you annoyed the living daylights out of me, you've exuded nothing but kindness and confidence. I'm very drawn to that."

Nora's had too much wine for sure, but she doesn't strike me as being so far gone that she won't remember what she said tomorrow morning. She might regret it, but she will surely remember—probably to her detriment.

"Thank you." Nora's hair is disheveled and her eyes watery.

"Maybe we can be friends after all." Maybe she'll actually talk to me next time I'm on the *Unbreak My Heart* set.

"We're friends already. I wouldn't still be here if we weren't." Nora lets her head fall back. "All that delicious wine is catching up with me." She heaves a sigh. "I'm sorry." She tries to get up. "I should get a car."

"I promised Imani I'd put you up in my guest room."

"Oh, no no no. I don't want to be a nuisance. I don't want to stay here. I need to go home."

"In that case, let me take you. My blood alcohol is zero point zero."

"You would drive me home? After having me over for dinner and putting up with my drunken ways?"

"I'm not putting up with you, Nora. I enjoy your company." It's fun seeing her like this instead of the usual buttoned-up Nora. "A lot."

"Oh."

"Surely that's not a huge surprise to you."

"Maybe a small one. Not many people actually like me after they get to know the real me."

I shake my head. "Well, I do."

"Hm." She huffs out some air, then sinks her teeth into her bottom lip. "Maybe I do want to stay here." She swallows slowly. "Maybe I—yeah." She pushes herself out of her chair and walks toward me. "Do you think I should stay?" Her face is right in front of mine. I can feel her warm breath on my skin.

"My guest room is all yours."

"No. I mean, do you want me to stay?" There's barely any space left between our lips.

"Nora," I whisper. "You're not thinking straight."

"Never have as far as I can remember." The corners of her mouth tilt upward. Her stare on me is intense and deep blue. She smells like wine and expensive perfume. And she clearly wants to kiss me. I want her to kiss me, but I can't let her. Not like this.

I put a little distance between us. "Why don't I drive you home?"

Nora shakes her head. "I don't want to go home."

"Then you'll stay in the guest room." I take another step away from her.

"Oh. I—" She brings her fingers to her un-kissed lips. "I'm sorry. I thought, um, yeah. Nothing."

"You're not yourself, Nora." I stop myself from putting a hand on her shoulder. "I'm not interested in any of this if you're not fully you."

"Wow." She expels some air through her nose. "In all my life, I never," is all she says. She sinks into a chair. "Okay. But just so you know, I don't do things like this when I'm sober. Ever."

"All the more reason to stop now."

"You're not even tempted?" Nora's probably not used to people saying no to her every whim.

"It's not about that. You've had too much to drink. You can no longer consent."

"Not even to a kiss?" she asks.

"Not even to a kiss."

"You're right, but… you're also a little bit wrong, you know."

"Guest room?" I draw up my eyebrows.

Nora shakes her head. "Nah. I need to go home. Imani will come and get me."

"Imani?" Poor woman. "She just left. I'll take you. It's not a problem."

"I have a car service. I'm not some precious cargo that needs to be dropped off in person."

I push that glass of water in her direction.

She knocks back a few large gulps, then buries her head in her hands. "Oh god," she mumbles. "I can already feel tomorrow's mortification."

"How about I promise you here and now you have nothing

to be mortified about. We're good. These things happen and, actually, nothing happened. So don't worry about it."

"If only it worked that way, but you can't absolve me in advance of what I'm going to regret later."

"Sure I can. I'm doing it now. If you feel the urge to apologize to me tomorrow, don't." I look for my phone. "I'm going to send you a text. Don't open it until tomorrow morning so it can serve as a reminder." I type a message, then show it to her before I press send. *No apologies required. Your friend, Mimi.*

Nora chuckles. "You're something else. *Friend.*"

"So I've been told." I finally feel comfortable enough to flash her a big, broad smile. "Come on. Let's get you home."

"Thank you, Mimi. I'm serious. For being so courteous and not taking advantage."

"That's what friends are for," I say.

CHAPTER 13
NORA

Mimi drives me home in silence. I'm ferried around in cars all the time, but never like this. To sit in the front with her is intimate, especially after the stunt I just tried to pull. I tried to kiss her. Why, oh why?

I don't understand. I'm not sure this is something I can rehash with Juan until I figure it out myself, seeing as Mimi is his boyfriend's mother. And poor Imani. I acted like such a diva with her. I made a real mess of things tonight, which is exactly why I decline most invitations.

It's late, and traffic's mercifully light. We turn into my street. I open the gate via a facial recognition app on my phone.

"I don't suppose you want to come in?" I want to get out of this car as soon as possible so I can start pretending none of this ever happened.

"Thanks, but I'll take a rain check on seeing the inside of your home."

"All right. I'm so sorry. What you must think of—"

"Nora. Stop. I don't think any less of you. Just let it go now."

"Okay." I think better of planting a quick kiss goodbye on her cheek. "Thank you so much for taking me home. I owe you."

"You're very welcome," Mimi says, a gorgeous smile on her face.

I could luxuriate in that soft smile of Mimi's for a good long while because it makes me feel instantly better. But I get out quickly and shut the door behind me. My dog sitter, Chad, appears at the front door, three excited creatures behind him.

Princess does that dance with her front paws she always does when she sees me. Izzy yaps until I pick her up. Rogue hangs out at the outskirts of whatever the other two are doing.

I thank Chad for his love and care for my precious babies and sink onto the couch. Princess and Rogue are at my feet, Izzy's on my lap. I text my assistant Mimi's address so she can send flowers. Then, I leave a message with my personal trainer asking for a grueling, punitive session tomorrow, even though Sundays are my only day off from working out.

"Mommy fucked up tonight, babies." Three sets of ears are perked all the way up, yet they don't understand me. That's the beauty of talking to pets. They always listen but they can never judge you. "Mommy tried to kiss another woman." Izzy looks at me as though I just told her I'm going to sell her to the highest bidder. "I know. I shouldn't have done that, but I had too much wine. Story of my life, right?"

I let my head fall back, and Izzy's body heat is so comforting and soothing, and the wine I've drunk all night is still very much in my system, and I've exhausted myself with all my stupid antics to such an extent, I fall asleep on the spot.

When I wake, I'm stretched out in the couch, with both Izzy and Rogue draped over me. Who needs a blanket when you have dogs to keep you warm? As soon as I stir, Princess brings me one of her toys. Instinctively, I reach for my phone. There are messages from my assistant and personal trainer, but also the message Mimi sent last night for me to read again this morning.

No apologies required. Your friend, Mimi.

My head hurts and my mouth is dry, but I can see things clearer now. This message is the very reason I'm drawn to her. I can't explain it to myself any further just yet, but I feel it in my core. I feel something. But I am myself again. I am sober, level-headed Nora Levine and this version of me doesn't go around trying to kiss people. How strong did I come on? Exactly how obnoxiously did I behave? I look at Mimi's message again and it stops my train of thought. What if she's right? What if, surprisingly simply, no apologies are required. She should get a nice bunch of flowers delivered to her doorstep soon enough. Then my phone rings. It's Imani.

"Good morning, sunshine," she says. "How's the head?"

"Oh, god, Imani. I'm so sorry about last night."

"It's all good, Nora. You're probably making it much worse than it really was, but, um… why on earth did you want me to leave so badly?"

"Argh. Don't ask," I groan.

"But I *am* asking."

"I tried to kiss her. I tried to kiss Mimi."

"Tried?" Imani asks, as though she could have easily guessed—or she already knows.

"She stopped me."

"That Mimi is real a class act," Imani says.

"Because she stopped me from kissing her?"

"Because she texted me after she dropped you home last night. And yes, also because she didn't take advantage of a tipsy Nora Levine in her house." Imani chuckles. "Now, would you like to tell me why you suddenly felt the irresistible urge to kiss this woman, aside from drinking too much wine?"

"Oh, I don't know. She's, um…" I can't explain it to Imani either. "I'm attracted to her. There's something about her that gets to me."

"Uh-hum." Imani sounds as though she's got me all figured out already. "She sure is an attractive lady."

"Did you really want to set her up with Simone?"

"Why not?" She clears her throat. "This was before I knew you were attracted to her."

Did I really admit to being attracted to Mimi? I hope this conversation doesn't open a can of worms I'd rather stay closed for the rest of my days.

"Can we keep this between us, please? Let's not involve Jay."

"Really?" Imani's voice drips with disbelief. "You want to keep the fact that you tried to kiss another woman from Juan? Good luck with that, girl."

"It's not as if he can read my mind."

"Maybe not your mind, but the man can read *you*. Besides, Mimi might tell Austin."

Somehow, I'm sure she won't—although I have no idea on what I'm basing my gut instinct and I could also be very wrong. But Imani's right. One scrutinizing look from Juan and I'll give myself away.

"Yeah, okay. I'll tell Jay when he gets back. Have you heard from him?"

"He sent a couple of pics of the view. It looks gorgeous out there."

"Hey, um, did I say anything that was too outrageous or out of line?" What I really mean is something I should be ashamed of, but I never phrase it that way.

"You were absolutely fine, Nora, although nobody can deny that you enjoyed that wine a whole damn lot." Imani chuckles.

"Argh. I know."

"But you were among friends, so you have nothing to worry about. Okay?"

"Yeah. Although Mimi's hardly a friend." I have a text in my phone categorically disputing that statement and the thought of it sends a jolt of something through me.

"But you are attracted to her."

"Yeah, but I was drunk, so it doesn't count."

"Are you saying that if she turned up at your doorstep today and tried to kiss you, you'd stop her?"

"What?" The prospect has me instantly frazzled. "No. I mean, yes. I'm still me. I haven't magically changed or anything."

"All right. Just checking, but Nora, just so you know. You are allowed to change. You are allowed to want whatever it is you want on any given day."

"You know what I want."

"Sure. Does that include the pleasure of my company this afternoon?"

"Yes, please."

A few moments after we've ended our call, my phone beeps with a message.

Thanks for the flowers, Friend. Completely unnecessary, but appreciated nonetheless. Hope you're feeling okay. M. xo

Something tells me I won't be forwarding Mimi's number to anyone else any time soon.

CHAPTER 14
MIMI

"Nora Levine came to dinner?" Heather sounds particularly miffed. "You just called her up and she came over?"

She did much more than that, I think, but I don't want my daughter's brain to explode.

"She and her friend Imani, and Stella Flack and her wife Kate."

"Come on, Mom. You can't keep on teasing us like that."

"Teasing?" Jennifer backs up her sister. "Holding out, more like."

"I don't have to introduce every work colleague to my family. Do I know everyone you work with?"

"You do, as a matter of fact," Jennifer says, and she's right, but her start-up is small, and her co-workers are also her best friends.

"Well, yes, but that's a completely different situation."

"It's okay, Jen," Heather says. "Our time will come. We just have to be patient. We've been waiting twenty-odd years to meet Nora Levine and we're closer than ever."

"I hope it's not that you're afraid of us embarrassing you in front of Nora. Unlike Austin, we know how to behave," Jennifer says.

"Speaking of. Did you see those pics your brother sent?"

"Don't change the subject." Heather fixes her gaze on the huge bouquet of lilies in the middle of the dining table. "What did you make for Nora, anyway? That must have been some meal if she sent you those after."

Nora trying to kiss me last night was wholly unforeseen. Last time I saw her, she barely paid any attention to me. I can only blame it on the excellent wine I served.

"Here's a change of subject for you," Jennifer says. "Guess who I ran into the other day?"

"Of all the people in Los Angeles?" Heather tilts her head. "Can you narrow it down, please?"

"Cathy." Jennifer's done playing the guessing game already. "I went to Palmetto's and there she was, having lunch with her girlfriend."

"Did you talk to her?" Heather asks.

"Of course. I could hardly ignore her."

"What did she say?" It's always hard to get a word in edgeways when the twins are on a roll. It's easier to just let them chat and get the information I want from listening to them.

"She asked how we all were." Jen looks at me. "How Mom was. If you were seeing someone."

"Is she doing well?" I ask.

"She looked like it. Her new girlfriend's at least ten years younger than her, if not more."

"Good for her." Cathy and I separated almost two years ago. I can honestly say I just want the best for her now.

"When are you going to put yourself out there again, Mom?"

Maybe I should try one of those apps Imani mentioned. But it's hard to think of that the morning after Nora Levine tried to kiss me. If it really was a drunken spur-of-the-moment kind of thing, I'm perfectly willing to banish it to the outskirts of my brain forever, but a small part of me would like to simply ask Nora about it in the sober and illuminating light of day. Maybe I should approach Imani and ask her what she thinks I should do.

"You can't force these things." I try to placate the girls so they don't try to set me up with some of their friends' 'questioning' mothers again.

"Of course you can," Heather says. "I wouldn't have two kids right now if I hadn't forced things ten years ago."

"But I already have you." I rest my gaze on my beautiful girls. Just sitting here with them warms me to my core. Most days, it's all I need. Although on other days, admittedly, I do crave a little romance in my life. Someone who makes me feel special. My gaze drifts to the flowers Nora sent. After the girls have left, I may give her a call—just to see how she's doing. To make sure she's not beating herself up on my account.

"Well, yes, we are the best children under the sun, but still…" Heather says.

"But still she won't introduce us to Nora Levine," Jennifer completes her sister's sentence.

"It's not just about what you want. Spare a thought for Nora. How she must feel when I ask her to come over to meet my kids."

"She's met Austin," Heather says. "That spoiled brat always gets everything he wants just 'cause he's the youngest."

"And because he's a man." Jennifer grins.

I shake my head. "I wish I could, but I'm not making any promises with regards to Nora. You're just going to have to find a way to live with that great injustice in your lives."

Jennifer purses her lips. "We'll let you off the hook for now, but, um, did Nora give you any juicy tidbits from her life? She must have revealed something about herself while she was here?"

"Let's just say she's rather fond of a glass of wine and leave it at that." I give them the kind of look that should indicate I'm done talking about this now, but they're not little girls anymore, and it doesn't have the same effect as it used to.

"Oh, my god, Mom. Did Nora Levine get drunk at your house?"

I shake my head. "We all had a bit too much. It was that kind of night," I lie.

"Surely you didn't."

I'm saved by the arrival of the rest of my family, distracting grandkids included.

After everyone has left, with my gaze on those flowers she sent, I call Nora. Heather was right. I can just call up Nora Levine whenever I want. And she did get drunk at my house.

It takes a few rings before my call is answered.

"Hi, this is Imani, answering Nora's phone."

"Oh. Hi."

"Mimi, hey, um, Nora can't come to the phone right now."

"Okay. I just wanted to check in. See how she was feeling."

"She's doing all right. She worked it out with No-Mercy Marcy."

"Excuse me?"

"Her trainer Marcy gave her the workout from hell to pay for all her sins." Is that Nora's voice I hear in the background? And a dog barking?

"That sounds like fun."

"Thank you so much for taking Nora home last night. We both really appreciate it."

"I know. I'm looking at the flowers as we speak." There's complete silence on the other end of the line. "Imani?"

"Yes. Sorry. Nora's being… Nora. Hold on."

I hear fumbling and whispering, followed by a loud thud. Just when I think the call has disconnected, Nora speaks into my ear.

"Hi, Mimi. Sorry about that."

"Thank you for the flowers. They're gorgeous." What I really want to ask is exactly how drunk Nora was and whether the irresistible urge to kiss me has left her completely. Whether it's true what she said—that she would never—*ever*—do something like that when sober.

"Thank you for last night. I had such a good time." This is not the Nora who was at my house last night. This is the Nora Levine with her walls all drawn up and all the windows and doors firmly shut. But last night, I did see a crack in that heavy-duty armor she wears. And drunk or not, she made a move. Maybe it's my turn now.

"Would you like to grab a coffee sometime this week? Maybe after you wrap for the day?"

"Oh. Um, you want to have coffee," Nora repeats.

"Say yes," I clearly hear Imani say in the background. So much for Nora having a private conversation.

"Imani's telling me to say yes."

"Imani's a good friend who only has your best interests at heart, maybe you should listen to her." I push a little because I think I've earned the right.

Nora chuckles. "Maybe, but I'm not really the coffee-grabbing kind. Why don't you come to my house?"

"I'd love that very much."

"Tomorrow after work?" Nora says, as though we work in an office together.

"I know the way."

"I'll text you when I'm home."

"See you then, Nora. Take care."

We hang up and, again, none of this has gone as I had expected. Nora's an expert at sending mixed signals, what with having her friend pick up the phone when I call, but then, pretty easily, agreeing to meeting up, even though she sounded as though that was the last thing on her mind. But hey, I'm going over to Nora's house tomorrow. And she did still try to kiss me. Some sort of progress is being made, although I'm not quite sure yet toward what.

CHAPTER 15
NORA

"Girls." Juan heaves his most dramatic sigh yet. "I'm so in love. What am I going to do? Why didn't you tell me this is what it feels like?" He's just arrived at my house after his weekend away with Austin and it's a welcome reprieve from what's been going on in my head since Mimi called.

"We're not exactly experts," Imani deadpans.

"You are." Juan looks into Imani's eyes. "Nora's a lost cause."

"A lost cause who—" I start to protest.

"I wouldn't be so sure of that," Imani cuts me off.

"What do you mean?" Juan straightens his spine. "Did something happen this weekend?" He knots his eyebrows together. "Weren't you having dinner with Austin's mom?"

"And Stella and Kate," I say, stalling. But I have to tell Juan. I want to tell him, but him dating Austin makes it awkward in a way I'm not used to.

Imani gives me a look.

"What did I miss?" Juan pushes a strand of hair away from his face. He looks tired and glowing at the same time.

"I had a little too much to drink at Mimi's and I stayed after everyone left."

"Imani included?" He narrows his eyes, drawing conclusions.

"Oh yeah," Imani says. "I was swiftly woman-handled out of the door."

"Whaaaat?" Juan tips his head.

"I got a little carried away and I, um, I tried to kiss Mimi. She turned me down gently."

"Okay. Wait." Juan inhales deeply, then slowly breathes out. "So much to unpack." He starts counting on his fingers. "One: you tried to kiss another woman. Two: that woman is my boyfriend's mother. Three: she turned you down? What the hell? I go away for a weekend and everything I once knew is no more."

I burst out laughing, partly out of nerves and partly because Juan is such an expert at defusing tension. All he has to do is turn up, really.

"Four," Imani adds. "Mimi's coming over here tomorrow." She flashes me a triumphant smile. If she hadn't been here, urging me to say yes, I probably wouldn't have.

"Oh my god, Nora," Juan fans his face with his fingers. "Are you going to be my mother-in-law?"

"Pull yourself together, Jay." Imani bumps her hip against his side and sits next to him. "It all started when I suggested introducing Mimi to Simone, and Nora protested a little too much."

"You like Mimi?" he asks me, then looks at Imani. "Did we see this coming?"

"We did not, Jay, but how could we? It has come completely out of left field. Nora has blindsided us, her two best friends. Her family."

It's precisely because Juan and Imani always find a way to make everything about themselves that I love them so much.

"Tell me about that kiss," Juan says.

"There wasn't one." I'm unsure whether I'm glad about that or not. I suspect, deep down, I'm not, but I'm not yet willing to admit it to myself. "I might have bridged some distance between our lips, but Mimi respectfully pulled away. Because I'd had too much to drink to consent."

"For real?" Juan asks. "What a woman. In a perfect world, that would be what any decent human being would do, but boy-oh-boy, is this world imperfect or what?"

"It wasn't just that she didn't take advantage of the situation. She was so nice," I say. "So... understanding and caring and worried. Even though I was behaving like an asshole, she still put me first. She put *my* feelings first."

"You are starring in one of her shows," Juan says.

"No. I mean, yes, that's true, but that's not why she was so courteous with me. She wasn't nice to me because I'm Nora Levine. She was nice despite... because of who I really am. I seem to amuse her instead of annoying her."

"Oh, Nora." Imani touches my foot with hers.

"Trust me, darling," Juan says. "Nora Levine or not, if you really were such an annoying bitch I wouldn't still be around after all these years."

"What he said." Imani points at Juan.

"It's different with you guys." I'm not going through the whole rigmarole of explaining to them how, since *High Life,* so many people have ended up bitterly disappointed after meeting me, simply because I wasn't the person they expected me to be —because I'm just me.

"Anyway, let's move on, because this is far from processed," Juan says. "You've had all day to come to terms with this plot twist in Nora's life, but I haven't. Why didn't you call me?"

"Because you were busy falling in love, darling," Imani says.

"Looks like I'm not the only one." Juan glances at me.

"Let's not get carried away." I like Mimi, but I'm not about to fall in love with her.

"The real question is," Juan says, wisely choosing a different direction for the conversation. "Do you still want to kiss Mimi now?" His gaze on me is piercing.

"That is the million-dollar question." Imani joins Juan in staring at me.

"I don't know, you guys."

"Bullshit," Juan says. "Of course, you know."

"You have to want to know," Imani adds.

"What's that supposed to mean?" I ask.

Imani purses her lips and gives me a look saying, "Girl, you know."

"I kind of look forward to seeing her tomorrow," I admit. "But it's just coffee. And actually, on the way home after dinner, Mimi and I kind of decided we can be friends. That we are friends. And friends meet up and chat, like we are doing right now. It's more like that. It's no longer about kissing her."

"Darling." Juan leans forward and puts his hands on my knees. "I'm only going to say this once." Even though I don't know what he's going to say, there's no way he will only say it the one time. It's not how he's wired. "Let yourself have this. Enjoy it. Whatever it is. Don't... stop it before it can be anything."

"I won't. Maybe a friend like Mimi is what I've been looking for."

Juan inhales sharply. "You can't just add my boyfriend's mother to the entourage."

"I can kiss her, but I can't be her friend?" My turn to stare at him intently.

"It's complicated. Give my poor old brain some time to absorb all of this. It's a miracle my brain's still working at all after the weekend I've had. If Mimi's anything like her son, I say, latch on right away and don't let her go any time soon." He bursts out laughing. "Listen to me. I'm terrible."

"Come on." Imani squeezes his knee. "Give us the downlow on your dirty weekend."

"It's not just that it was dirty, although it sure was." Juan grins. "Austin's just so kind and wholesome, as if he doesn't have a bad bone in his body. As if he never even has a negative thought. He's so upbeat and gorgeous, it's infectious. I can barely stand to be away from him, but, you know, we're not lesbians like that." He winks at Imani. "No offense, darling."

"None taken." Imani huffs out some air. "Looks like I'm the only one in the entourage without a love interest. I never saw that coming."

"Guys," I say. "Mimi's *not* my love interest."

They both look at me as though I might as well have just said I'm not really Nora Levine.

I'm tired after a long day on set and, especially on a Monday, I normally wouldn't meet up with anyone in the evening—not even my two closest friends. Somehow, over the weekend, I lost my senses enough to agree to have Mimi come over 'for coffee', whatever that really means. I'm about to find out. I've just let her car through the gate. I take a few deep breaths. Just friends, I remind myself, we are just friends.

Mimi might not be movie-star dazzling—no one is, for that matter—but she has style and grace in spades. She's wearing one of those tight skirts again, so tight they make her hips sashay as though she were on a catwalk. She's carrying a bunch of flowers, which dangle from one hand as she places the other gently on my shoulder.

Her lips brush my cheek, then she holds up the flowers. "I thought it only polite to return the favor."

"Thank you so much." It's hard to say whether the flowery scent engulfing my nose only emanates from the bouquet. When she leans toward me, Mimi smells divine, like the freshest bunch of spring blooms.

I usher her inside, but she's taking her time.

"Fuck me, Nora." She gazes into the living room from the doorway.

Already? I want to joke, but I'm not sure we're at that level where I can.

"I need a moment to take in the splendor."

I'm proud of my house, but it's not as though I built it myself, nor am I responsible for most of the interior design choices. But it is my personal cocoon, the place where I spend most of my time, and where I regain my inner peace after a long day on set. It's also my private hiding space, and not many people actually set foot in here.

Princess, always the most curious and forward, greets Mimi. Izzy and Rogue are more wary and keep their distance.

"I forgot to ask if you're okay with dogs."

"Sure." Mimi gives Princess a good scratch between the ears. "No problem." She attempts to crouch down to greet the other two, but it's a hard thing to do in a skirt like that. "I'll meet those other two cuties later."

She walks forward slowly, letting her gaze linger on a few objects, until it's irresistibly pulled to where it's designed to go. The massive patio off the living room. The windows are folded all the way open and beyond and below, Los Angeles sparkles in the dusk.

"I totally get why anyone who lives here would be a homebody." She turns to me with a smile on her lips. "Let's never meet at my house again." She makes a beeline for the frameless glass railing at the end of the patio.

"It's only the house that *High Life* bought."

"*You* bought it and *you* earned it, Nora." She turns to the spectacular view again. "Thank you so much for inviting me."

"My pleasure." It really is. As much as I like to crash into the couch with my dogs on a Monday night, it's lovely to have her here, to invite her particular energy into my home. "Have you talked to Austin?"

She nods. "I didn't tell him about what happened."

"I told Juan and I thought it unfair to demand he keep my

scandalous behavior from Austin, with you being his mother and all."

"Okay." She nods pensively. "I'll give him a call later. It's better if Austin doesn't tell his sisters. Their poor fangirl brains might not be able to take it."

"But as we agreed, nothing really happened. Right?"

"Exactly." Mimi pins her gaze on me. The smile disappears briefly from her face as she, perhaps, tries to read me.

"What can I get you?" I double my own smiling efforts. "Any kind of coffee or something else?"

"I'd ask you for one of those complicated coffee beverages for the sheer pleasure of watching you make it, but I'll just have some water, please."

Mimi must be the most well-hydrated person in all of LA. Maybe that's the secret of her smooth skin—constant hydration from the inside out.

"Coming right up. Make yourself comfortable."

"I'd love a peek at your kitchen."

"Of course. Follow me."

The dogs saunter behind us as we head to the kitchen.

"I don't want to sound like a broken record, but, fuck me again." She briefly holds two fingers in front of her lips—the ones I tried to kiss last Saturday. "And pardon my French, of course."

"It's all right. The doggies can take it." I flash her a smile. "And so can I." I pour us both some of the lemon-and-mint water my fridge is always stocked with.

CHAPTER 16
MIMI

We're sitting on Nora's patio, the magnificent view in front of us, a large pool to the right. Next to the pool house, I spot a gym with all sorts of equipment. That must be where Nora sculpts that almost impossible body for someone above fifty.

"Austin's going to lose it if you ever invite him here." Even water tastes better when you drink it in this environment. I've been to a few spectacular Hollywood mansions over the years, but there's something extra dazzling about Nora's house—maybe because this is her most-private territory. Or maybe just because she lives here, and she has invited me to spend time here with her—although, technically, I suppose I invited myself.

"I guess that's the next step in his and Juan's relationship." Nora tucks a leg underneath her. "I really like Austin, and not just because my best friend is crazy about him. He's such a nice guy."

A compliment about one of my kids is always going to improve my mood. "Austin's my baby. Odds were he was going to turn out a spoiled brat, but it never happened." The twins were thirteen when their little brother was born, on the cusp of puberty, but still they couldn't help but dote on him, despite all the hormones raging in their bodies. Lauren was eleven and, at least for a few years, couldn't get enough of the real-life doll that was suddenly living in her house.

"Surely, that's a credit to your talents as a mother."

"I'll take it." Nora's looking delicious and relaxed tonight. Her pug—Izzy, I believe—is snoring in her lap. Nora caresses her little head. "As much as I've always loved work, for the past thirty-nine years, I've always been a mother first. Everything changes, just like that and forever, when you have your first child. Or in my case, children."

"Twins, yeah. That must have been something."

"You don't have any siblings, do you?"

Nora shakes her head. "Just parents I don't really talk to." She says it as though it's something she has accepted a long time ago.

"May I ask why? Tell me if I'm being too nosy."

"I did try to kiss you, so I can hardly play the discretion card any longer."

"I'm glad you're not being hard on yourself for that any longer."

"Someone sent me a text saying I shouldn't." Nora grins at me. Her magnificent upper arms gleam in the light of the setting sun.

"Sounds like a wise person."

Nora nods. "You could be right."

"So? Your parents?" I urge, before we go off track again.

"My parents… They… Compared to Juan and Imani, I got very lucky with my parents. They tried their best and they love me, that much I know, but, um." She takes a sip of water. For all the glorification of alcohol, I've always thought it a million times more fascinating to talk to a non-intoxicated person. Nora comes across as so much more sincere than when she was drunk at my house. "I guess the problem between me and my parents is that we're too alike. None of us excel at communication. We don't know how to really talk to each other so, over the years, we've kind of stopped."

As a mother, that sounds horrifying. "You don't check in once in a while?"

"Maybe the odd text now and then."

My heart sinks as I empathize with Nora's parents. It must show on my face, because Nora looks at me and asks, "What?"

"I'm not judging you, but I'm a mother and…"

"Being someone's mother doesn't entitle you to anything. Look at Juan and Imani's mothers. What does it mean to Juan's mother that she has this amazing man as her son? She doesn't even know what a great person he is."

"Okay. Sure." I touched a nerve.

"Some women shouldn't be mothers," Nora says.

"Agreed." We're being a bit harsh, yet it's true.

"Yet so many are."

"Most people do their best, of that I'm convinced," I say.

"Not Juan's mother. Not Imani's, either."

"Are you okay, Nora?" The dog stirs in her lap, picking up her sudden agitation, no doubt.

"I am." She calms Izzy down. "I know I'm one of the lucky ones. The stories I've heard from some of the people at the LGBT Center." She shakes her head.

"Yeah." I can only imagine.

"And age is hardly an excuse. You're what? In your fifties?"

"A lady never tells." I wave off my own comment. "Actually, I'm not one of those women who is hung up over her age, just because the patriarchy tells me to be."

"You're not past your sell-by date just yet." Nora's smile lifts the mood instantly. "As we established last Saturday."

"Hell no. I'm sixty-five, by the way."

Nora just nods in response, then she breaks into a grin again. "I'm not going to lie, that was the first time I've tried to kiss a woman in her sixties."

"How about a man in his sixties?" Maybe Nora referring to that non-kiss a few times has thrown me.

Nora's eyes go wide, but then she regroups. "Can't say I've tried that either."

"I'm sorry. The kids were grilling Juan mercilessly about you when he came to brunch. He didn't give much away, just so you know."

"I'm bisexual, but I haven't been in a relationship, by choice, for years."

"Okay." Nora trying to kiss me, albeit under the influence, was already quite flattering, but hearing it's such a rare occurrence, feels like I just sprouted a set of wings. "Austin did say that you might be a bit like Jennifer." If she's really like Jennifer, I'll know not to expect any more attempts at kissing me ever again.

"Oh, yes, your self-partnered daughter." Nora nods. "I told you, didn't I? The other night? Being single is so underrated."

"Hm. I can't say I fully agree."

"Oh, yes. You're *looking*. Did you talk to Imani about any of those apps?"

Does Nora know she's driving me a little crazy with this? Referencing the kiss that never happened one minute while alluding to her firm choice of being single the next? Maybe she's so out of practice with flirting, she doesn't even realize she's doing it.

"Not yet." Izzy heaves a big sigh in Nora's lap, adequately expressing how I'm feeling right now. But I'd be a fool to expect anything from Nora. Maybe it's me who wants her signals to be mixed. But what if I hadn't stopped her from kissing me? What would we be doing now?

"I'll nudge her tomorrow," Nora says.

"Please, don't. You don't have to do that."

"Oh, you're not looking anymore?" Izzy has suddenly had enough of her nap and jumps out of Nora's lap. She joins the golden retriever on the floor by Nora's feet.

"One of the reasons I asked you for coffee was because I thought we should talk about the other night," I say. "I don't want you to feel bad about it. That's not what I'm after. I just want to… know, I guess, if it was all because of the wine or if there was something more to it than that."

Nora looks away briefly. It's getting darker but I can tell her cheeks have pinked up. "I'm very bad at this," she whispers, so I can barely make it out. "Which is why I prefer to simply stay away from romance. I'm really bad at all of it. Luckily, I'm very fond of my own company. I'm not looking, like you are. I—um. Yeah." She runs out of steam. "Earlier, when I said that everyone in my family sucks at communication. This is exactly what I meant by that."

Having raised four children through the big and small dramas of adolescence, I happen to know a thing or two about flawed communication. About words that come out all wrong and about saying the opposite of what you really want to say.

"I don't think you're bad at communication at all, Nora. You did a pretty good job of conveying to me that almost-kiss was a mistake."

"No," Nora says. "You're jumping to conclusions."

"Okay. I'm sorry about that. So you did really want to kiss me?" I've always had a special talent for coaxing secrets out of my children—and I've had plenty of time to practice. Although I don't want to compare Nora Levine to any of my children when they were teenagers and their brains weren't fully formed yet.

"Yes," she blurts out. "Because I like you. A lot. But I would never do anything like that when I'm not tipsy. Like right now, fully sober, I'd never pull a stunt like that. Because of how I am and because of what I want in life. But I understand that it's confusing for you, Mimi. I really do. For that, I am really sorry, even though you'll probably tell me that no apologies are necessary."

"So, what is it that you want in life exactly?"

With every time I make her repeat things, I hope she'll reveal a bit more valuable information to me.

"I don't want a relationship." Nora shakes her head vehemently. "But… I am attracted to you."

Right. That's the rest of my conversation strategy successfully torpedoed. Nora Levine is attracted to me. My body can't help but react. Heat washes over me. Because, damn, if I'm not very much attracted to her in return. But, as it stands, there's not much I can do about it. I also don't know how to respond to that.

"Oh, Nora," I say on a sigh. "Just so we're clear, I'm attracted to you as well. It's only fair that you know that."

"I don't do one-night stands either," Nora blurts out. "God, sorry. I'm not saying that's what—Argh. Fuck."

This situation is completely different than trying to get a child to confess a minor sin to their parent. It couldn't be more different. I have skin in this game, too. And Nora is an adult woman with some serious issues.

"It's okay. It's all good." I should have broached the subject in a less direct manner, perhaps. But I truly believed I could be direct with Nora—that she would appreciate it.

"I'm not good with emotions either, so now you know why I'm the worst relationship material you'll ever meet."

Poor Nora. Is this really how she feels about herself? I have to stop myself from going to her, from wrapping my arms around her and making sure she knows she doesn't owe me anything—that being friends with her is more than enough, if that's the boundary she's setting.

"That's why I became an actor. Everything I have to say is written out for me, and so is everything my character has to feel. It's the perfect job for me."

"You're damn good at it." Time for me to bottle my own feelings. I might be looking, but I'm not looking to persuade anyone into something they don't want—no matter what

Nora's reasons are for not wanting a relationship, I have to respect them.

"Yeah." Her voice breaks. She looks at the floor, where her dogs are gathered at her feet—and my heart breaks a little for her. But it's not for me to jump to any conclusions, despite it being very tempting. I can only let Nora be who she wants to be. It's not up to me to try and change her—or her views about herself.

"As I said before, we can be friends." I try to keep my voice level. It's not so much sadness for myself I feel—although part of me was hoping to have this conversation go in the opposite direction—but for Nora.

"That would be nice." She reaches down and scoops up Izzy. She holds her dog close to her chest. "Although Juan said we can't just add his boyfriend's mother to the entourage."

"Entourage, huh?" I send her my warmest smile.

"I get it if you want to leave now that things have become awkward."

"What kind of friend would that make me?" I try to look into her eyes, but Nora keeps glancing away. "Unless you want me to leave."

Nora shakes her head. "I would like it very much if you stayed a while."

CHAPTER 17
NORA

I royally fucked everything up again, Nora-Levine style. I shouldn't have allowed Mimi to get under my skin, but how do you stop something like that? I haven't met anyone who makes me feel the way she does in such a long time, it seems I've forgotten how to protect myself. Now, here we sit, in the sort of dreadful silence that makes me doubt everything about myself and my life. But I asked her to stay. I might have only drunk water, but I'm not sure I have full use of all my faculties. Mimi's so sweet and such a good sport—no wonder I'm so drawn to her.

"Of course, I'll stay," Mimi says. "And I won't consider myself a member of your entourage just yet."

I chuckle and bury my face in Izzy's fur for a moment, before putting her down next to her sister again.

"Speaking of," Mimi continues. "Juan regaled me and the girls with the story of how he met you."

"At the LGBT Center?" I smile at the memory. "You should have seen Jay back then. Despite his history, he was full of bravado already. He changed my life, you know, that guy. He's the closest to having a husband I'll ever come." What a strange thing to say to the mother of the man Juan is actually dating. "I mean, um, we've never, obviously. He's not interested in me that way, and vice versa."

"I get it," Mimi says. "What about Imani?"

With all the verbal mishaps I've had with Mimi, she's never made me feel bad for any of them. She just moves on as if it's a normal conversation, as if I'm as fluent in the art of chitchat as anyone else.

"Juan met Imani at the Center, not long after we met. I think he saw a lot of himself, of his own story, in hers. Shared parental rejection makes for a strong bond. He introduced us and it's been the three of us ever since." I stretch out my legs, relaxing a little. It's always easier to talk about other people than about myself. "It's not all been hunky-dory. All three of us have come a long way, but here we are. On the other side of a lot of bull-shit, and ready for whatever else life will throw at us. I know, for an absolute fact, they will always be there for me. That all three of us will always be there for each other, no matter what. Their friendship is the best part of my life. It's the most precious thing to me." I'm about to well up. Juan and Imani are that special to me.

"It's lovely that you found each other."

"Yeah." I blink back a tear. "I really hope it works out between Jay and Austin. He might not be your first choice for a boyfriend for your son. He's a lot, but he has a heart of gold." And the attention span of a very horny goldfish, I don't say out loud.

"Austin's smart enough to make good choices," Mimi says. I've heard her say plenty of things with much more conviction in her voice. "He's made a few what I might call mistakes, but are they really mistakes if these men made him happy at the time? What's a mistake, really?" She holds up her hand. "For the record, I don't regard Juan as a mistake. I've really taken to him. So have the girls." She pauses. "They keep nagging me about meeting you, by the way. But don't worry. I won't put you through that."

"I can, you know? I can meet your daughters. If we're going to be friends, maybe I should."

"You don't have to do anything that makes you uncomfortable. Not for my sake. Really."

"You're a very unlikely TV executive. You seem entirely too nice for your profession."

"We come in all shapes, sizes, and personalities."

"You look the part, which had a lot to do with my first reaction to you that day you crashed our table read. You're all gloss and expensive clothes, which really suit you, by the way. But getting to know you, you're nothing like the image you portray."

Mimi wriggles around and smiles at me. "I'll take that as a compliment."

"Also, how can someone like you be *looking*?"

Mimi bursts into a chuckle now. "For a friend, you're awfully flirty, Nora."

"Oh. Sorry. That's not what I meant. I'm just trying to understand." My never-ending quest for an explanation for every little thing is messing with my conversation skills again. I wasn't deliberately flirting. I'm just incorrigibly curious.

"I had a long-term relationship end about two years ago. It takes a while to get over something like that. To find yourself again."

"How long were you and this person together?"

"Nearly eight years."

"That's a long time." I can't even begin to imagine what that's like.

"Given that I was married to a man for much longer, and had four kids along the way, it's not that long, but yeah…" She squares her shoulders. "I guess what I'm really trying to say is, if it had been up to me, it would have lasted a lot longer."

"Did she dump you?" I assume her ex is a woman.

"Dump?" Mimi scoffs. "I hate that word. As though I'm a

piece of trash to be discarded after use." She clears her throat. "I guess, technically, Cathy broke up with me, yes."

From where I'm sitting, it's hard to imagine why anyone in their right mind would break up with the likes of Mimi St James. Right now, she comes across as some unattainable goddess any human should be so lucky to be with. But I should really get a grip. I'm not going to throw away my desire to remain single even for Mimi, no matter how amazing, interesting, and lovely she is. I let her talk—let her be the judge of what she's comfortable sharing.

"People change over time," she says. "I'm not always the easiest to be around either. No one is."

"Are you still in touch?"

Mimi shakes her head.

"I would like to meet your daughters." If I can't give Mimi anything else, apart from what I can offer in the friendship department, I'll give her that. "I've met Austin and I'm curious to meet your other kids. I really am."

"There comes my multiple mother-of-the-year award." Mimi smiles from ear to ear. "Thank you so much. It will make them so very happy." She holds up her hand. "I'm not kidding. They won't just be happy. They will be beside themselves. There are no limits to how much these girls adore you. If you think Austin was something else, that's nothing compared to how the girls will react."

"In that case, are you sure you want me to meet them?" I can really only be a disappointment in the face of that level of fandom.

"Absolutely."

"Bring them around this weekend. I'll have Ricky, my chef, set up the grill by the pool. We'll make an afternoon of it."

"Are you sure?" Mimi sounds as incredulous as that time Stella and Kate told her how they met.

"Yeah. Juan and Imani will be here. It'll be a proper St James pool party." It's easy enough to say. On the day itself, I might have to knock back a glass or two of wine to get through it, but as long as I don't try to kiss Mimi again, things will be all right.

"Whatever plans my kids already have for this weekend, consider them canceled." Mimi's smile has reached her eyes. "Thank you so much. Nothing makes me happier than seeing my kids happy, no matter how silly they're behaving."

"What am I doing?" I complain to Juan. "Have I lost my mind completely?"

"You might have." He gives me a once-over. "This is very un-Nora-like behavior. First you try to kiss Mimi and now you've invited her entire family over for a pool party. At your own house." He peers into my eyes. "Has the real Nora Levine been abducted by aliens, and are you an imposter?"

"I think she might have been. I don't know who I am, anymore." Although I was very much myself when I was talking to Mimi last night, explaining in my very stunted ways, that I don't do relationships.

"You know I'm always up for a party, and it kind of feels like my family is going to hang out with my boyfriend's family," Juan holds out his hand. "But let's break this down, darling. Let me analyze this for you." I put my hand in his. "You told Mimi you're attracted to her, but that you're not interested in her, after which you proceeded to invite her family to a party at your house. Talk about some serious mixed messaging."

"Argh. I know."

"Could it be"—Juan gently rubs his thumb over my wrist—"that you're simply scared? That you are interested in pursuing something with Mimi, but you feel it's not true to yourself. To whom you've become."

"Jay." I try to pull my hand away, but he doesn't let me. "She thinks she likes me, but… she can't really like me. She's still dazzled by my name and what it stands for."

"It's so insulting to me when you call yourself unlikeable when I've been your best friend for two decades. If you're as unlikeable as you always claim to be, what does that make me? Some stupid star-crazy fool?"

"You're an exception. So is Imani."

"So what you're saying is that Imani and I are the only two people in the world who can like the real Nora Levine? I know you don't believe in therapy, girl, but you should really reconsider."

"That's not what I was trying to say."

"Uh-hum." Juan drums his fingertips on the palm of my hand. "Sure, darling."

"What I'm really trying to say is that my reasons for wanting to be single haven't changed."

"Sounds to me as though they have and, for the record, that's completely okay. As I've said a thousand times before, it's okay to change your mind. It's okay to be attracted to another human. In fact, it's very human, and in case you've forgotten you're human too, Nora."

"I don't need a therapist as long as I have you." I've had enough of this now.

"True. By the way, I decided not to inform Austin that you tried to kiss his mother."

"You didn't tell him?"

Juan shakes his head. "I'm not going to tell him anything about that until something… more happens. Until there's actually something to tell."

"Thanks, Jay. I appreciate that."

"I did it for Austin most of all. Imagine him finding out his own mother is fooling around with Nora Levine." He puffs up his cheeks. "His mind would be too blown."

Did he just say 'until something more happens'? When I first met Juan, I had a few tries at a relationship, but it never amounted to anything. *High Life* had properly screwed me up by then. Twenty years down the line—twenty years of being a recluse and trying to find my real self again—nothing much has changed. But still, when he puts it like that, a part of me wants to find out what the 'more' in what he just said could be. If it could be delightful instead of mortifying. Thrilling instead of terrifying. Wonderful instead of doomed from the very start.

CHAPTER 18
MIMI

Jennifer in particular is glued to Nora's side. She doesn't have a significant other to pay attention to or children to keep an eye on—although both Heather and Lauren are doing a good job of ignoring their husbands in favor of Nora as well.

Bobby and Gus have taken up residence by the grill, where Nora's chef is preparing tasteful bite after tasteful bite—and a non-stop buffet of sliders for the kids.

Imani is in the pool with Wyatt and Lucas, teaching them some sort of complicated somersault dive.

"I'll never forget you did this for us, Mom." Heather has sidled up to me. She even puts her arm around me. I'd expect this kind of gratitude after babysitting her boys for a full weekend and giving her some much-needed time off. But to them, Nora is so special, this is the treat of a lifetime.

Apparently, Juan didn't tell Austin about Nora trying to kiss me last weekend, so he's none the wiser, which is for the best.

"Don't thank me, darling. Thank Nora."

"Can you believe this place? That view is to die for." Her gaze is pulled to the cityscape below us. "Does this mean Nora and you are the kind of friends who hang out at each other's houses all the time?"

"We'll have to see about that." I glance over at Nora. Jennifer is talking her ear off about something, but Nora doesn't seem perturbed. They look like they're having a pleasant chat. My mind is pulled back to the conversation I had with Nora on this very patio a few days ago.

"She's so nice. So... down-to-earth." All my daughters sound as though they have a massive crush on Nora today.

"I could get used to this." Austin joins us. "Nora's the closest thing to family Juan has, so I think I will get used to it, thank you very much."

"Oh, yesss!" Lauren shouts from the side of the pool. "Turn it up, please. It's the new Other Women tune." I'll need to keep my eye on her. Someone's been a bit heavy-handed with the champagne—I suspect Juan. "Time to dance!" Someone must have heard her, because the music's suddenly a lot louder. Lauren jumps up and starts dancing.

"I knew Lauren would embarrass herself," Austin says. "I've got this." Instead of having the music turned down again and coaxing his sister into a chair, he joins her. They're dancing in front of the pool and I can only be filled with joy as I watch them. Juan starts shaking his hips as well.

I glance over at Nora to gauge how she feels about this sudden rowdiness. Our eyes lock for a split-second. She seems okay. Jennifer gets up and joins her siblings on the pool-side dance floor.

"I'm going to check on Nora," I say to Heather.

"I'm going to dance." Jennifer's already pulling her toward the others.

I join Nora on a lounge chair a few feet away from the make-shift dancefloor.

"I hope this is not too out-of-control for you."

"It's absolutely fine." Nora reaches for her champagne glass. "In fact, I might join them. Your kids are so sweet, Mimi. Just like you." She chuckles. "And they sure can bust a move." This is the version of Nora who came to dinner at my house—who tried to kiss me. She's not the only one to have had too much champagne this afternoon—it's the kind of event for it. "Do you want to dance with me?" Her eyes are pleading and watery as she looks at me.

"No, I'm going to leave that to my kids." I lean toward her. "Are you sure you're okay?"

"Oh, yeah. I can't get through an afternoon like this without some liquid courage. But I'm fine. Perfect. I just had a very interesting conversation with Jennifer about the joys of being single. I like her and what she has to say. A lot."

"I think that feeling's fairly mutual."

"Please excuse me, but I'm a huge fan of The Other Women. I simply have to dance to this song." Nora jumps up. She's wearing nothing but a bikini and it's hard not to look at her perfectly sculpted body. I've caught glimpses, mainly of her arms and impressive shoulder line, but Nora in a bikini is something else.

The kids go berserk with Nora dancing between them. The smiles on their faces are like the ones they sported on Christmas morning when they were younger.

"Come on, Mama." Juan shuffles toward me and beckons me to him. "Dance with us."

When Nora said pool party, I wasn't expecting this. But the kids are elated, champagne's been flowing freely, and everyone's having a wonderful time. Imani has helped the boys out of the pool and even my grandsons are doing something that looks like dancing. Bobby and Gus still can't get enough of that state-of-the-art grill—they couldn't be more stereotypically heterosexual if they tried.

The girls and Austin have formed a tiny circle around Nora, who seems to enjoy being the center of attention for once. I let Juan pull me up, because why the hell not? I can let my hair down. And I made this happen for my kids.

Juan twirls me around and it's easy, riveting even, to dance with him and my kids and Nora. I have no idea who has taken control of the music—just like it's hard to say exactly how many people have been working behind the scenes of this party this afternoon—but everyone keeps going as the songs change. I let myself be carried by the vibe of the afternoon, of this impromptu dance party, of being here at Nora's house, surrounded by the people I love the most.

"And she can dance as well." Nora flings an arm around my shoulders. "You are a woman of many talents, Mimi." She holds up a glass of water. "Don't worry, I'm done with the strong stuff."

"Nora." Jennifer joins us. We've been here all afternoon, but none of my daughters have had enough of Nora yet. "If you ever need a house sitter, I volunteer my services. I love dogs, too, so I've got the furries covered as well."

"I'll keep that in mind," Nora says.

"Don't let her talk you into anything." Lauren turns up, Gus hot on her heels. "I wish we could stay longer, but we have to get back to the babysitter."

"Maybe we can do it again sometime," Nora says, to my surprise. "It was great having you over."

"Someone's phone is blowing up over here," the chef shouts from the grill. It's been the kind of afternoon that had everyone not care if they were a few feet removed from their phone—not a mean feat for my kids.

"That might me be." Jennifer kisses her sister and brother-in-law goodbye and goes to fetch her phone.

Bobby stands next to me. "If we don't take those boys home, I'm afraid Imani might not survive."

"I don't want to go home!" Wyatt shouts from the pool.

Imani whispers something in his ear. She's indefatigable, or maybe she's just good at hiding it. I glance at Nora from the corner of my eye, to see how tired a raucous afternoon with my offspring has left her. She doesn't have the same freshness of face about her than she did a few hours earlier, that's for sure. Juan and Austin are canoodling in the far corner of the patio.

"Oh, shit. I'm really sorry," Jennifer rushes toward us. "There's something going on with our server. I have to go put out some fires. Damn it." She looks at Nora as though she might never see her again. "This afternoon was a dream, Nora. Seriously. You have no idea." She clutches her hands to her chest. "I know I'll never be able to return this favor, but if there's ever anything I can do for you, just hit me up."

Everyone's saying goodbye in quick succession. Meeting the idol from their teenage days or not, my daughters are women in their thirties with busy lives and, in Heather's case, worn-out children.

Juan and Austin say they're taking this party elsewhere and depart, leaving just me, Imani, and Nora. And a few people cleaning up behind us.

"How about one final glass of champagne?" Nora says. "Just the three of us."

"Seriously, Nora, I think I need to lie down," Imani says. "Those kids have worn me out."

"Do you want to stay here?" Nora asks.

"I'm going home if that's okay with you. I have the early shift tomorrow, but I'll come by in the afternoon."

Nora and Imani hug each other tightly. By the time Imani leaves, it's as though the entire patio has been cleaned of any remnants of the party that just took place here.

"I know better than to offer you champagne." Nora has wrapped herself in a colorful sarong against the evening chill in the air. She moves her elbow backward and presses her fingertips into her shoulder blade. "I think I pulled a muscle while dancing with your kids. Truth be told, I don't dance a whole lot." She grimaces. "Does the *Unbreak My Heart* insurance policy cover injuries sustained while entertaining one of the producers?"

"I'd have to look into that, but you have a full day to recover tomorrow."

"I'll get a massage and I should be good as new. Issa, my massage therapist, has hands of gold."

"My ex used to be a massage therapist. She taught me a few tricks. Would you like me to…" I nod at her shoulder. "Have a look at that?"

"Um, sure."

I rise and take a deep breath. But isn't this the friendly thing to do?

CHAPTER 19
NORA

"Jesus, Nora." Mimi's thumbs skate along my shoulders. "When was the last time you had a massage? Your shoulders are incredibly tight."

"A couple of days ago," I say.

"You're so tense."

Maybe because Mimi's hands are dancing across my skin. "In case you missed it, I'm not really a people person."

Mimi's thumbs dig in and it hurts so good.

"I really couldn't tell by looking at you this afternoon."

"I'm a highly paid actor." I lean into her touch. "Not that I was pretending. I do like your family. But that party was exhausting."

Mimi's thumbs slide gently along my neck into my hair. My skin breaks out in gooseflesh.

"Sore shoulders are the price I pay for pretending to be social for a couple of hours," I mumble. "My god, that feels good."

"I'm glad."

"Your ex didn't just leave you with a broken heart, then." I'm just saying things. I've used up all my common sense and acceptable conversation skills this afternoon.

"Indeed, she left me with some serious skills." Mimi's thumb pushes onto a particularly painful point at the base of my skull. "Skills I haven't practiced in too long."

"Are you some sort of renaissance woman who can do just about anything?" It's easier to chat when I can't see Mimi's face.

"I can't act to save my life, so I wouldn't call me that." There's plenty of glee in Mimi's voice. Her hands on me are increasingly divine.

"We all have our strengths, but right now, you're definitely winning if we're tallying up our individual ones."

"It's not a contest." Mimi's just stroking my skin with her fingertips now, and that feels the most divine of all. "Besides, I think you won everything there is to win today. I told you my kids wouldn't adore you any less after meeting you."

"Well." I'm of half a mind to just let my head drop back against her belly and have her caress me wherever she wants. "The format of the party was genius, of course. A pool party is not like a dinner party where conversation is much more formal. It's also easy enough to retreat from when needed." Not that I could go anywhere unnoticed this afternoon. A St James had eyes on me at all times. "And when there's dancing, you can just let the music speak for you."

"Smart move." Her thumbs dig in again. "It worked like a charm." She massages my shoulders in silence for a while.

"I take it you don't have a hot date tonight?" I ask after a few moments of blissful quiet.

"Not after a pool party at Nora Levine's house."

"What are you doing tonight?"

"It's almost nine. It's evening already. This is what I'm doing tonight." Her fingertips scoot downward, along my spine.

"I guess I lost track of time." A rare occurrence in my universe. "You can do this all night long as far as I'm concerned."

The sound of Mimi's laughter is delightful. "Is your shoulder feeling better?"

"Oh, no. It's still very sore," I lie. "Please, don't stop."

"All right." Mimi lowers the straps of my bikini and I'm glad I'm sitting down. "I'm using some of this sunscreen to smooth things so I can give you a proper massage."

"That wasn't a proper massage until now?"

"Not a proper Mimi St James massage." I hear her squirt lotion into her palm. Then I feel her spread it over my shoulders.

I heave a deep sigh. What a day. It's not as though I didn't have a good time, but it takes a lot of mental energy to entertain a group of people like that—although it helps when every one of them turns up loving you already, even for no good reason at all. I'm glad I was able to do this for Mimi—and she's paying me back, more than plenty, in kind.

Mimi wasn't kidding. It's as though I can feel her fingers everywhere now. Even when she kneads the toughest knot out of my shoulder, and it should be hurting, it feels right—like her hands are exactly where they're meant to be. That ex really did teach her a trick or two.

"I think I'll have to fire Issa," I groan when her touch loses intensity. "Are you available to do this twice weekly?"

"I'll have to renegotiate your *Unbreak My Heart* contract first. Massages by executive producers are most definitely not included. Quite the opposite."

"You have my full consent." Fatigue hits me like a ton of bricks—always the aftereffect of a skilled massage. "I can give that to you in writing as well."

Mimi gives my shoulders one last squeeze. Did her fingertips just linger? It's not just fatigue I'm feeling, that's pretty much all I know at this point. For a brief moment, I allow myself to wonder what it would be like to let those magic hands roam across my entire body instead of them being confined to my shoulders.

"I'm going to wash my hands. I'll be right back."

"Thank you so much," I shout after her.

I'm so tired, I can barely still string a sentence together, but I don't want Mimi to go home. Luckily, she seems perfectly content to sit here in silence with me, overlooking the glowing lights of the city below.

"It's so peaceful here," Mimi murmurs. "I don't feel like I'm in LA at all."

"Yeah. It's pretty magical. So restorative to come home to after a long day."

"I can imagine." Her eyes glisten in the half-light of the patio.

"Are you hungry? Thirsty? Can I get you anything?"

"I'm absolutely fine, Nora. I can see why you would never cook a meal yourself with a chef like that."

At my feet, one of the dogs heaves a big sigh. All three of them look as exhausted as I feel—exhausted but strangely happy.

"I'd offer you a shoulder rub but I can still hardly move my arms." For dramatic effect, I pretend I can no longer lift my arms.

"You've given plenty today. I really can't thank you enough."

"You have thanked me enough," I say.

"I've probably overstayed my welcome. I'll get a car and let you rest now."

"You don't have to go. Stay as long as you like. I enjoy sitting here with you. You're excellent company, Mimi, and that's not a compliment I give lightly." There's something so calming, so soothing about being around her.

"I won't take it lightly, then." She sinks her teeth into her bottom lip. Then we're both startled by the loud and disturbing ring of a phone. "Sorry. That's me." Mimi shuffles through her bag. Her brow furrows as she looks at the screen.

"Feel free to take that," I quickly say.

"I don't think I will." She rejects the call. "It's my ex. The one who taught me a few massage tricks." Her eyebrows knit together. "It was probably a misdial. We haven't spoken in a long time."

A few seconds later, her phone chimes again with an incoming message.

"Do you mind if I quickly listen to this? Otherwise, I'll keep on wondering whether it was a mistake or not."

"Be my guest."

I try not to watch Mimi as she listens to the message from her ex. I'm curious enough to try and find out this person's full name so I can google her and see what type of woman Mimi spent eight years of her life with. It's hard to look away from the intriguing expressions on Mimi's face.

"It was a drunk dial instead of a misdial." Mimi puts her phone away. "Apparently, she and her partner broke up and she had to let me know." Mimi huffs out some air. "I'm glad I didn't pick up." Worry tightens her features. "I'm a little concerned, though. Wondering if someone's looking out for her." She shakes it off. "Even though that stopped being my concern years ago, when she told me she no longer felt that spark."

The phone rings again.

"It's her again. What the—" Mimi stares at her phone, clearly in two minds whether to pick up or not. She has too much goodness, too much sheer kindness, in her heart to ignore it, even though the person calling her broke that very heart years ago. "I'm sorry, Nora. I need to take this."

She takes her phone to the other side of the patio. She whispers when she speaks, and I can only make out a few words.

"I'm so sorry," Mimi says as she walks back to where I'm sitting. "She's in a really bad way. I'm going to, um, go meet her."

"Of course. Yeah."

"Thank you so much for a lovely day. Sorry to cut it short so abruptly." She opens her arms. "Can I give you a hug?"

Please do. I nod and walk into her embrace. Her arms around me are tight, her skin soft against mine. As she pulls away, I realize that the last thing I want Mimi to do right now is leave—especially, and this might be the most irrational feeling of all, to go and save her ex from something.

CHAPTER 20
MIMI

I find Cathy in some dive bar off Sunset Boulevard. The bartender looks pleased to see me, but not as much as my ex-partner who greets me as though we haven't been completely estranged the past two years. Cathy has plenty of friends. Why she had to call me of all people—and ruin my evening with Nora—is a total mystery to me.

"Mimi, you came. I can't believe it."

I can't quite believe it either, but here I am. Loving someone for as long as I loved Cathy will always leave me with a sense of responsibility toward them.

"What's going on?" I settle on the stool next to her.

The bartender shoves two glasses of water our way.

"It didn't work out. I had to break up with Ravi, and do you want to know why?" She sounds more coherent than she did on the phone. She doesn't look half as disheveled as I had expected her to, either.

"Please, enlighten me." I came all this way already—and probably, in Cathy's inebriated view, with the sole purpose of listening to her telling me what she's about to.

"Because, Mimi, she's not you."

"Excuse me?" That's a good one.

"She wasn't you, Mimi. For two years, I've been trying to find someone like you. Someone as classy and at the same time as warm as you, as nurturing and caring. As sexy and kind as you at the same time, but you know what I've learned? It's very rare to find that combination in a person."

"All right." I make no bones about hiding my dismay at this little speech. I'm certainly not about to take it seriously because all it tells me is that Cathy must have been drinking all day and she has reached the ultra-nostalgic, everything-was-so-much-better-before stage of her drunkenness. "Let's get you home, shall we?" I ask the bartender if she has an outstanding bill. He slides Cathy's tab my way and while I pay, she puts a hand on my knee.

"Does that mean you're taking me home? Because nothing would make me happier."

"Thank you and good luck," the bartender says, before I fold an arm underneath my ex's shoulder and walk her out of the bar.

"I know you think I don't mean it. That I'm just a drunk woman saying things, but that's not how it is," Cathy mumbles.

The Uber pulls up and the driver looks a bit wary at the sight of my tipsy co-passenger, but I assure him everything will be all right, although I have no way of knowing this. I haven't spent time with this woman in two years. Yet, it's easy enough to let time fold in on itself, let the years collapse between us and go back in time—to when we were a happy couple and often shared an Uber home after a night out.

"I made a big mistake two years ago," Cathy says. "And I know. I know! My very bad for taking two years to realize it. But there are no other women like you out there, Mimi. Believe me, I've looked and looked. I've swiped right until my thumb nearly fell off. And then I found Ravi and I thought, yeah, you know? I can work with this. I can fall in love again. And I thought I had, until I wasn't so sure anymore."

I wish I could close off my ears so I didn't have to listen to this. This woman dumped me—to use Nora's word for it, because, sometimes, it does sound appropriate. This woman told me she fell out of love with me. That she needed more excitement in her life than being with me provided. That she was so desperate for something to change, she would sacrifice the most important thing to me: our love; our relationship. To have to listen to this now is more than just a nuisance. Although it's a fool's errand to expect a drunk woman to show me, her ex-partner, a modicum of respect.

"I ran into Jen the other day. Did she tell you?"

I give a terse nod.

"That's what kickstarted this whole thing. I mean, I must have gone to Palmetto's for a reason. It must have been some subconscious thing steering me there because of the odds of running into you or one of the kids, because we used to go there all the time. It made me think about you and our life together so much, so intensely, I couldn't stay with Ravi any longer. It would have been so dishonest." She reaches for my hand and grabs it tightly. "Thank you so much for coming to get me."

Cathy doesn't live far from the bar I picked her up from and, mercifully, the car comes to a stop. I ask the driver to wait before hauling Cathy inside.

"Who can I call?" I ask, once I have her safely sitting in her living room couch.

"No one." Cathy attempts a smile but it looks more like a sneer. "You're the only person I need."

"I'm not staying."

"Oh, Mimi. Please, stay a while. I've missed you so much. Like you cannot possibly believe."

"Cathy." I sit next to her. "Listen to me. You're drunk. You're feeling vulnerable. You don't mean any of this, and even if you did, it wouldn't make any difference. Okay? You and I ended a long time ago. I've moved on."

"But you're not seeing anyone. Jen told me. I asked her because I just had to know."

"That's irrelevant."

"It's so not. Look, I'm not asking you to pick up where we left off. I'm not that delusional. But just… I don't know. Maybe you would consider going on a date with me? If we're both single, what's the harm?"

"Cathy." I rise swiftly. "I'm not going on a date with you. I only came out tonight because you sounded distressed. But you shouldn't have called me. I'm sure you will agree in the morning."

Cathy shakes her head. "I won't. I know what I feel."

"Feel whatever you want to feel, just leave me out of it." I blow out some air. What the hell did I walk into? "I have a car waiting outside. I'm going now. You're home. You're safe. I'll call Monique on my way home and ask her to check in with you."

"Monique? Monique and I are no longer in touch."

"Tell me who to call, then. Please, Cathy."

"I'm sorry. You don't have to call anyone." She waves her hand at the door. "Go. I'll be fine. And thank you, Mimi. I know you didn't have to come and get me. You didn't have to take my call. But I knew you would, because that's who you are." She gets up. "Can I give you a hug at least?" It reminds me of the words I spoke to Nora less than an hour ago. How different can two invitations to hug be?

"No. I'm sorry. I'm leaving now. Yeah?"

"Yeah. Okay. Bye, Mimi."

I'm still processing everything that happened yesterday when Austin arrives.

"Stop whatever you're doing right now," my son says. "I'm taking you out to lunch."

"I wasn't doing much of anything." After yesterday's last-minute pool party, most kids have other plans today than come to Sunday brunch at their mother's. Not Austin, though.

"Juan's volunteering, and I don't know what to do with myself after yesterday." Austin pretends to shake it all off. I kind of know how he feels. "Did you stay long after we left?"

"A while, until I got a call from Cathy."

"Say what?" His eyes nearly pop out of his lovely head.

"She and her girlfriend broke up. She got drunk and couldn't think of anyone better to call than me." I sigh. "I went to meet her and took her home."

"Oh, my god, Mom. After what she put you through? You did that for her? After all this time?" He shakes his head. "I should really teach you how to be more selfish. You don't owe Cathy anything, okay? Not after how she treated you."

Even though I tried to hide it from my kids as best I could, my separation from Cathy was painful and upsetting—and children always know, Austin most of all.

"Why didn't you tell her to go eff herself? It's what she deserves."

"Darling, calm down. It's okay. I made it perfectly clear how I felt about the whole thing."

"But you went to meet her? That says so much more than all the words in the world."

"I had to go. I couldn't just leave her in some sketchy bar in Hollywood on her own. You know I wouldn't do that."

"You're such a mom, Mom." He flashes me a smile. "And you were still at Nora's when she called? You left Nora's exquisite palace of a house to go pick up your drunken ex?" He clicks his tongue in disapproval.

"Yeah. My bad, really." Nora and I were having a lovely, relaxed, friendly time together. And what about that shoulder massage? Once I got past how incredibly taut and full of pent-up tension Nora's shoulders felt, it was equal parts treat and challenge to touch her skin like that, to drive my fingers into her flesh over and over again. And that shoulder line, my god. To look at it is one thing, but to have your hands all over it is another thing entirely. During that massage, I felt much more than friendly toward Nora, but that'll be my secret. I'm not telling anyone. Not my son, and certainly not Nora.

"Can you believe yesterday, Mom? To have Nora host a party like that for us. You and her must be pretty tight?" He holds up his hand. "And before you implicate Juan in this. I know he didn't have anything to do with it. He's way too protective of Nora for that."

"They have an interesting relationship, that's for sure."

Austin slants his head and stares at me for an instant. "Did you just avoid my question?"

"What question, darling?" Surprisingly, playing dumb often works with my kids.

"You and Nora? You're friends? Which wouldn't be so weird if it were anyone else, but I have it on good authority that Nora doesn't make new friends that easily."

"Yes. I think we are friends. Getting there, at least."

"You do realize how unique that is? She must really like you then."

"What's so special about someone liking me? I'll have you know I'm a very likable person." I bat my lashes at him, feeling rather silly.

"You don't have to tell me. You're my favorite woman in the whole wide world."

"Thank you, darling. Now where are you taking me?"

"The Tasting Room." Austin puts his hands on his hips.

"How did you swing that?"

"Courtesy of my boyfriend. He said to take you somewhere nice today."

"He's a keeper, that one."

"Hell yeah, Mom." He turns so I can hook my arm through his. "Have I told you how much I like him?"

CHAPTER 21
NORA

"I'm sorry. Oh, god. I'm so sorry, Nora," Stella says. "Fuck. I can't get it right today."

"Take five," the director says. "It's okay. It happens to the best of us."

"What's wrong?" I ask.

"Silas didn't sleep a wink last night and no one could pacify him. Not me, not Kate, and not the nanny. It's been like this all week. All he does during the day is sleep, sleep, sleep. Then once we all go to bed, he decides to wake up and have a party in his crib." She rubs her palms against her eyes gently so as not to ruin her makeup. "I'm going to try some breathing exercises in my trailer." Stella walks off set, holding up her hand in apology to everyone for keeping them waiting.

During short breaks, I prefer to stay in the zone as much as possible, to linger in the vibe of the scene we're shooting. I've worked with most people on this set for almost three years, so they know not to bother me in between takes. But from the corner of my eye, I see someone approach who doesn't necessarily belong here. Instantly, at the sight of her, I'm pulled from my state of flow. I wonder how things went with her ex—and what hold that woman still has over her after all these years that she can just call Mimi and have her drop everything.

My focus is ruined, so I walk over to Mimi.

"Hi, Nora." Her smile is dazzling and connects with something deep inside me. Maybe Stella won't be the only one messing up today. But when you're shooting a show, you can't just take a personal day. This entire production relies on Stella and me showing up every single day. If we're not here, the production company bleeds money. "How are you?" It's as though the studio lot disappears, and it's only Mimi and me. I'd best get a grip. I shouldn't have let her massage my shoulders last weekend. For the life of me, I can't get the memory of her hands on my skin out of my head.

"Good." Next thing I know, I'm giggling like a school girl. "You?"

"Fine. Wanted to check in on my favorite show. Looks like Stella's having a rough day."

"She didn't get much sleep last night."

Mimi nods. "I remember what that's like." She looks around the set. Our show runner, Jo, is lurking in the distance. "Do you think it would be too obnoxious of me to demand that Stella has time to take a nap?"

"You want to overhaul the schedule?" Surely Mimi knows that delaying a shoot will have a knock-on effect of further delays.

"I just feel for Stella. I know what it's like and I'm sure a lot of other parents here do as well." She pins her gaze on me. "It will give us a chance to catch up."

Catch up? We spent almost an entire day together only last weekend. Yet, the prospect is enticing.

"I'm not the boss here. You do what you think is right."

"Don't pretend you have no say in this, Nora. This affects your schedule and I know you don't like that."

"It's okay. It's better for me as well if Stella takes a nap." She has been pretty hit-and-miss all morning.

"Okay. I'll take care of it." Like a boss, Mimi calls Jo and a few other people to her. Five minutes later, a message is spread that shooting will resume this afternoon.

"Way to throw your weight around." It's kind of sexy that Mimi can just show up here and have all these people do whatever she wants—and what's best for us, actors. "Do you want to have an early lunch?"

"Um, yes, definitely." She taps her phone against her palm. "Let me just rearrange a few things."

"Please, Mimi. Don't change your schedule on my account."

"I just changed yours. It would be rude not to follow suit, really."

"If you say so." While she makes a few calls, I ponder our lunch choices. I usually have a poké bowl—hold the rice—in my trailer while I go over my lines for the next scenes.

"Can I take you somewhere?" Mimi asks. "Unless you're very attached to craft services."

I chuckle because surely she knows that I'm not. "Somewhere private?" I'm not going to a restaurant in the middle of a day of shooting, although I get the feeling I'll have trouble finding focus again this afternoon.

"I promise."

I follow Mimi to her car. While she drives, she orders lunch to be delivered at an address I don't recognize. Less than ten minutes later she parks in front of a glitzy office building. The huge sign at the front says 'Gloves Off Productions'.

"Your office?"

"It has perks," is all Mimi says. "We'll go in the back so no one asks any annoying questions."

I follow Mimi to the back of the building. She escorts me to a bank of elevators. When someone walks up to us, she just holds up her hand and gives a shake of the head. The person slinks off like my dogs do when they know they've done something wrong. She's the boss, all right. And fuck if it doesn't excite the hell out of me. As we go up in the elevator it hits me that, even though we've decided to just be friends—on my insistence—this feels a lot like dating. Her showing up and whisking me away. Her staying after her family left my house on Saturday. Sending each other flowers. That utterly blissful massage.

I glance at her. She's wearing a pants suit today instead of one of the pencil skirts I've gotten used to seeing her in. She still looks gorgeous as ever. Elegant and in command, but also infinitely kind toward me—and Stella, earlier. Over the weeks that I've known her, and gotten to know her better, it has become more and more obvious that Mimi St James is a rare gem of a person, especially in Hollywood. The CEO with a heart of gold. The career woman with four children who adore her. The executive who puts people's wellbeing over money. The kind of person who drops everything to pick up her drunken ex even after she broke her heart.

The elevator takes us to the top floor and it's as though, even though the ride was swift, the journey upward has given me a new perspective—some new insight into what this might be.

She walks us to a glass door that leads out onto the roof. Someone rushes toward us with a paper bag held out in front of them.

"Thank you very much, Adam." Mimi takes the bag. "That's lunch." She holds the door open for me. I walk out and look out over downtown LA.

"With where you live, I figured you weren't afraid of heights."

"Wow." We're so high up, traffic down below sounds like the soft buzz of a fly. "You weren't kidding about those perks."

"Come." Mimi walks to an area shielded off by plexiglass walls. It boasts a wooden table and a couple of chairs—and even a few plants. "First thing I had installed when I became the boss. I can think much more clearly up here. I never make a difficult decision without coming out here."

It's so rare for me to be impressed with another person, let alone this impressed. But I can see what has happened here. I've given Mimi the chance to impress me—not a kindness I allow many strangers. I've left the door of my usually airtight heart ajar and, over time, she has inched her way in. That also explains the kiss-that-never-was. And yes, I'm still me. I'm still convinced a romantic relationship is out of my reach and that I will fuck things up at an astounding speed but, right now, it doesn't really matter. Right now, I would very much like to kiss Mimi again—and too much wine has nothing to do with it.

Mimi grabs a tablecloth and napkins from a cabinet against the wall. She removes our lunches from the bag and sets the table. Eating is the last thing on my mind, but it's a joy to see her do this—to have her make this effort for me.

"I hope water's fine?" She puts two bottles on the table. "Although if you want something else, I can call for it."

"Water's perfect. All of this is absolutely perfect." Instead of taking a seat in the chair she just pulled out for me, I stand next to her. "You… are absolutely perfect."

Mimi turns to me. "We both know I'm not, but I'll take it."

"Mimi, I—um." It's much harder to do this without a good dose of liquid courage. "Thank you." I touch a finger to her hand, hook my pinkie into hers. She doesn't flinch, doesn't retreat.

"It's just lunch." Her voice has dropped into a lower register.

"I don't think it is." I swallow hard.

"Maybe it's not, then." By the tone of her voice, and the intense look in her eyes, I can tell she's right here with me—not only on this rooftop, but in this moment. In this pause before I'm about to do something I vowed—and I told her—I would never do in the sober light of day. But the sky stretches blue and endless beyond us. It's the middle of a workday. I'm in full possession of all my faculties. I have no mitigating circumstances, only the acute, irresistible desire to do this.

What's the protocol these days? Do you have to ask someone's permission before you kiss them? I don't know, so I do.

"Can I?" I ask.

"Can you what, Nora?" Mimi's fingers tighten around my hand.

"Can I kiss you?" I look straight into her dark eyes.

"You can if you want to. Do you want to?"

"I wouldn't be asking if I didn't."

Mimi doesn't reply with words. I bring my hand to her cheek, caress it with the back of my fingers. She leans into my touch. I slide my fingers to her chin, tilt it toward me.

I lean in and I don't think about the consequences. I only think about Mimi's lips. About how it will feel to finally kiss her—because if I'm being honest, I've been wanting to do this since long before today. Since long before she brought me to this romantic rooftop.

It's time to find out. I brush my lips against hers and even though we've barely touched, even though it was only the prelude to an actual full kiss, a dam inside me starts crumbling already. My stomach flip-flops. My legs go wobbly. That's what happens when you deny yourself the pleasure of a fellow human's touch for as long as I have.

Mimi exhales a ragged breath, before she leans closer to me again. Before our lips meet again, properly this time, lingering, the tip of her tongue skating along my lower lip.

Her hand rides up my arm and comes to rest against the back of my head. Her fingers push into my hair. The next brush of our lips is filled with intention and, judging by what I feel coursing through me, a whole lot of lust. Does she feel this too? I briefly open my eyes and all I see on Mimi's face is open-lipped desire. I curl my arms around her waist and pull her close. Our lips meet again and again and, each time, they open wider. Each time, I let more of her in—not unlike what I've been doing since I met her. Since she invited me to dinner at her house just after we met.

Juan and Imani's words bounce around my head. It's okay to change your mind about things. But this isn't about changing my mind. It's about being in this moment with Mimi and kissing her over and over again. About exploring her soft, pillowy lips and never wanting this kiss to stop. It's about this magical space she carved out for herself on this rooftop and where she brought me so we could have a quiet lunch. But any food is off the menu now. My stomach is tripping over itself. My body has no clue what's happening because I haven't kissed someone like this in decades. Because this is not how you protect yourself and your fragile little heart.

CHAPTER 22
MIMI

Even though I'm surprised, Nora's lips on mine feel right. As though my lips are the only sensible place for hers to settle. As though, despite everything she has said, it was inevitable that, eventually, they would.

I certainly didn't bring her up here to kiss—to have her kiss me like this. I just wanted to hang out, luxuriate in her company because the opportunity presented itself. But now what? What happens after this kiss ends? If Nora's tight grasp on my back is anything to go by, I don't have to worry about this kiss ending any time soon. So I let her kiss me. I enjoy the exquisite sensation of Nora Levine's tongue dancing in my mouth for as long as she'll let me.

I can easily predict what will happen next. She'll be all bashful and want to pretend it never happened. If she were anyone else, I wouldn't let her get away with more of that nonsense, but I have such a soft spot for Nora. And we're still kissing. I keep pulling her to me, keep planting my lips on hers, keep her close to me.

Our bodies press together and to run a hand over her strong back again, and give my fingers free rein over the skin of her neck, is divine. One thing I do know: I'd like to do much more with Nora than just kiss. But there's no point in getting ahead of myself. Knowing what I know about her, she'll probably pull back again. She'll make herself go through a completely unnecessary song and dance again; she'll push the limits of logic again to justify why on earth she ended up kissing me on this rooftop. She'll blow hot and cold again and Nora can do whatever she likes, of course, but I need to make sure I don't get pulled in past the point of no return. I'm not going to twist myself in knots to accommodate someone who is emotionally unavailable.

Although, as this kiss deepens, I'm also more than willing to give her the benefit of the doubt. Maybe she'll be so blown away by it, she won't have room in her heart for regret. But that my mind is even going there in the throes of this kiss is evidence enough of Nora's boundaries. I'm a good sport, but I'm not in the habit of convincing people to try dating me. Either they want to, or they don't. And I won't be taking the next step. The ball's still firmly in Nora's court.

That doesn't stop me from prolonging this kiss, partly because I don't want it to end and partly because I'm afraid that once it does, it will be all over forever. She'll retreat back into her shell.

But my skin buzzes and my blood beats hard in my veins. A tingle spreads from my belly to between my legs. How can she be this good a kisser? Shouldn't she be out of practice? But it's not the skill that counts, it's the two people doing the kissing. Right now, it feels like Nora and I were made to kiss, to have our lips find each other time and time again. To have our tongues twirl into each other's mouth. To have our bodies this close to each other. But even the best, the most rapturous and addictive kisses must come to an end.

Our faces retreat, but our hold on each other remains. I'm not letting her go and she's not letting go of me either.

"I—I don't know what to say," Nora says.

"You don't have to say anything."

"We can't just stand here in silence." Her body moves against mine as she chuckles.

"We can for a little bit."

"Do you, um, want to come to my house tonight?" Nora asks.

I nearly do a double take. "Yes." I nod vigorously. "I would like that very much."

"Me too." She sucks her lower lip between her teeth.

"Are you thinking dinner? Should I bring anything?"

"I'll make sure there's food in case you're hungry." She runs her fingertips along the side of my shoulder.

"Do you want to have that lunch now?"

"I can't do food right now. I'm, um… No, that's not going to work." She pulls back a bit and puts her other hand on her belly. "Things are all over the place in here."

"I get it."

"I want you to know that… I haven't done this lightly," Nora says. "Not that I planned it. I didn't. How could I? But, um, it means something to me."

I swallow something out of my throat. "It means something to me as well."

"I'm of half a mind to kiss you again." Nora surprises me again. Maybe, once she lets go, she's all in. There's no stopping her.

"Only half?" I joke.

She shakes her head and leans in again.

I'm more nervous than ever when I ring Nora's doorbell. It's not something either one of us would explicitly say out loud, but we both know why she invited me to her house. More kissing, and whatever else follows.

Nora opens the door dressed in jeans and a tank top that makes her shoulders look extra alluring.

I can tell she's on edge as well so I occupy myself briefly with greeting her dogs, so they—and I—can calm down a bit. When she ushers me in, my gaze lingers on the staircase to the second floor, and I can't help but wonder if I'll be shown around the upstairs of Nora's gorgeous house tonight.

"How did it go this afternoon?" I follow her to the jaw-dropping patio. Tonight, though, I only have eyes for Nora.

She rubs her palms on her jeans. "Better. I mean for Stella. That nap did her the world of good. She's lobbying to have a daily lunch-time nap instated on set."

"Excellent idea. And you?" We haven't even kissed hello yet, but I don't reach for her. It's important to let her come to me.

"It was all right. I did a good enough job. For myself, I mean."

Because I know Nora better now, I know what she means.

"Are you hungry? There's food if you want some," she asks.

"Have you eaten at all today?" Lunch, unlike our lips, remained untouched.

"I had something when I got home earlier, but yeah." She makes a funny noise, like a failed giggle. "Fuck, Mimi. I'm so nervous. Can we just talk for a bit, please? Maybe have a glass of wine?"

"Of course." I walk over to her. "It's okay. There's no pressure to do anything. You know that, right?"

Nora nods. "I'll get you some water. Please, make yourself at home."

"Thanks." I watch as two dogs follow her into the house. One of them, the cocker spaniel whose name escapes me, stays with me. I release some of my own tension by scratching him behind the ears. He looks up at me with begging eyes. "What do you want from me?" I ask. "What can I get you? If it's more hugs, you've got it."

"Rogue likes you." Nora's back already. "Which is rare, because he's a lot like me. He doesn't like a lot of people. Unlike these two attention whores." She puts the drinks on the table and pets her other two dogs.

The dogs settle and we lean back in our chairs, beverages in hand.

"I feel like…" Nora folds one legs over the other. She's not wearing any shoes and even her feet look perfect, her toenails painted a deep red. "Maybe I owe you an explanation after what I said last time."

"You don't have to explain yourself to me."

"No. I do. Because I sat here, in this very chair, and told you I wasn't interested in anything romantic, after which I proceeded to kiss you." She grins at me. "Even felt you up a little."

"That's the part I've decided to focus on."

"That's a good part to focus on." She stretches out her leg and touches her toe against my foot. "I can't," she says on a sigh, "promise you any fairy tales. My track record in relationships is bad to non-existent and I don't see how that could magically change just because years have gone by."

"No promises are needed, Nora. All you have to do, if you want to, is give it a try."

"The thing is, with you, I really want to try. So very badly. But I'm so scared I'm going to fuck it all up." She holds her thumb and index finger a fraction apart. "This is how much faith I have in myself when it comes to this."

"Try not to think about the future or what could go wrong. Just focus on what you want right now. On today. On tonight."

"I can't get you out of my head." She says it as though she caught some nasty virus instead of, perhaps, a little crush on me.

"You don't have to."

"Also, when we first met, you said you'd never ask someone who works for you on a date. And I know we agreed that I don't really work for you directly, but still."

"I still stand by that, but that rule doesn't apply to you,

Nora. It's a power balance thing and a control thing and you are not in a position where you can't say no to me out of fear for your job. In fact, you're the one with all the power in this particular equation."

"Really? I hold all the power?" The glimpses of playfulness that break through her facade are delightful. I wish she'd feel comfortable enough to always be like that—to just be herself.

"You do."

"I kissed you on that rooftop." Her toes climb up my ankle. "Thank goodness I asked for permission."

"Would you like to ask permission for anything else?"

She grins at me. "How about another kiss?"

"That can most definitely be arranged."

Nora leaps out of her chair and bridges the distance between us. She plants her hands on the armrests of my chair and gazes down at me. "Christ, Mimi. What have you done to me?"

"As far as I know, I didn't do—" Before I can finish my quip, Nora's lips are on mine. They're much hungrier, much less shy, than earlier today. Maybe because dusk is falling, and we both knew this was coming.

She lowers herself onto my lap. Her hands skate along my neck, into my hair. I guess she didn't invite me over to take things slowly.

I pull her to me, wanting to feel as much of her as I can in this position. I press my fingertips into the flesh of her magnificent shoulders, then run them over the enticing bulge of her biceps. I've seen Nora in a bikini. Her body belongs on the cover of all the magazines, inspiring countless articles on how to stay fit after fifty. Mine, not so much. The only workouts I get these days are running after my grandchildren. But neither one of us is perfect. Nora might hide in her perfect house with her perfect body, she's made it clear she has plenty of other issues. My body might be far from perfect, but I have other strengths. And I think Nora's drawn to them. She wouldn't be kissing me the way she's doing right now if she didn't.

CHAPTER 23
NORA

I'm trying to follow Mimi's advice and not dwell on the future before it even has a chance to happen, but it's hard not to wonder what the immediate future has in store for us. This is not the kind of kiss that will just end here, that can end without consequences. I try to let myself be carried away by the insistent pulse between my legs, by the butterflies in my stomach, by the divine sensation of Mimi's lips on mine and her fingers all over my skin—exactly where I've wanted them all week. But when you haven't done this for such a long time it might as well be a new sensation altogether, it's impossible not to worry.

This was always going to be like a war raging within me. Because of course I'm terrified, but I'm also turned on and desperate for so much more.

"You've probably been dying to see my bedroom," I say, trying to sound sultry, but failing miserably.

Mimi looks at me as though I can never fail at anything ever again in my life. Her eyes are all hunger, all raw desire. She can't seem to get enough of my upper arms—I spend enough time working on them so it's good that someone's finally enjoying them. I flex my biceps a little, pushing myself up on the chair, and I swear to god, she's moaning in the back of her throat. There's no end to the ways in which she delights me.

"Absolutely dying," she whispers. "If you're sure?"

I'm not sure of anything except that I don't want this night to end. I nod and slip off her. I hold out my hand and walk us upstairs. My dogs follow suit. They're not going to be happy about being locked out of my room. I should have called Chad, but what should I have said? *Odds are I'm having sex tonight. Can you take the dogs somewhere else?*

"They're going to make a fuss for a little while, but they'll get over it soon enough. They have each other." I crouch down. "Sorry, babies. Mommy's doing—" I catch myself before I finish my sentence. Mimi's standing right next to me, a big smirk on her lips. I rise. "Sorry about that."

"It's okay. They're your babies." Mimi holds out her hand to me.

"To say they're not used to this is a great understatement."

Mimi turns to the dogs. "I promise I will return your mistress in one piece and fully satisfied." She says it with such conviction, something inside me gives again. Her easy confidence has that effect on me.

We go into my bedroom, and I close the door. The dogs whine, as expected, but it's easy enough to shut out the noise because when Mimi kisses me, she also brushes the left strap of my tank top off my shoulder. Next, she kisses me right above my collarbone.

"Jesus," she whispers. "Your shoulders are like a work of the finest art."

Mimi's obvious appreciation of my body turns me on. I work on it every day—a remnant of my *High Life* days, when the producers, mostly out-of-shape men, demanded the cast hit the gym because we had to look a certain way for the show. There are days that I wonder why I go through the grueling effort—because it is grueling—but Mimi's words are more than enough reason for all the pain I've put myself through.

Her lips travel up my neck, leaving a hot trail of kisses. I need to find a way to stay in this, to not let my ever-churning thoughts get the better of me. Because I want Mimi, for many reasons, and I want to enjoy every single second of this. Odds are, I will screw up sooner rather than later. I can tell myself I will try, but I honestly have no idea what that even looks like. Maybe I should cast a quick glance into the mirror—that should give me a good enough idea. But I can't possibly look at myself right now.

Mimi's lips find mine again and we kiss, but only briefly, before she pulls away. She looks me in the eye. "Are you nervous?"

"Yeah." Maybe she felt my heart hammering in my chest, or saw my pulse flutter raggedly when she kissed my neck. I swallow hard.

"We'll go slow. And even though it goes without saying that we can stop any time, I'm saying it anyway." Her eyes narrow. "Do you want to stop? Is it too much?" She gives my arm a gentle squeeze.

I shake my head. "Definitely not."

"Okay." A hint of a smile. "Do you want to get into bed and just lie down together for a while? To calm our nerves?"

"Sure." Her caring is one reason we've made it to my bedroom in the first place. Against my better judgment, I trusted Mimi, and sensed somehow she would be like this. That she would give me the time I need and respect the boundaries I've never even thought of having.

"I'm going to take some of my clothes off because they're not very comfortable to lie down in," Mimi says. "That doesn't mean you have to do the same."

"Can I?" I reach for her neck, slide my hand along the back of it. I wait for her consent. When she nods, I use my other hand to unbutton her blouse. To slowly tug it out of her pants. I'm overcome with the overwhelming urge to feel her skin, to put my hand on her warm belly. So I do. She shoulders off her blouse and stands before me naked from the waist up —except for her bra. She does it so confidently, without any qualms about her body, she might as well have abs for days and biceps like mine. To not care how skin stretches over your muscles is a foreign notion to me. I spend too much time caring about it and for what? Granted, Mimi does respond to it exactly the way I had hoped her to. At times, when her gaze rakes over my body, she looks more baffled than impressed.

I can't take my hand off her belly. It's as though now it has made contact, that contact can never be broken again. My gaze is pulled to her bra, to her porcelain skin curving out of the cups. She wiggles against me as she slips out of her pants.

"Sorry. I'm just going to hang these up—they wrinkle easily."

I take a step back and miss the touch of her skin instantly. I watch her fold her clothes and drape them over the nearest chair. Before I take her hand and let her pull me onto the bed, I quickly step out of my jeans.

We lie on the covers, facing each other.

"Hi," she says, her voice low and soft.

"Do you like what you see?" I ask, referring to my bedroom, but quickly realizing how that actually sounds.

"Very much." Her lips pull into a grin.

"I mean my bedroom." My cheeks flush.

"I'm sure it's a lovely room, but I only have eyes for you, Nora." She shuffles a little closer, closing the small distance between us. She slides her hand under the tank top I'm still wearing.

Her lips find mine again, and we fall into a long, lingering kiss. Her hand rides up but keeps a respectful distance from my bra. She's probably waiting for more permission. Is it okay to give her permission for everything right now, just to get it out of the way?

She pulls away from our kiss again.

"I can feel it, you know?" Her voice is all gentleness and understanding.

"Feel what?"

"When you start to get lost in your head. Your touch loses intensity."

"Sorry."

"Don't apologize, but I want you here with me, Nora. We have time. We can take all the time we need." Somewhere in the back of my head, the thought of my alarm clock going off at five tomorrow morning pops up. But this is exactly what she means —it's also the hardest proposition for me. It's probably the main reason why I'm so bad at being in a relationship.

"I was just wondering how to, um, make you aware that I enthusiastically consent to everything."

Mimi laughs and the sound of it is almost freeing—and makes me realize exactly how tense I've been.

"Noted." She removes her hand from underneath my tank top and cups my jaw. "And likewise."

"Let me take this off." I start pulling up my tank top. She moves away to give me the space I need.

"Let's use the words 'tank top'," Mimi says. "In case 'stop' is too hard to say."

"What?"

"If either one of us wants to stop what the other's doing, or what we ourselves are doing, at any point, we say 'tank top' instead of 'stop'."

"Sure." I look into her sparkling eyes and it's as though I'm injected with a fresh dose of confidence, or maybe just the absence of second-guessing my every move, even for an instant. I slide on top of her, slipping my knee between her legs. "But Mimi, I'm not going to want you to stop." I wonder if I should say more. If I should assure her that even though it seems I'm pulled out of the moment, and she may notice, I always come back to it. She has that effect on me.

But I don't say anything else. I'd much rather kiss her again than do more talking. So I do. I kiss her over and over again. Her hands roam across my back and, as though finally unleashed, slide to my buttocks. She cups my behind in her palms, softly at first, but then much more insistently. I gasp for breath, because this is what I want. The reason why I've been so drawn to Mimi from the beginning is that she displays so many of the characteristics I look for—if I allowed myself to look—in another person. She has unlocked something in me, found a secret key, and it's only just beginning.

Next thing I know, she unhooks my bra and topples me onto my back. She doesn't ask if she can do things anymore. She just does them—to my great delight. She runs her fingertips from my throat to the swell of my breasts, then hooks them under my bra cup. She pulls it down and slowly reveals my breast. Unlike other parts of my body, my breasts are one hundred percent natural. My nipple aches for Mimi to wrap her lips around it, but she looks stunned. She swallows slowly, briefly looks up at me to catch my glance. If she called my shoulders a work of art earlier, I wonder how she feels about my breasts. But I don't have to ask. Her admiration for my body is written all over her face and while it turns me on, I'm pretty certain Mimi's not in my bed because of the promise of my body, or because I'm Nora Levine. I'm pretty convinced she's here with me *despite* me being Nora Levine—because the Nora Levine shield is always up, and it's hard to get past that. Many have tried and failed. But here is Mimi St James.

I didn't know what to make of her in the beginning, and look at us now. She's about to take my nipple into her mouth. When she does, the sensation reverberates throughout all my cells. Decades of being single have left me adept at taking care of my own sexual needs, but feeling another person's lips around your nipple is not something you can simulate. Feeling her tongue against my rock-hard nipple, the soft warmth of it, is exquisite and ratchets up my level of excitement. The years have only strengthened my belief that being single is highly underrated in our society, but there's a lot to be said for the soft touch of a woman's tongue against your nipple. And what a woman Mimi is.

She bares my other breast and treats my other nipple with the same reverence.

I wriggle with delight under her touch. Without lifting her lips from my nipple, she tosses my bra into the room behind her. My skin sizzles. Between my legs, a bomb is about to explode. She skates a finger from my breasts to my belly button, leaving nothing but goose bumps in its wake. While she licks my nipples, she draws a circle around my belly button. I'm squirming now. How did this happen so quickly? How did I go from lukewarm to sizzling hot like that?

People think of me as cold and distant, and I am those things, but I'm also this. Just like anyone else, I'm not just one thing. And that's the priceless gift Mimi has already given me. The knowledge that this kind of pleasure is still within my reach. That with the right person, I can be this version of myself as well. I can share intimacy. I can use my body to create it. To delight her and lift myself up onto a cloud of pleasure.

Mimi's lips are still firmly wrapped around my nipple. Her finger scoots down, drawing a line along the waistband of my panties. My clit throbs for her. Oh, will she put her lips between my legs? The mere thought of it ignites a fresh round of wild throbbing.

My breath stalls in my throat. I'm so beside myself, I start pushing my panties down. I want her so much and the desire for her hasn't only taken over my body, it's taken over my mind as well. I couldn't care less why this is happening. I couldn't care less about anything other than what Mimi is doing with her tongue and her hands right now.

She lets go of my nipple and helps me remove my panties.

"Fuck, Nora," she says on a lusty sigh. "You're so fucking gorgeous."

And I believe every word she says. Although, right now, I'd

believe her if she told me my name was Juan Diaz instead of Nora Levine. Then, it hits me that I'm totally naked in front of someone else. But again, my mind can't focus on how out of the ordinary that might be or how that makes me feel, because my body is too busy wanting more. Wanting Mimi, who's pushing me down again.

She can't get enough of my nipples. She licks and sucks on them, while her hand drops between my legs. Her fingertips dance across the inside of my thighs.

I spread for her. I'm so ready for whatever she has to give. For the pleasure that awaits me. But Mimi takes her time. Her fingertips only skirt the edges of my clit for a split second here and there, but every time they do, every cell in my body lights up.

She looks up at me, my nipple softly clamped between her teeth. Her eyes are dark, stormy almost. I can't look away from them, from her, but then I have no choice, because she's kissing her way down. She feathers kisses around my belly button, on my lower belly, on my—oh, fuck. She plants a kiss right on my clit. It's close-lipped and light as anything, but I'm right at the edge of whatever awaits me on the other side already. She's driving me crazy in ways that have been too unfamiliar for me for too long.

Mimi glances up at me again and I look back. With my gaze, I try to urge her to do that again, but more this time. But I can't make Mimi do anything. Mimi does exactly as she pleases.

I'm panting as though Marcy just made me do fifty push-ups, but my body doesn't feel as spent. My flesh is on fire, my synapses ready. My body might be trained like an athlete's and be able to take a lot, but it can't take this. Every fiber of my being screams for release. It's not just the tension created here tonight between us that I need to let go of. It's years' worth of pent-up emotions, denials, and doubts. It's a layer of myself I'm ready to shed, the hard, outer one that I didn't let anyone get through for too long.

Mimi's lips touch down on my clit again and wrap themselves around it like they did to my nipple earlier. My dream has come true. I allow myself to enjoy every single second of this—as though I have any other choice. Her tongue is warm against me, her fingertips are suddenly everywhere. Mimi licks me, caresses me, makes love to me. I know this for certain because this love we're making is turning me into someone else. After this, I won't be the same Nora Levine. At least not for a while.

I come at Mimi's tongue and I let it all go. All the love I denied myself. All the possible friendships and acts of human kindness I rejected because it was the only way I knew to hold on to the last shred of myself. To not let the fame and being Nora Levine crush me completely. And I don't blame myself for what I did and the choices I made because, in my head, they've always only been the result of simple cause and effect.

And I cry. Of course I cry. This might be divine, the pleasure of a depth unknown, but it's not painless. To be shaken to your core like this never is.

CHAPTER 24
MIMI

I hold Nora close. I let her cry on my shoulder, let her dig her fingertips into my flesh, as though she's clawing at something—or holding on to something, perhaps.

Before she can start apologizing—because I know she will—I say, "Remember that text I sent you a few weeks ago? No apologies required." I kiss her on the crown of her head. "Especially not for being who you are."

I'm not unmoved by this. Nora basically collapsed at my touch. After she climaxed—loud and howling—she folded in on herself, and I had to wrap myself around her. But I'm used to keeping my wits about me in all sorts of circumstances.

"It's like you..." is all I can make out from what she mumbles against my shoulder.

She takes a deep breath, and another, then looks up at me. "Like you pulled me apart or something."

"It was my pleasure." I'm not being facetious. I mean it from the bottom of my heart. To see Nora like this is a privilege.

"You're like a dream." Nora runs her fingers underneath her nose, but they don't even begin to catch her tears.

It's a huge thing that she's not crumbling even more right now, that she's still managing to have a conversation.

"I need about a million tissues." She pushes herself up.

"Are you okay?" I ask.

Nora nods. "I will be. I am. I just… it was overwhelming." She nods again.

"It must be." I hear her dogs becoming nervous outside the door. Maybe they can sense Nora's going through something in the next room. "Do you want to talk?"

"No." She grins at me. "Just give me five and, um, I'll be ready."

"Ready for what?" I know what she's getting at, but I do need that conversation.

"You know." She rakes her gaze over my body. Unlike her, I'm still wearing my underwear.

"We're not going to do that right now." I make sure to meet her gaze.

"We're not?" Confusion crosses her face. "Don't you want to?"

"Of course, but I want something else more." I already feel so close to Nora, the vibe between us is so intimate, that whether or not I have an orgasm is of little importance to me. What matters is this moment between us.

"You want to talk?" she asks.

"Or just lie here with you, hold you in my arms."

"Is this… um, I mean, is there something I should know about your, um, preferences in bed?"

I chuckle. "No. I don't think so." I hold out my hand to her. "I want you. Have you seen yourself? You look like a swimsuit model—no, better actually, because you defy age by looking the way you do—but it's not about that for me right now." My usual eloquence has deserted me at the sight of Nora's naked body.

Nora takes my hand. Her fingers are moist, her palm clammy.

"I appreciate that, but um…" Nora has recovered already, because the corners of her mouth lift and she looks at me as though she only has one thing on her mind—devouring me. "I'm not sure how I feel about that." She lifts my hand to her lips, plants a quick kiss on it, then hops off the bed. "I'll be right back." She disappears into the en suite. The bedroom is only lit by the light that spills in from the outside. I hear a pitter-patter outside the door and the sound of Nora splashing some water on her face.

"I think your babies are getting antsy," I say when Nora walks back into the room. It's hard to look away from her body. It defies all logic, all laws of being human. I know she's had Botox to her face, and some filler in her lips, but the rest of her looks totally natural. When I had my hands all over her earlier, I couldn't believe how rock-hard her abs are. As far as I know, no surgeries have been invented to provide people with six-packs.

"They can wait a while longer." Nora jumps back into bed with me. "I know you want to talk, but I'm not in a big talking mood right now." She drags her finger over my belly.

"That climax you just had might catch up with you, emotionally and physically, very soon. I think I should be there for that."

"You're not going anywhere, are you?"

"I sure hope not, but Nora… Listen to me. Your body's just been shocked, basically. Your body and your mind. I don't take that lightly. I want to be here for you."

"Mimi, honestly." Her finger skates up along the cup of my bra. "I have no idea what you're talking about."

I'm flattered by her insistence as well as turned on.

"Maybe," Nora says, "I'm not the only one who needs to learn to let go."

Maybe she has a point. Maybe we're both control freaks in our own way.

"All right, well… If Nora Levine's asking, who am I to say no?"

"That's what I thought."

Before she can kiss me, I ask, "I have a crucial question first."

"Sure." Nora kisses me on the cheek.

"Do you have any lube?" Of all the things to ask Nora Levine.

"I'm fifty-one," she says. "I have a large supply of it."

Now's not the time to ask what she does with that large supply.

"Good." I tilt her chin toward me and kiss her. Then I forget I ever wanted to have a conversation instead of doing this, instead of kissing her again, and of trying out Nora's large supply of lube.

Nora's lips drift to my neck, then find my ear. "You're fucking spectacular, Mimi St James," she whispers. Her hand snakes to my back. With one hand, she unclasps my bra—how on earth do you practice a skill like that? But I still have lots to learn about Nora.

She guides my bra off my body and pins her gaze on my breasts. I'm sixty-five and I've had four children so it would be an exercise in complete futility to compare my body to Nora's. I've never been in a situation like this—I've never been in bed with someone as blatantly fit as Nora, someone who looks so perfect. But even though this town, and the heartless machine that Hollywood can be, is a constant reminder of the opposite, I'm not one to hold the course of nature against myself. You can't raise children in good conscience, teach them to be happy in their bodies as well as their minds, if you're going to let that nonsense dictate how you feel about yourself. My body is the result of sixty-five years of living, of all the ups and downs, of all the nurturing it has done, of the tiny bodies that grew inside of it. It still serves me very well because, right now, my flesh is pining for Nora's touch. My clit pulses in sync with my amped-up heartbeat. And I'm ecstatic we're doing this instead of talking.

Nora runs a finger over the C-section scar on my belly. Some women may hate their scars, but mine will always remind of my beautiful son. It's because of that scar he's been brightening up my life for twenty-six years now, so how could I possibly hate it? Nora doesn't say anything. She caresses me in the half-dark of her bedroom. I've been in this room a while now but I still have no idea what it looks like—I only have eyes for Nora. And yes, her body is spectacular, but it's not what has bowled me over the most. Nor was it taking her into my mouth, or even that magnificent climax. It was the fact she surrendered. That we're in her bedroom in the first place. That she asked me here with the purpose of doing this. That she let me in and showed herself to me completely. That she trusts me on some level.

That's another reason not to have any qualms about my body, or compare it to Nora's. This isn't a competition. This isn't even just sex—not by a long shot. We are here to express with our bodies what is too early for our mouths to say. There's a commitment in what we're doing, in the act of it, that defies words or promises. It's intimate and special.

I'm trembling under her touch, but it's the good kind of trembling. It's anticipation mixed with desire and a lot of emotions. And it's easy enough to claim I like the version of Nora that the world doesn't get to see—and I do—but she's still, also, very much Nora Levine.

Right now, Nora Levine's finger is slipping inside my panties. I gasp at her touch. She doesn't let it slide all the way down. I look up at her, into her sparkling eyes. She kisses me while we work in tandem to slip my panties off me, and then I'm naked on Nora's bed.

She takes my hands and pins them above my head. She slides her body on top of me and kisses me, her tongue hot in my mouth. All those divine sensations blend together into a cocktail of pure pleasure. Nora's all over me in a way I hadn't expected, although I'm not quite sure what I had expected. Walking through her bedroom door was like taking a leap into the great unknown.

One thing I do know. I haven't been this turned on in years. If it's like this for me after only two years of celibacy, what must it have been like for Nora? Although that, too, I don't know for certain. Yet, I kind of do. Still, we have so much left to discover about each other, a long journey to go on together.

Nora's going on her own special journey right now. She kisses her way down my body. She licks my neck, tugs at my nipples with her teeth, slides her warm hands across my belly. Until she settles between my legs.

We haven't asked each other what we like—my bad for forgetting earlier. For getting too carried away by the circumstances. I wonder if Nora's going to ask me. I glance at her from underneath my eyelashes. She looks like a different person now, like yet another version of herself. More free and uninhibited than I've seen her before. Like she's in it, fully sunk into this moment with me. And she doesn't have to ask me anything.

Nora bows down. I feel her breath between my legs. Her hair tickles my belly. At the very first touch of her tongue, I'm about to implode. Heat flares up in my belly. My clit ignites. My body tries to hold on because I don't want this to ever end.

Nora's tongue is gentle and soft. She's in no hurry. Neither am I, but my body doesn't agree. My body can't wait to release all the tension it's endured since I met Nora. That massage. Her drunken attempt at kissing me. All the mixed messages. It has all led to this, to her tongue between my legs, and an inevitable climax roaring through my bones.

"You didn't even give me a chance to bust out the lube," Nora says after she has crawled up and wrapped her arms around me.

I can only laugh. I can only be over the moon, and thrilled to my core, by this moment—and by her.

It's the middle of the night when a hell of a noise starts blaring in my ear. My brain has barely caught up with where I am when the light switches on. Nora sits up beside me in the bed. She doesn't look alarmed at all, just very tired.

"What the hell is happening?" I rub the sleep from my eyes.

"It's morning," Nora says matter-of-factly. "But please, do go back to sleep."

"What time is it?" Judging by the fatigue in my body, it must only be two or some other ungodly hour.

"Five. Marcy will be waiting for me."

None of this makes any sense. "Who's Marcy again?"

"My personal trainer." Nora flashes me a smile. The dogs shuffle around the bed. "This body isn't a fluke of nature, Mimi. It's two hours of hard graft every single morning."

"Jesus."

"Jesus has nothing to do with it either." Nora kisses my forehead. "Go back to sleep. Come downstairs whenever you feel like it. My chef arrives in an hour. We can have breakfast together at seven thirty." She hops out of bed. "Unless you want to join me. I'll ask Marcy to go easy on you, although she's ex-army and she really doesn't have an easy mode."

For a second, I wonder if I'm in the middle of a nightmare. This is how our night together ends? No warm snuggles in bed. No hot morning kisses underneath the sheets. None of that, apparently.

"You can't take a day off?"

"No."

I crash onto my pillow. I need to get some more sleep. How is she this awake?

"Enjoy your workout."

"I will." Mercifully, Nora switches off the light before she disappears into the bathroom.

Fully showered and dressed, I make my way downstairs a bit before seven. Despite being bone-tired, sleep was hard to come by after that rude awakening.

In the kitchen, Ricky, the chef who was here when Nora had her pool party, welcomes me with a big smile on his face.

"Good morning, Mimi," he says. "Please sit." He gestures at a stool at the kitchen island. "Can I get you some coffee?" It's like being in a hotel where I'm the only guest.

"I'd love some coffee. Thank you so much." I sit in my designated spot.

"Did you sleep well?" he asks before he turns to Nora's fancy coffee machine.

"Yes, until Nora's alarm went off at five a.m."

I'm not sure whether I was supposed to say that, but my brain's not fully operational yet. Nora must have the odd house guest over, but they wouldn't necessarily be woken up by her ruthless alarm—I can still hear it ringing in my ears, that's how shocking and loud it was.

"Marcy gives her hell if she's not in the gym five minutes before they're supposed to start. Marcy's a bit loco like that, but I think Nora secretly likes it." Ricky puts a steaming mug in front of me. "Enjoy. Can I get you anything else?"

Seeing as I barely ate all of yesterday, I'm famished. "I think Nora would like us to have breakfast together, but if you could sneak me a slice of toast already, I would be forever in your debt, Ricky." I make sure to flash him a big smile.

Ricky's eyes go wide. Is he that surprised that I remembered his name? "Don't say the b-word, Mimi."

I didn't even say anything that starts with a b.

"This house is a bread-free zone." Ricky plants his elbows on the counter between us. "If you don't know this yet, then consider this absolutely vital information."

"What? No bread?" Is he kidding me. "Don't tell me you only make egg-white omelets for breakfast.

"Of course not. The yolk's reputation was restored years ago."

"What do you have on offer?" I suppose pancakes are out of the question as well.

"Lots of delicious goodies like a protein smoothie." He checks his watch. "I need to start on Nora's now. She'll want it before she showers. Do you want one?"

"No. Thank you." I drink from my coffee instead.

"It's going to be loud for a few minutes. Cover your ears, please, Ma'am."

While Ricky blitzes the ingredients of Nora's smoothie, I wonder if I've woken up to an alternate universe.

Ricky pours two glasses of the liquid he prepared and, for a minute, I fear he's going to give me one of them and make me drink that vile-looking concoction, but he doesn't. He looks at his watch again.

"They're late, which can only mean one thing. Marcy's giving Nora hell." He shakes his head and smiles.

To make conversation, I almost ask what he has put into that smoothie, but I have no desire whatsoever to find out.

"How long have your worked for Nora?" I ask instead.

"Coming up to three years now." He leans against the counter. "Best time of my life." He nods pensively. "I didn't have much of a life befo—"

The glass door to the kitchen slides open. Nora walks in with a towel draped around her neck. Her work-out gear is completely drenched in sweat. Hot on her heels is a tall woman with a buzz cut who has the kind of presence that sends an instant chill up my spine.

"You're up." Nora grins at me.

Ricky hands Nora and Marcy the smoothies he prepared. "Drink up, ladies."

While she sips, Nora introduces me to Marcy, who appears to be a woman of few words. She glares at me while she drinks, towering over me. Drill sergeant doesn't even begin to describe her. This is the person Nora spends two hours with every day first thing in the morning?

Nora downs that drink in no time. "As you can see, I need a shower. I'll be right back."

"Are you staying for breakfast, Marcy?" Ricky asks.

"Nu-huh." She gives me a once-over, as though she's been told that she should eat breakfast somewhere else today and it's all my fault. Or maybe she just really disapproves of my body. "I'm just going to arrange some stuff in the gym and head out. See you tomorrow, Ricky." She blows Ricky a surprisingly coquettish air kiss. "Ma'am." For me, she only has a terse nod on offer, as though she doesn't agree with me keeping Nora up past her usual bedtime. I don't agree with being woken up so early, so I guess that makes us even.

"I wouldn't want to spend any time with her in the gym, but Marcy's actually a sweetheart once you get to know her." Ricky sends me an apologetic smile. "Now, tell me. What can I make for you. Eggs? Avos? Buddha bowl?"

"You know what, Ricky, you can make me whatever tickles your fancy. As long as it's not one of those smoothies."

"I'm making avocado and black bean eggs for Nora. Shall I make that two portions?"

"Sure."

I watch Ricky as he gets to work. He's a chatty guy and pleasant company.

"I met Nora at the LGBT Center," he says, after we've been exchanging small talk for a while. "She only employs people she knows through there. People like me, who really need a job, you know? It's like adding rocket fuel to your résumé when you can say you worked for Nora Levine."

"Really?" All this time I've spent with Nora, and she's never breathed a word about this—she's usually too busy putting herself down.

"Except for Marcy." Ricky giggles. "She's straight out of the army."

Nora joins us. Apart from a soft pink color in her cheeks, you can't tell she just did god-knows-what in the gym. She's dressed in jeans and a pale-blue sweater. Her wet hair is pulled back in a ponytail. "Hey, did you get some more sleep?" She briefly puts a hand on my knee.

"A bit."

"I should have told you last night that I'm an early riser. Sorry. It slipped my mind due to… circumstances."

"Now I know and I will never, ever forget." That alarm clock might have scarred me for life.

"I only get up this early when we're shooting and I have to be on set early. So it's just for a few months each year."

"Breakfast's ready," Ricky says.

"Let's eat outside. It's a beautiful day," Nora says.

After we've sat down and Ricky has gone back into the kitchen, I glance up at Nora. "I could get used to this. Well, minus the five o'clock alarm."

Nora tucks into her food with the kind of gusto I've not seen from her before. "You're welcome here any time," she says in between greedy bites.

CHAPTER 25
NORA

Marcy has worn me out completely. My arms tremble as I cut up my eggs. Ricky makes them just how I like them, runny but not to the point of slimy. I usually spend this hour before going to work recovering from my workout in complete silence, some much needed peace and quiet before another crazy day on set, but not today—not that I mind, I just need to adjust a little.

"Am I welcome here again tonight?" Mimi asks.

"Sorry. I can't tonight." I need to tell Juan and Imani about last night, after which I need to catch up on the sleep I missed. My alarm will be going off at five again tomorrow—and Marcy really has no mercy. "Just so we're clear, I can tell Juan about, um, this? About us? It's not a problem because of Austin?"

"Of course you can tell your friend, Nora."

"Are you going to tell Austin? Juan won't say anything to Austin if I ask him not to, but... it's a bit of an awkward situation to put him in."

"It's a bit early to tell my kids," Mimi says. She's totally right.

"I get it. It is way too early." I have no clue what I'm doing yet—I haven't even fully grasped that I'm doing it. "But I can't keep this from my friends. Not even if I wanted to. They'll read it off my face as soon as they lay eyes on me."

"Let's not worry about that," Mimi says. "This is delicious, by the way."

How can Mimi not stress about this? "Aren't you worried your kids will find out?"

"If they do, they do. I can handle it."

"I think I'll ask Jay not to tell Austin."

"Nora." Mimi puts her fork down. "It's not a secret. At least, I'm not in the habit of keeping secrets from my kids. If Juan tells Austin, I don't have a problem with that."

"Okay." For now, I decide to take her advice and not worry about it. I have work to focus on. Then, I have the expressions on Juan's and Imani's faces to look forward to.

"You met Ricky at the LGBT Center?" Mimi asks.

"Oh. Yeah. Ricky's amazing. He's so talented." I lick my lips. "His eggs are to die for."

"Was he a chef and you met him just as you were looking for one?"

"My previous chef trained him. Didn't she do a wonderful job?" I look at my empty plate. I sure wolfed down those eggs. A workout with Marcy always has that effect on me.

"That's extraordinary," Mimi says.

"It's really not. You know what's extraordinary? That I get paid millions to act, to do the thing I love the most. To play this character for a few hours each day. That doing something like that earns me all that money while people like Ricky come to the Center with nothing. That's extraordinary, because it's not how things should be. So I help where I can. It's only normal." I shrug. "I throw a huge Christmas party at the Center every year. Just so that people who are away from their family can experience some of the Christmas spirit. You should come. Bring your family." Maybe I'm getting a little ahead of myself. I'm not one for parties, but the LGBT Center's annual Christmas bash is one of the highlights of my year.

"I'd love to." Mimi takes a sip of coffee, then rests her gaze on me. "What about your family? Do you go home for Christmas?"

"Not usually, no. I spend Christmas with Juan and Imani."

"Oh, you go home for Thanksgiving? Or does your family come here?"

"What? No." What is this? Why do I suddenly feel as though I'm doing something wrong whereas mere minutes ago, Mimi was calling me, or at least my actions, extraordinary? "I told you. I'm not close with my family."

"All right." Judging by the disapproving look on Mimi's face, it's not all right at all. "It's not my business. I'm sorry for prying."

"My family's complicated, okay? I'll try to explain it to you some day, but I don't have time right now." I make a big show of looking at my watch. "I need to get ready."

"Nora." Mimi holds out her hand. "I didn't mean to upset you. Family is such a big and joyful part of my life, I sometimes forget not everyone is that lucky. I'm sorry."

"It's okay. I'm a little touchy when it comes to certain subjects." And I never promised this would be easy, I think, on the contrary. I take Mimi's hand in mine. "If you play your cards right, I might spend Thanksgiving with you." I run a fingertip over her palm. "As long as you realize I come in a package of three." What am I saying? Surely, I'm overcompensating for being so imperfect in Mimi's eyes earlier.

"And I come in a package with four children, their partners, and three grandkids." Mimi catches my finger in her palm.

"Looks like fun times ahead," I joke. What have I gotten myself into? Why does the first person I fall for in such a long time have to have such a large family? And what are we doing discussing Thanksgiving and Christmas after spending only one night together? I'm going to have to let Mimi take the lead on whatever this is because I'm out of my depth already and I have no clue what I'm saying or doing.

Juan's jaw slackens. "I can't believe you, Nora." He jumps up, then sits again, encouraging Izzy onto his lap. "You slept with my boyfriend's mother."

"Don't say it like that. You make it sound so sordid."

"I'm going to need more wine." Imani refills our glasses. "I'm so happy for you, Nora."

"I sensed that this was coming." Juan looks straight ahead, as though he's genuinely stunned. "It's not a surprise, really, yet it still shocks me."

"It's a shock to me as well," I admit. "Honestly, I don't quite know what to do with myself. I want to keep seeing her, but..."

"No, no, no." Imani wags her index finger. "No buts, Nora."

"Let her speak, darling," Juan says. "This is my boyfriend's mother we're talking about. We have to take all the possibilities for drama into account."

"Jay." Imani's tone is not one Juan will argue with. "This is not about you and Austin."

"No, he's right," I say. "It is also a little bit about them."

"Please don't tell me I have to keep this a secret. That boy adores his mother. Mama's boy doesn't even begin to describe Austin. If Nora Levine breaks his mother's heart, he might end up hating me for it."

"Jay, for crying out loud." Imani's not one to shout, but she can put plenty of menace into her voice.

"I know I'm a drama queen. I own it, girl," Juan says. "And yes, this is about Nora, but that doesn't mean we can just ignore Austin and me."

Izzy looks up at Juan with adoring eyes. He looks back at her and gives her another scratch behind her ear. Juan takes a deep breath. "Also, Nora, are you going to enlighten us on how it was with Mimi? I take it things were a bit rusty down there?"

Both Imani and I can't help but break into a chuckle. We are family, after all. We can go from tension to laughter in the space of a second.

"Everything's in full working order, thank you very much." I shake my head. "You know I'm not going to give you any details, so best forget about that now."

"Even though this is a monumental occasion and I would normally interrogate you until the sun comes down, I won't," Jay says. "Mimi's like… well, let's just say that if I were the marrying kind, she could become my mother-in-law."

"Jesus, Jay. How long have you known Austin?" Imani asks.

"About as long as Nora's known Mimi."

"And you're still crazy about him?" While embarking on my own romantic adventure, I've forgotten to ask my friend about his. "After all those weeks?"

"Five weeks and six days, to be exact," Juan says.

"That must be some sort of Juan Diaz record," Imani says.

"It's not, but I feel like with Austin, I could break all former records. I'm nowhere near sick of him. My heart jumps in my throat every time he simply texts me. He does this cute thing with his fingers when he's nervous that just cracks me up. And when he looks into my eyes, I swear I might just drown."

"Wow. You've got it bad, darling." Imani grins at Jay.

Listening to Juan describe his feelings for Austin makes me wonder if I should be feeling all those things as well. I'm definitely not sick of Mimi—I'm the one who kissed her on that rooftop. When we slept together last night, there were a few times when I believed I could no longer come up for air, that's how overwhelming it all was.

"I'm so in love with that man," Juan says. "I want to do it right. But if you tell me not to talk to him about you, Nora, then I won't. You know my loyalty is always to you first." He clasps a hand to his chest.

"It's okay." I remember what Mimi said this morning. "Let's not worry about it too much. You can tell Austin. He's your boyfriend, and she's his mother. You can't keep something like that from him."

"Thank you," Juan says, as though I've just given him Izzy instead of permission to tell his boyfriend his mother's sleeping with Nora Levine.

"So, it's a thing?" Imani asks. "You're… dating Mimi"

"Yeah." A warm glow speeds through my chest. "Looks like I am."

"I'll be fucking damned," Imani says. "She must be some woman."

"She is," I say. A short silence falls as, perhaps all three of us, ponder how utterly out of the ordinary this is.

CHAPTER 26
MIMI

Although it's not unusual for one my kids to drop by unannounced, my heart skips a beat when Austin walks in.

"Mom." He seems out of sorts when he kisses me on the cheek. "I had to come by because I wanted to do this in person." Has Juan told him already? "Guess who called me."

For a split second, I think it might be Nora—although she's really not the type to do that out of the blue.

"Cathy!" Austin says. "Can you believe that woman?"

"Cathy?" This will be a different conversation than the one I thought I would be having. Good—although it's not acceptable that my ex called my son. "What did she want?"

"She wants you back, Mom. And she's making sure I know all about it."

"Was she drinking? Did she sound drunk?"

Austin shakes his head. "Stone-cold sober. She told me she made a huge mistake and asked if she and I could meet. To catch up and talk about… things. Is she completely delusional?" He glares at me. "Nothing happened, right? When you went to meet her at that bar?" He rakes his gaze over me from head to toe. "I don't know. There's something different about you tonight. It's not her, is it?"

"If there is, it has nothing to do with Cathy." I boil some water for a cup of tea. Two years of nothing, and all of a sudden my ex is back, and I slept with Nora Levine. "I'll make sure she doesn't contact you again."

"I told her that myself. Don't get in touch with her. I'll warn the girls they might get a call from her. Tell them not to pick up."

"That's very sweet of you."

"Yeah, but seriously." He tilts his head. "I can't put my finger on it, but… I don't know. I'm probably imagining things." I've often wondered if my son and I aren't too close—that I can read him like an open book is only normal because I'm his mother, but it shouldn't be like that the other way around. "Unless there's something you'd like to share." He bats his lashes.

I'm in two minds about telling him. It's still so early and this is Nora Levine we're talking about. I'm not sure he can handle the information. On the other hand, do I want him to find out from Juan instead of me? But if I do tell him, I can't ask him to keep it a secret from his sisters. Or can I? Maybe Nora was right, and this is more complicated than I thought.

"Mom?" The kettle boils. "You're being awfully quiet."

"Let me make the tea and then we'll talk."

By the time I sit, the huge expectation is visible on Austin's face.

"Who is it, Mom?" Clearly, he has no idea.

"Listen, darling, the thing is that I shouldn't be telling you anything yet because it puts way too much pressure on something that is only in the very early stages and delicate and fragile—"

"Mom." This is my son I'm talking to. "You're killing me."

"I've been, um, seeing Nora and yesterday, things got more serious very quickly."

His brow furrows. "Nora? Nora Levine?" He says it as though I just told him I'm dating the pope or someone else completely inconceivable. "Are you and Juan pulling a prank on me? Because Nora doesn't date. She's like Jennifer. And even if she did date, why would she..." He scratches his stubble instead of saying what he's about to say—before insinuating that I'm the very last person on earth he would expect Nora Levine to be involved with.

"I'm telling you because I wanted you to hear it from me. Juan must know by now and I'm sure he can keep a secret, but I'm your mother and it doesn't feel right to keep this from you, what with you and Juan dating"

"Is this serious?" He sinks back in his chair. "I didn't notice anything when we were at Nora's."

"You're suffering from a small bout of tunnel vision at the moment, darling."

"How long has Juan known?" He shuffles in his seat.

"There hasn't been anything to know before today. I think Nora's telling him tonight."

"That's why he couldn't make dinner. He had to go see Nora." He brings his hand to his mouth and shakes his head. "This is humungous news." His face goes a little pale. "Did you, I mean... I can't even go there. But you and Nora, it's, um, sexual?"

"We're seeing each other, and I think it's serious." It's probably a pretty safe bet because Nora's not the type to strike up anything not serious with anyone. "I spent the night at her house last night."

"Mom. Come on. You're seeing Nora Levine? *The* Nora Levine? I know we've been to her place and it was cozy and wonderful, but it was still out of this world." He rests his chin on his palms, covering his cheeks with his hands. He looks as flabbergasted as I've ever seen him—rivaling that time, more than ten years ago, when he told me he had such a crush on his male lab partner. "Nora Levine likes my mom."

"I suppose it's too much to ask you not to tell your sisters?"

"I'm having lunch with Lauren tomorrow," he says, as though that says it all. As though sitting across from his sister physically makes it impossible not to tell her. "Besides, if I don't tell them and they find out that I knew all along by the time you're ready to inform them, they will not be happy sisters. I don't need that kind of aggravation in my life." He beams me a smile.

"Look, Nora, she's... well, as you just said, she doesn't date a lot. I'm her first in a very long time. Surely, you understand that this whole thing can still go so many ways."

Austin huffs out some air. "You want me to keep it a secret?"

"I would very much appreciate that. You can talk about it with Juan all you want, but don't tell your sisters yet, darling. Do it for Nora."

"I can keep a secret for Nora." He slides his hand in my direction. "And for my other favorite person in the world. I get it, Mom. I don't want to be the one to screw this up for you." He gives my hand a quick squeeze. "I might have to skip Sunday brunch, though. I'm strong, but not that strong." He chuckles.

"Bring Juan. It will distract them."

"Fuck me, Nora Levine is going to be my stepmom."

"This is exactly why you shouldn't tell the girls yet. You do realize that?"

"Oh, Mom." He ignores my comment. "I'm so happy for you I could cry." He gets up. "I need a hug from my mama."

I rise and hold my son tight. I'm glad I told him, but whether I can trust him to keep his mouth shut remains to be seen. "I love you, darling."

"I love you too, Mom." He puts his head on my shoulder. "And I love Nora, too."

It's late when Nora calls. I'm half asleep in front of the TV, both my body and mind catching up with the last twenty-four hours.

"Hey," Nora says. "How was your day?"

Since I became single again, it's been rare that someone asks me that question at the end of the day.

"Not bad at all. Yours?" It's good to hear her voice.

"I told Juan and Imani about us. Jay was shocked. Imani not so much."

"I told Austin. He dropped by and I couldn't keep it from him. So it's okay. He and Juan can process together."

Nora inhales sharply. "How did he react?"

"That boy thinks you walk on water, Nora. He was astounded, actually. He probably can't quite believe that his mother gets to be with someone like you."

"Surely he does. You're his mom. He has first-hand knowledge of how special you are."

If it's her intention to make me melt, it's working. "But I'm parent-level special in his world, which isn't really that special at all. You're Hollywood special. It's not exactly the same for him."

"You know that doesn't mean anything, right? Being on TV doesn't make me special, and definitely not more special than you."

"I may need you to pass on this information to my children at some point."

"Don't worry, Mimi. I'll talk to them." I can't help but wonder whether Nora ever will, not to tell my kids that she's no more special than I am—they'd never buy it, anyway—but just in general, as my new partner hanging out with my family. "Do you want to come over tomorrow evening?" she asks.

My heart flutters in my chest. "Depends," I say, while I actually want to scream a very loud 'yes' through the phone. "What time is your alarm going off the morning after?"

Nora laughs and it's such a joy to hear her laugh like that, to have her lower her inhibitions. "I sleep in on Saturdays."

"Good, because so do I. But just to be sure, what's your definition of sleeping in? Is it setting your alarm for six instead of five?"

"No alarms. Not even the doggies. I'll have Chad take them on a long walk and I'll make sure we have the house to ourselves."

"Sounds like heaven."

"Marcy will be coming around before lunch, though."

"Really?"

"I only take Sundays off from working out."

"What if I make you an alternative proposition?"

"Like what?"

"I'll give you a different kind of workout before lunch."

"You can do that on Sunday," Nora says matter-of-factly—no room for negotiation in her voice. "Remember when we first met and you made me change my schedule for you?"

"Sure, but that was different and we know each other much better now."

"I told you. My body needs a lot of work to look this way."

I swallow what I'm about to say—that her body doesn't need to look like an elite athlete's. "I'll stop complaining then."

"See you tomorrow, Mimi. Sleep well." Without further ado, Nora hangs up.

CHAPTER 27
NORA

I'm both nervous and excited when Mimi arrives. When shooting, I wouldn't usually entertain guests on a Friday evening because I'm mentally drained after a week on set, but I gladly make an exception for Mimi.

I walk her into the house and before I can guide us to the patio, she grabs my hand and pulls me to her.

"Hey," she says, while looking into my eyes. "It's *really* good to see you." She leans in to kiss me and the plans I had for us threaten to go out of the window already.

"And you." I wrap my arms around her shoulders. "I was thinking that, if you feel like it, we could watch my favorite movie together. I haven't shown you my home theater yet."

"Is that a euphemism?" Mimi asks.

"No." I chuckle.

"Oh." Mimi kisses my neck and I go weak at the knees already. "Pity," she whispers in my ear.

Excitement is winning out over the nerves I feel about this, about jumping into whatever this is with Mimi headfirst—because I'm not a headfirst kind of person. I need to examine a proposition from all sides so I can make an informed decision—and after that much careful consideration, my answer's usually no. I don't yet know why I keep saying yes to Mimi. Why I let her waltz in here and kiss my neck like that, when I'm bone-tired after a week of work. But I do. And it feels good to do this, to not let the other part of me win for once. To throw caution to the wind and allow myself this heady feeling of falling in love. Because that's what it is. It may have been a long time since I experienced it, but the sensation is unmistakable.

"I guess we can watch that movie any time," I say.

"How about tomorrow?" Mimi's hand snakes into my hair. "Or next week."

All three dogs, even Rogue, do a little dance around our legs. "You haven't said hello to the babies yet. They take great offense when you don't."

"I'm so very sorry. It's hard to tear myself away from their mistress." Mimi kisses my neck again, then pulls away and bends downs to pet the dogs. Izzy's jumping up and down like a little lunatic. "Hello, you." Mimi crouches all the way down and picks her up. "Is Izzy short for something?"

"She's only named after the greatest singer of our time."

"Isabel Adler?" Mimi asks.

I nod. "I love her so much."

"Isabel Adler's amazing." Mimi looks into my dog's face. "I bet you can't sing like her."

"She tries, but to no avail."

Mimi puts Izzy down. "I used to know her manager. Back in the day, before Izzy hit the big time, Ira spent some time in LA. I met him a couple of times."

"Really?"

"We're of the same generation." Mimi shrugs. "Have you ever met Isabel Adler?"

I shake my head. "I wouldn't dream of it."

"Why not?"

"Because of my name, I could have something arranged. I could go to one of her concerts and meet her backstage. I've let myself be talked into things like that before. But some heroes, I believe you shouldn't meet." What would I even say to someone like Isabel Adler? Especially after what happened to her?

"My kids surely don't regret meeting you," Mimi says.

"I truly hope I'm not their hero the way Isabel Adler is mine."

"What do you mean?" Mimi was about to come for me again, but she seems to have changed her mind.

"Nothing." It's my go-to reply when I've gone as far as I can go regarding a certain subject, or I don't want to get into a conversation I know will be difficult to get out of due to my limited communication abilities. "Where were we?"

"I'm just curious, Nora." Mimi takes my hand in hers. "Trying to figure out how your brain works."

"Good luck with that." I smile at her.

"I'm enjoying every single second of it."

Once again, Mimi kisses away my doubts. If I had known it was this easy, I would not have stayed single for so long. But maybe it's only Mimi's kiss that has this power. That has me forgetting all about my hang-ups because her lips are so damn soft and she grabs the back of my head with just the right amount of firmness in her grasp.

"I've been thinking about you non-stop," she whispers in my ear. "All very unchaste thoughts."

"Like what?"

"I'd much rather show than tell."

Didn't we agree to take things slowly? My mind is so frazzled, so filled to the brim with desire for her, I don't remember. Maybe I only had that conversation with myself in my head—not an uncommon occurrence, either. "You'd better come upstairs, then."

Mimi's nose tickles my neck, her breath is hot on my skin. "How about we take this outside instead?"

I swallow the immediate 'no' I have at the ready out of my throat. She also has that effect on me.

"I have a very specific scenario in mind," Mimi says.

"Okay." I'm more excited than reluctant—and also rather curious.

A few minutes later, Mimi's dotting kisses along my collarbone while my back is pressed against the patio's glass railing, the city lights blinking below me. But I can't see any of that—nor can I actually see the point of doing this here, but I've learned to play along with other people's whims to a certain extent.

For this to work, I have to say yes once in a while. That's how relationships thrive. Not that I'm objecting, because Mimi has a way with me. There's something in her touch that I respond to, in how she looks at me that makes me want to say yes more often than before.

Her hands slide under my top and go straight for my bra clasp. Before I know it, Mimi's cupping my breasts, her fingertips stroking my nipples, and I start losing my mind to her a little more still. If I've lost it so much already that I'm okay with this, where on earth will it end?

She gazes into my eyes. Her glance is full of desire, full of the lust I feel inside myself as well. When I look at her, I forget the parts of myself I prefer to ignore. When she looks at me like that, I simultaneously feel more like myself and like a complete stranger. It's disconcerting, but thrilling. And fuck, I just really want her and, for once, I'm okay with that. For now, I can banish all the reasons why this might end badly—and there are many—to a corner of my brain where my consciousness can't reach.

One hand remains on my breast, while her other travels lower. She unbuttons my jeans and her fingertips skate along my panties. She kisses me and I open myself up to her again. Her finger dips lower and—we're interrupted by the loud ring of a phone. It's not mine.

Mimi stiffens. "Sorry." Both her hands retreat instantly. "It's probably one of the kids. I'm sorry, Nora. I really have to get this. You never know."

"It's okay." I take a breath and center myself.

"Hi, darling," Mimi says into her phone. "No, don't stop by. I'm not home." A pause. "Late. No. Lauren, I'm sorry. I'm the middle of something. Can I call you back?" Clearly Lauren is not having any of that, because the call's not ending. Maybe I should take the opportunity to run up to my bedroom and fetch some supplies, if Mimi's planning on spending a lot more time outside.

It takes a few more minutes before she hangs up.

"Sorry." She sends me an apologetic smile. But there's nothing to pull you out of a moment like the one we were just having than a call from your lover's kids—like reality calling and ruining the magic of the moment. "My weekends are usually pretty taken up with kids and grandkids. It's always something with a family that big."

"Hm." I stand against the railing with my bra hanging off my shoulders and my jeans flipped open. "I wouldn't want to keep you from anything."

"Let's talk about it later." Mimi puts her phone away. "Where were we?"

"Can you put your phone on silent?"

"I'd rather not."

"Oh." Is she serious?

"I choose to be reachable to my kids all the time."

All the time? Aren't they adults? "Sure." Mimi's family is so picture-perfect and wonderful, who am I to comment on how she runs it?

"Don't worry." Mimi presses her body against mine. "I'll have you back where you were before in no time."

Mimi kisses me again but the magic of how she arrived here and nuzzled my neck and made me forget about myself, made me want the same thing as her, has evaporated. I'm too much in my head to enjoy it to the same extent as I did before, to go with the flow she was suggesting, follow the pace she was setting.

"I'm sorry," I say, because I really am. Because this is where my neurotic side is about to take over. "It pulled me out and… I need some time."

"That's totally okay."

"I shouldn't have assumed you could just spend the weekend." I don't even want to spend the weekend with Mimi. I need some time on my own to recharge before Monday.

"I have a car. I can go places and come back." Mimi straightens her clothes. She does have a way of putting things that makes what I say sound pretty ridiculous.

I button up my jeans and try to close my bra, but my fingers feel too clumsy, and I can't be bothered anymore. Suddenly, I feel deflated more than anything else.

"Do you need some help?" she asks.

"No, Mimi." I walk to a chair and sink into it. "I'm sorry. I'm really tired and…" *Don't say it.* "Maybe this was a mistake."

"What's a mistake?" Mimi asks. "I don't know what you mean."

What must I look like to her? Moments ago, she was all over me. Her fingers were about to dip into my panties. And now I've gone all hot-and-cold on her again. How can I pull myself together quickly?

"There will be a lot of times when you don't know what I mean." I can't get a grip on myself.

"Nora." Her tone's suddenly clipped. "What's going on? We were having a good time, weren't we? Or did I read that so wrong?"

"No. We were, but… I shouldn't have invited you tonight. I'm so tired. Exhausted, really. I don't have the kind of energy you have. I need to rest."

She pulls her chair close to mine, our knees almost touching. "How about that movie, then?" She puts her hands on my knees. "Because I'm not going anywhere."

"Yeah. Okay." Am I fucking this up already? Just like that? I look into Mimi's patient face. I'm not like you, I want to say, but I don't, because it serves no purpose—and I'm sure she knows by now. I don't know how to do this. To let someone in and just be me. I've never known. If it's supposed to come naturally—which is what Jay and Imani would have me believe—then why is it so damn hard?

I take her into my home theater and we watch Faye Fleming and Ida Burton fall in love on the big screen. Their chemistry is out of this world and this movie, *A New Day*, is my favorite for a reason. It always makes me feel at least ten percent better, no matter how hard my day has been.

CHAPTER 28
MIMI

After waking up together on Saturday, Nora and I agreed to spend the rest of the weekend apart until Sunday evening. As usual, I have my children over for a long, luxurious brunch on Sunday. I can only hope that Austin hasn't told his sisters, because I'm beginning to see why Nora doesn't do relationships. It's like she doesn't have a clue what they are and how they work. I can tell she has feelings for me, though, and for now, it's enough. For now, I can work with whatever she has to give me.

"Hey, Mama." Austin hugs me tightly. "Look who I brought."

"Hey, Mama," Juan echoes, and he's so charming, I let him get away with it. "What an absolute pleasure to see you again." He pecks me on the cheek—unlike most of Austin's friends who prefer air kisses over real ones.

"Don't worry," Austin whispers in my ear. "I haven't told the girls."

"Good for you, babe." Juan blows Austin a kiss, then turns to me. "Between us, he's been insufferable since he's known. Like Nora's in love with him instead of you."

Nora's in love with me? She certainly hasn't told me that, or maybe she just didn't say it with words. There was a moment on Friday night, when I genuinely thought she would ask me to leave. If she'd actually asked, I would have, of course, although I'd like to believe she wanted me to stay. One thing's for sure. This isn't going to be a whirlwind romance. That's not an option with Nora Levine.

The rest of the family arrives, and whenever Nora comes up, as she does in my family—especially after last week's pool party—Austin shoots me a look. If he keeps that up, the girls will find out in no time. They're not stupid. Luckily, they're not that observant either. Heather and Lauren's main focus is on their kids and Jennifer has always been more focused on herself than anyone else. They also have no reason to suspect that their mother would be romantically involved with Nora Levine.

When I get a moment alone with Juan, I can't help but ask him. "Have you spoken to Nora this weekend?"

"I speak to Nora every day." He quickly wipes the grin off his face. "I know your movie night didn't really go as planned. Nora told me she freaked out."

"Is she okay?" Those damn butterflies flutter in my stomach again.

"She's a bit embarrassed, I guess, but otherwise, she's fine." He sends me a gentle smile. "Our girl's a tough nut to crack. It's all well and good when you're a gay man like myself, with no romantic designs on her whatsoever." He sighs. "She's not going to change just because she has feelings for you she doesn't know what to do with, but I promise you, Mimi, she's so worth it. Even though she's convinced she's not, and that's by far her biggest issue. That's my promise to you and something I want you to remember when things get a little dicey, because they will. Nora's her own worst enemy and she just can't help herself."

"You obviously love her very much." Juan's plea is so heartfelt, you'd think he was begging me to take Nora back after an actual break-up.

"Love her? She's like my sister. She's my family. She might as well be my blood." He glances at me. "Do you? Love her?" His voice is soft and sweet, but his question is clear.

"I like her a lot and I'm taking my chances with her. But, um, she's not straightforward, is she? She's a challenge, but one I can handle." At least I think I can. Any doubts I express to Juan will probably go straight to Nora's ear, so I have to watch what I say.

"For the record, she likes you a lot as well. You could be so good for her, Mimi. You could be exactly what she needs."

"We'll see."

"You're seeing her tonight, aren't you?" Juan asks.

"Who are you seeing?" I got so caught up in listening to what Juan had to say about Nora, I didn't hear Heather walk up.

"Nora," I say truthfully. We're friends. It's perfectly plausible for Nora and me to spend time together.

Still, Heather's eyes go wide. "Is she coming to the house?"

"No, darling." I make a mental note to not invite Nora here until I've told all my children. They have a habit of dropping by at the most awkward moments. "I'm going to hers."

"Lucky you." Heather pulls up a stool and sits with us. "Are you and Austin also going?" she asks Juan.

"Austin and I have much better plans." Juan waggles his eyebrows.

"Oh, god. Way to make me sorry I asked." Heather chuckles. "I was going to ask if you could take the boys tonight, Mom, but I don't want to foist those mini gangsters onto Nora Levine."

"Austin and I can babysit," Juan is quick to say. Maybe he's worried I'd say yes to taking Wyatt and Lucas over to Nora's.

"Really? After what you just said about your plans for tonight?" Heather doesn't sound convinced.

"It's not because we're gay that we don't know how to

behave." Juan straightens his spine and pretends to be greatly offended.

"Austin *used* to babysit his nephews all the time, for your information," Heather says. "Until a certain man came along and monopolized all his time."

Juan nods, then calls for Austin. "We're babysitting your nephews tonight, babe," he says.

When I meet her that evening, Nora looks like a different person. Well rested and as upbeat as I've seen her. Not a hint of Sunday evening blues about her.

She asks me about my weekend, and I regale her with some tales about my family.

"Heather got Juan to babysit her kids," Nora says, reminding me of her close connection with Juan. "That's a first for him. If I were Heather, I'd pick Imani as a babysitter over Juan any day of the week."

"The boys are crazy about their Uncle Austin and the feeling's entirely mutual, so I'm sure everyone will be all right."

"I'll let you know how Juan survived the night." Nora smiles. "They do seem to be getting awfully serious. Juan's quite involved with your family. That's usually not his thing."

"There must be something about my family." I look into Nora's eyes. They sparkle as though she's hiding some great mischief. "That keeps both Juan and you coming back for more."

"There's certainly something about you." Nora reaches out her hand and I take it. "I'm sorry about last Friday. I was shattered. I always am after a week of shooting." She narrows her eyes. "And that for the younger party in this... affair."

"I have a lot of experience with actors. I don't take what you do for granted even a little bit, Nora. You don't have to apologize for being tired. I get it."

"Is there anything you don't get?" she asks.

The ninety percent of your true self you insist on hiding, I think, and the reasons why. "Fuck, yes. But let's not get into that tonight."

Nora nods. "For your information, I need to get up at five tomorrow."

"Oh, god," I groan. I don't know how to prepare myself for another brutal wake-up call like that. "There goes my beauty sleep."

"You don't have to stay if it's too much."

"I want to stay."

"It's up to you. Either way, I won't be offended. As long as you stay a good long while now."

"Want to watch another movie?" I waggle my eyebrows.

"I want you." Nora tugs at my hand. "I really do, Mimi."

I put any notions of feeling her up on the patio out of my head—maybe I can save them for later—and let Nora take me to her bedroom. We kiss and it's perfect. Nora's desire for me is obvious in the press of her lips against mine, in how her tongue darts deeper into my mouth. Nora Levine wants me, that much is clear. And I want her too—I do. Ever so slowly, I'm beginning to scratch the surface. She's allowing me a peek underneath her carefully orchestrated facade. I'm infinitely intrigued, so I'm exactly where I need to be.

We peel off our clothes because we have no time to waste. That wretched alarm clock is going to blare way too early. But before that, Nora is all mine, and I want her squirming underneath my touch.

I lie next to her, my body glued to hers. My fingers dance across her skin. I can't tear my lips away from hers just yet, even though I'm dying to taste another part of her. Nora spreads her legs for me, eagerly, and my hand slides down. To touch her there is everything. To make her feel like this. Not only because I'm well on the way to falling in love with her, but because of how she is. Of how unlikely this is for her, and how privileged that makes me.

My fingers skate through her wetness as I gauge if it's enough, if she's ready for me. We're magically in sync because Nora pauses our kiss and reaches for her bedside table. She hands me a bottle of lube and the intimacy of the act touches me. She must both trust me and have prepared for this. The preparedness is very Nora—the trust, I'm not so sure.

I make certain Nora's plenty wet before I enter her. She reaches for me, wants to pull me in for another kiss as my fingertip slides inside her, but I need to see her face. Her breath stalls as my finger slips in deeper, as Nora wraps herself around me. She doesn't look away, although her eyes flutter shut as I slide my finger all the way in.

She opens her eyes when I start to move inside her. Nora looks at me with her gaze full of surrender and I have to swallow a lump in my throat. My own emotions threaten to spill over, but this moment is about her. I focus on my finger. I slide out of her and add another. I slip deep inside of her, my gaze firmly on her, on her gorgeous face, on how she gives herself to me. Nora doesn't have to tell me in words that this isn't something she does regularly. That this is special to her—it's special to me too.

I touch the heel of my hand to her clit as my fingers move inside her. Looking her in the eyes like this is almost too intense for me. I cast my gaze down to her magnificent breasts and the subtle curve of her biceps as Nora's hand curls around my free wrist.

We may have many hiccups in whatever we're doing, in what we're trying to build together, but we'll always have moments like this to come back to. If things get dicey, the way Juan predicted they surely would, all I have to do is remember the magic of this moment with her, my fingers deep inside her, her pelvis writhing under my palm.

Nora gasps for breath. She groans at my touch. She lets go of everything that in other circumstances might hold her back. She gives herself to me completely. Nora tightens around my fingers. Her muscles spasm, before her body relaxes fully and she expels a moan so guttural, it engulfs me with a huge wave of happiness.

Silently, she pulls me near. I disappear into her warm embrace. Without words, she tells me everything I need to know.

CHAPTER 29
NORA

I can barely lift my fork to my mouth after this morning's workout with Marcy. Mimi's glance burns on me, but she doesn't say anything. I don't ask what she's thinking because I'm not in the mood to hear the answer. I'd much rather bask in the afterglow of our amazing night together. Of what she makes me capable of.

"How about," Mimi starts, "the three of you celebrate Thanksgiving at my house?"

"Hm." Is she serious? Despite what I blurted out the other night, that's a big step. "I don't know."

"I'm asking you now, so you have time to think about it and discuss it with Juan and Imani."

Smart move. "Is it just your kids and their families or is anyone else coming?"

"My ex-husband and his wife will be there."

"For real?"

Mimi nods as though this is how all divorced people spend the holidays. "Eric and I are still friends. It was important to us to keep that intact for the kids' sake."

"You want me to spend Thanksgiving with your ex-husband?" I can't think of a more horrible way to spend the holiday, unless, perhaps, spending it with my own family.

"I'm just putting it out there that it would mean a lot to me to spend it with you, but I acknowledge that my family is a lot. No hard feelings if you decline. If you think that makes things move too quickly."

"Your daughters don't even know about us yet. I'm an excellent actress, but certain things, I really can't hide."

"We'd have to tell them beforehand. I won't ask you to lie."

"Maybe we can have a mini-Thanksgiving the day after, just the two of us?" I offer.

"Sure."

"Wait." I drop my fork. "Are you really asking me whether you should tell your other kids about us?"

"No." Mimi shakes her head. "I'm simply inviting you to Thanksgiving. You, Juan, and Imani. What do you usually do?"

"We're very good at pretending it doesn't exist." I pause to think. "Juan might want to spend it with Austin this year, though."

"Even if that's what he wants, something tells me he'll spend it with you and Imani, anyway," Mimi says, and she's right.

"I'll be sure to tell him that's not necessary. I don't care, either way. Neither does Imani. Although the last couple of Thanksgivings, she was with her ex. She might need a little emotional propping up this year."

"Please know you are all very welcome at my house for the day." Mimi sends me a smile. "No problem whatsoever if you're not up to it, for any reason."

"Thank you, and I'll think about it."

"Good. Now, when will I see you again and, depending on your answer, what time do you have to leave this morning?" She eyes me as though she hasn't eaten in days and I'm the tastiest bite of food she's ever seen.

"What are you asking?" I wish Mimi didn't have this effect

on me. That I wasn't actually considering letting her have her way with me. I'm working. I need to focus and I need to prepare.

Mimi pushes her plate away. "I'm implying that I can make you come again before your car arrives."

I swallow hard. "I'm not really one for quickies."

"Wanna bet?" Mimi walks over to me and pushes my chair away from the table. She leans over me and kisses my neck.

"I just got ready," I protest, but my heart's not in it. I don't even know who I'm pretending for. "I'm still recovering from my workout." Mimi doesn't know how hard Marcy is on me—how ruthless I allow her to be.

"It's your call," Mimi breathes into my ear. "Yes or no." She clamps my earlobe between her lips, then trails a path of kisses down my neck.

"Fuck, yes." I can't believe this—I can't believe myself. This isn't me, and if it is, it's a part of myself I haven't been in touch with for a long time, maybe forever. All Mimi had to do to unearth it, is turn up. Be her glorious, exquisite self.

"Music to my ears." She kisses me full on the lips, her tongue slipping inside my mouth.

I hear noises from inside the house. Ricky's still here. Chad will arrive soon to take care of the dogs. I run my household on a tight schedule. I have strict rules in place to maximize my time alone, although most of them went out of the window the moment I let Mimi into my life.

When we break from our kiss, I say, "Ricky's in the kitchen. We can't do this."

"I'm sure Ricky's seen a thing or two." Mimi leans in again, but I push her away.

"No, Mimi. I can't. It's not right."

"Don't worry. I'll talk to him. Tell him to step outside at his own peril." Mimi winks at me, grabs our empty plates, and rushes inside. Jesus Christ. My cheeks have barely cooled off post workout, and now they're burning up again.

A few moments later, Mimi's back. She struts toward me with that confident stride she has. Who is this woman, anyway? Who the hell does she think she is to turn my life upside down like this? "It's all taken care of. You can relax." She holds out her hand. "Come here."

Without giving it any further thought, I take her hand. She leads me to a lounge chair at the other side of the pool.

"Maybe you'll feel more comfortable here," Mimi whispers as her hands roam across my body. If only she didn't make me feel so damn good, then I could put a stop to this madness. These sensations wouldn't overwhelm me to the point there are no rules anymore. My life has descended into chaos, which might be fun for a minute or two, but will surely come back to bite me in the ass later. I've learned that the hard way.

Mimi's already unbuttoning my jeans. She tugs them down. I help her get them off, because there's no way back now. Part of me strongly believes this isn't going to work, that there's no such thing as a quickie for a woman my age, but Mimi has proven me wrong before, and I don't want to deny her a try.

She looks into my eyes as she slides my panties off me. Then, there I lie. Legs spread wide on a lounge chair in the back of my yard. What has my life become? I don't do things like this —nor do I fall in love like this. But fuck, that soft rush of air between my legs feels amazing. It's quiet up here. It's just Mimi and me. She lowers herself toward me, kisses the inside of my thigh. She doesn't waste any time. Before I know what's happening, her tongue is soft on my clit, and a wave of heat and lust spreads through me.

It's surprisingly easy to give myself to her because I want it so much. Or maybe she's just a magician with her tongue. Or maybe a bit of both. Mimi's tongue on me there always unleashes something spectacular inside of me, nudges at the parts of me that have been stuck for decades. If I'm not careful, if I don't shield myself enough, she may loosen me up completely one day. God knows what will happen then.

But that's for later. This is now. My body is still tired from my workout, my muscles mellow, my blood vessels dilated. Mimi might be a magician, but it's not just that. I'm so in love with her, I'm seriously considering spending Thanksgiving with her and her family. I'm considering bending all the rules I've lived by for so long. Look at me, knees wide, at her mercy. How did she even do this? Because it's no longer a question of not believing in quickies, either. Not if the dizzy feeling in my head and fluttering sensation in my gut are anything to go by. I can't get enough of her tender tongue on my clit, how it stands for everything she is. How she makes me do things I would never otherwise consider with that soft but insistent touch she has. How she makes me see things differently. How she makes me come like this before eight o'clock in the morning. It's all so inconceivable, yet it's happening all the same.

"I vote yes." Juan holds up his hand. "But I guess you saw that one coming a mile away."

"I'm not sure." Imani sends me a quizzical look. "I'm not a fan of big family gatherings. And Nora, I didn't think that would be your thing either."

"Nora's in luuurve," Juan says. "She just wants to spend time with her lady."

"It's not my thing," I confirm. "But Jay's right." I let my head fall onto my shoulders. "Argh. I am in love." I huff out some air. "I don't have a fucking clue what's happening to me anymore."

"I'm so proud of you, girl." Juan suddenly sounds very solemn. "For letting this happen. I know that's not really your thing, either."

"It's Mimi." Even just talking about Mimi makes me feel all funny inside. "There's something about her I can't resist."

Imani peers at me, head tipped.

"Yes?" I ask, because I know that look.

"It's not exactly rocket science," Imani says. "I'm not judging." She brings her hand to her chest. "We all have some serious mommy issues, and Mimi happens to be this absolutely amazing mother. Subconsciously, you're drawn to that aspect of her."

"Objection!" Juan shouts. "That's my mother-in-law you're talking about."

"So?" Imani nods at Juan. "Don't tell me that Austin's big, happy family isn't part of it for you as well."

"I honestly don't care," Juan says. "I'm just baffled that I'm still so crazy about him. That his family's so welcoming and wonderful is a big plus, sure, but that's not why I'm in love with Austin." He pauses. "I'm just saying that there's no need to analyze why Nora feels this way," Juan continues. "Why can't we just be happy for her?"

"Oh, but I am." Imani looks at me. "Nora, you know I am. I'm over the moon for both of you. But a little extra insight never hurt anyone."

I nod, but don't say anything. Maybe Imani's right, but Juan's right as well. What does it even matter? I haven't felt like this in such a long time, it might even be too risky to analyze it —although analyzing, in the greatest possible detail, why things happen a certain way is one of my favorite pastimes. But I can't apply the same process to my relationship with Mimi. I don't want to pick it apart and assign subconscious feelings to it. I just want to enjoy being with her—and who I am when I'm with her. I quite like that version of me.

"Maybe we should just go. Just do it, without spending an evening debating it," I offer, surprising myself once again.

"Damn, girl," Imani says. "You've got it bad."

"Yeah." I glance at the chair in the corner of the yard where, earlier this week, Mimi made me come so hard so swiftly, I believed I had become someone else altogether.

CHAPTER 30
MIMI

The basket of bread I'm holding trembles in my hand. I make sure not to put it too close to where Nora's sitting—it's like she's allergic to it.

Thanksgiving is next week and we have to tell the girls today. I'm surprised Nora agreed to be here for this, but come to think of it, she hasn't ceased to surprise me since we met. The past few weeks have been like a dream. Thanksgiving or not, I want all my children to know about us. The risk of some major freaking out is high, but that's why I thought it would be a good idea for Nora to be present. They're all on the edge of freaking out already around her. And they might be more inclined to believe me if Nora can confirm our relationship to their faces.

"Okay." I stand behind my chair, hands gripping the back. Why am I so nervous? Telling Austin wasn't this stressful. Maybe because Nora and I have moved to the next stage. Informing Austin had more to do with him being Juan's boyfriend whereas this is really telling my family. I wonder if Nora's family even knows that I exist. She must talk to them sometimes. "I have some news." I glance at my kids and their partners. "*We* have some news." I put a hand on Nora's shoulder. She shifts in her seat. "Nora and I, we, um, we've been seeing each other."

"Rub it in, Mom," Heather says.

"Shut up, Heather," Jennifer shouts over her. "Let Mom talk."

"You *really* want to let her talk," Austin butts in. I wish he would wipe that smirk off his face, but of course he's going to feel smug about being the first to know.

"What do you mean?" Lauren turns to her brother. "What do you know that we don't?" She heaves a sigh worthy of the most obnoxious teenager, then looks at me. Her gaze rests on my hand squeezing Nora's shoulder. "Oh. No." She shakes her head.

"What?" Heather looks at her sister, then at me.

Nora helps things along by putting her hand over mine. "Your mother and I are in love."

I could die right here and now. And I'm slightly concerned about the stunned silence. It never happens when my family is together. Even the grandkids are shocked into silence.

"Don't all congratulate us at once." Nora breaks the tension —again. I didn't know she had it in her but, in the end, she is a performer. I don't blame her for calling on her acting skills to get through this. In fact, I love her even more for it.

"Is this a joke?" Jennifer glares at us. "You and my mom? That's just… not possible."

"Why not?" Austin's tone is combative.

"Of course, you knew." Heather shoots daggers at her brother.

"Girls, please." Nora gets up and stands next to me. "This is not bad news. And yes, Jennifer, it is very much possible." She folds an arm around my waist and pulls me close. If the girls weren't still absorbing the shock, I'd kiss Nora right in front of them.

"But you're Nora Levine," Bobby stammers. "And Mimi is my mother-in-law."

"So?" I love how Nora's not taking any of their antics. To think I was considering telling my kids without her. But I never would have guessed she'd be like this—so proud and open. "I hope you're not questioning my taste in the people I fall for."

"But Nora," Jennifer says. "I thought you were, um, like me."

"Being self-partnered is out of fashion already." I do wish Austin could be a bit less obnoxious to his sisters sometimes, but he's probably just blowing off steam. He's kept my secret beautifully.

"Babe. Come here." Juan pulls Austin to him. I witness how he shoots a quick wink at Nora. "Time for you to butt out of this," Juan says to Austin. "Let your sisters process in peace."

"How long has this been going on?" Lauren seems to regroup the fastest. "Were you already together when we came to your house?" There's no more room for deference toward Nora. It's inquisition time.

"No, but it started not long after," Nora says.

The memory of that massage still sits at the forefront of my mind—and we've made so many new, thrilling memories since.

"What's happening?" Wyatt yells. He's amped up as though he just ate the most sugary donut in the universe.

"Granny and Nora are, um, a couple. Like me and Daddy," Heather says.

Wyatt scrunches up his face. "But granny's so old," he says.

I can't possibly be offended by my grandson. Instead, I crack up.

"She's not that old," Bobby says.

I am rather offended by that.

"Your granny's a fabulous woman," Nora exclaims. She doesn't have a natural way to talk to kids—not like Imani—but I definitely like what I'm hearing.

"We just wanted you all to know," I say. "Shall we eat now?"

Nora and I take our seats at the table. Heather, who's next to me, leans over.

"I'm so happy for you, Mom." She plants a kiss on my cheek.

"Me too, obviously." Jennifer is always quick to follow on her twin's heels.

"Of course, we're happy." Lauren raises her glass. "I'm ecstatic that Nora Levine is going to be my stepmom."

"Nora, Imani, and I are crashing your St James Thanksgiving next week," Juan says. "So you all better get used to the idea by then. Nora's not the only new addition to this family, you know."

"Imani's coming!" Wyatt balls his little fist. "Yessss!"

"See." I lean into Nora's ear. "Everyone's happy."

She turns to me and amps up the wattage in her smile. "I'm happy, too," she says.

Bobby and Gus have been educated well. They're always the ones who help me clear the table. The girls flock around Nora. I have to trust I raised them well enough to behave—besides, they're adults. But famous people can have a weird effect on even the most level-headed person.

As I clean food off the plates, it hits me—not for the first time—that I've barely seen Nora put any food in her mouth. The only times I've seen her eat with any gusto and intention is after her morning workout. If any of my kids ate and exercised like Nora, I'd be having a serious conversation with them. But Nora's not my kid. She's my… girlfriend? Partner? I've gotten to know her body intimately over the past few weeks. As far as I can tell, she's in excellent physical condition, all her body parts functioning optimally.

"You and Nora, huh," Bobby says. "I didn't see that one coming, Mimi. But good for you."

"Thanks." What else can I say? I didn't really see it coming either, but here we are.

As usual, Gus is quieter and more pensive. He's always been a man of few words. Juan joins us. He's the opposite of Gus. When Juan's in your space, the space is all his.

"Hey, Mama. Let me do that." He all but snatches the plate I'm scraping off from my hands. "What is it with these kids of yours that you cook them a meal and then they pretend that washing up doesn't exist?"

"That's why she has sons-in-law," Bobby says.

We all chuckle, then I say, "It's my bad as a mother. I should have been stricter when it came to chores."

"No way." Juan's not having any of it. "Listen up, St Jameses!" He clanks a spoon against a dirty pan. "Mama Mimi is going to put her feet up and we are going to make this kitchen look spic and span." Is he including Nora in this admonition? I highly doubt it.

"But the cleaner's coming tomorrow," Jennifer says.

"How dare you, child." Juan beckons them over. "Everyone likes a tidy kitchen after a meal." I wonder who cleans up Juan's kitchen after he's made dinner. Come to think of it, I wonder who pays his bills. As far as I know, he volunteers a lot at the LGBT Center and he spends a lot of time with Nora. "Come on."

Nora sits there grinning. Her special skill is arranging for her staff to make her house look perfect while she's not there. I've only met Ricky and Chad—and Marcy, of course.

Juan holds out his hand to me. "Let's get you out of here, Mama."

"Jesus, Mom," Heather protests. "Is it going to be like this all the time from now on?"

"Control your man, Austin!" Lauren adds. "I have a one-year-old. This is the only time I get to put my feet up."

"Everybody into the lounge." I make sure my voice is heard above the hubbub. "Out you go, all of you. That includes you, Juan." His intentions are good, but I run my house how I see fit.

"Only trying to help." He's not the kind to take offense easily—he's probably been through so much worse.

Nora stays behind with me. Instead of helping, she sinks onto a stool at the kitchen island.

"You were really great with them." I stop what I'm doing and take her hands in mine.

"They love me already, so it's really easy."

"Do you maybe… want to stay here tonight? Spend the night?"

Nora's eyes go wide, as though I just popped a very different question. "I've got Marcy tomorrow morning. Or shall I ask her to come here?" She paints on a grin.

"Please, don't ever do that." I rub my thumb along Nora's palm. "Would it be completely inconceivable for you to skip one workout?"

"Yes." Her tone is curt. "I don't skip workouts. That's simply not something I do."

"Nora." I try to make my voice sound as sultry as possible. "Maybe things are a little different now." I squeeze her hand.

"Yeah, but, um… But still." She sighs. "Skipping my Monday morning workout is going to throw off my entire week."

"Is it really?" I'm only pushing slightly, only nudging at the edges of her boundaries—and only because I think Nora needs a little push from time to time.

"Yes." She pulls her hand away. "I don't expect you to understand, but that's how it is for me."

Clearly, I pushed too far. "Fine. Do you want me to come home with you?"

Nora shakes her head. "I'm going to need some alone time to unwind after this. It's a lot."

"All right." She's nothing if not straightforward. I pretty much know what to expect when I ask her a question—I just don't always get the answer I personally hope for.

"I'm sorry. I know I'm difficult." She looks at the dishes. "And spoiled. You should really have let your kids take care of those." The grin she sends me is so disarming, I don't have it in me to protest.

CHAPTER 31
NORA

It's the Monday before Thanksgiving, and we're not shooting this week. I'm in heaven because I'm lying with my head in Mimi's lap, Izzy happily snoring on my belly. Mimi's stroking my hair and we're just enjoying each other's company in silence.

"Can I ask you something?" Mimi breaks the blissful silence.

"Sure." I glance up at her. "Anything."

"Really?" She grins at me. "Even something that will most likely annoy you?"

"Who? Me? You know I'm not that easily annoyed," I joke.

"Just gauging your mood."

"You've done an excellent job of relaxing me. I may need you to follow me around permanently and run your fingers through my hair like this all the time."

"Great, and just so you know, after I've asked the question, and I might or might not have annoyed you, feel free to avail of my incomparable massage skills. Okay?"

"Okay." What is she going to ask me? "Just ask me already."

"I will, but I'm trying a new approach where I tell you beforehand that you're not going to like my question and I know you're going to get all defensive, and I'm ready for your reaction. I'm prepared and I'd like you to be prepared as well. But—" She slants to me and kisses my forehead. "I love you and I only want good things for you."

"Jesus." Way to kill the mood. At least she's not breaking up with me—she just told me she loved me. I pick up Izzy and push myself out of Mimi's lap. "Same," I say, and even though it sounds a bit lame, I mean it from the bottom of my heart.

Mimi looks at me, her features soft. "Are you planning on calling your parents this week? To wish them a happy Thanksgiving."

My muscles tense, but I can't just rebuff her after her extensive preamble. She has outsmarted me by predicting my reaction.

"My mom will probably call me on the day," I say.

"How about… you call your mom first," Mimi says.

"Why are you doing this?"

"Because, Nora, I am a mother and, no matter how strained your relationship with your parents may be, this must be killing them. Not being in touch with you. Not hearing from you. Do they even know about me?"

I suppose I can't say this isn't any of Mimi's business anymore. We're together now. She just told me she loved me—or was that just a sly means of manipulating me?

"For the record, I am extremely annoyed by this," I say.

"Oh, I know."

"It's too hard, okay? So I just don't do it. I don't call. I text now and then. Half the time, they don't even text me back. Half the time, I don't even know whether they care or not."

"Of course, they care."

I shake my head. "Just because you love your kids more than anything in the world, doesn't mean every parent does. Far from it."

"I know that. But do you have any evidence that *your* parents don't care?"

"Evidence?" What is she even talking about. "No. Things just are how they are, and I've made my peace with that."

"But you have the power to change things."

"Power and desire are not the same thing."

"But don't you want to talk to them? Or at least talk to me about them? I don't know the first thing about your parents, Nora. There are no pictures of your family in this house."

"Why are you so adamant on me changing things?" I point from her to myself. "This. You and me, is already enough of a change. I've told you from the very start not to expect too much from me, yet you keep pushing. You keep trying to change me." I shuffle backward, away from her. "This is who I am. If it's not good enough for you, you're free to leave any time." Come to think of it, she should go. Whenever Mimi starts scratching at my surface, she clearly finds something she doesn't like.

"I'm not trying to change you, Nora."

"Could have fooled me."

"I get why Juan and Imani have broken with their families. What I don't get is what your family has done that makes you want to ignore them." She holds up her hand. "Please, don't say that I won't understand. It's not a valid argument."

"I *have* explained it to you."

"Not sufficiently."

"This is so unfair." What the fuck is happening here? From blissfully lying in Mimi's lap to this? "What does it even matter? It's my business. It's my past. It doesn't concern you."

"It hurts me that you would just shun your family like that."

"Mimi, you don't know anything about it."

"So tell me."

"I don't want to talk about this stuff. It bums me out and I don't have the words for it."

"I know it's hard, Nora. I get that. But sometimes, you have to do a hard thing. All I'm asking is that you try and explain it to me so I can begin to understand. That's all."

"Oh, really? Because two minutes ago you were asking me to call them."

"Let's just start with you trying to explain."

"I don't owe you an explanation! What the fuck?" Every cell in my body screams no—I'm not doing this. I'm not being manipulated into this. "First, you think I should work out less. And I see how you look at me when I refuse to eat something. Now you want me to call my parents, because it hurts you in some inexplicable way. What's next? Hm? Basically, you want me to be someone else—someone I'm not." This is spiraling out of control quickly. I can see it happening, but I'm powerless to change it. I jump out of the couch. "I made myself vulnerable for you already, Mimi. I have—" The power to string a coherent sentence together swiftly escapes me. "This is why… I don't do this. Why I don't do relationships. This is exactly fucking why. Forget it. I'm done. Go. Please. Just go."

Mimi gets up. She walks to me and takes my hands in hers. "Nora, take a breath, please." She tries to look me in the eye, but I can't look at her now. "Remember how this conversation started? We both knew it could go this way and it's okay. I'm here and I'm not going anywhere."

I so wish that were true, but in my head, the next few moments are unspooling already. I can already see her walk out of the door, never to return. I can taste the relief that will wash over me when she does.

"It's not okay," I manage to say. "It's really not."

"Remember what I said?" Mimi's nothing if not persistent. "I love you, Nora. I only want what's best for you."

"That might be so, but you clearly have no idea what's best for me. You think you know, and you think you can start judging me just because we've been sleeping together for a couple of weeks. And fine, judge me all you want, but if this is how it's going to be, I'm out." I pull my hands free from her grasp.

"I'm not judging you. I'm trying to help."

"Help with what? I don't need your help." I most certainly don't need this. The barbed wire around my heart that Mimi so patiently, so carefully, dismantled is back. She can only hurt herself now, whatever she tries next. "I don't need any of this."

"Come on. Please. Be reasonable," Mimi pleads. The confidence in her glance is being replaced with hurt, with the dawning that, even though she tried to go about it gently, even a bit whimsically, it has all backfired.

"I am difficult. I know this about myself. There are things I do and things I don't do. Things I don't compromise on, for anyone. That includes you. Clearly, this is a problem, because you're already trying to negotiate with me. And I get it. I wish I wasn't like this either, but I've had to accept it about myself. And sure, you may think you love me, but guess what? You don't. You love some version of Nora Levine you wish I was. Just like everybody else." And that's how it always fucking is. "This…" I awkwardly wave my hands about my body. "Is not a lovable person. Now you know."

"Don't say that about yourself, Nora, please."

"I made a mistake. I thought I could do this because you're just so… kind and loving and…" My voice breaks, but I continue. "But I can't do this. I'm done putting on a show for you. I want to be alone."

"Nora, I'm not leaving you like this."

"Oh yes, you are." The first tears trickle down my cheeks. "It's over. I don't want to do this anymore." If only she wasn't so damn patient. If only she would leave already.

"I do love you." Mimi swallows hard. "In fact, I think I may love you a whole lot more than you love yourself."

Oh, Jesus. Not that again. "Please, I'm begging you. Go."

"Okay. But this doesn't have to be the end, Nora. It really doesn't."

Maybe if she said she was sorry for pushing too hard, but there's been no hint at an apology. This *is* the end and we are so over. Yes, we fucking are. Tears stream down my cheeks as my prediction comes true, after I've successfully chased her off, and Mimi leaves my house—hopefully never to return.

"What happened?" Juan asks.

"I really don't want to talk about it, Jay. I just need you to be here with me."

"Sure." Juan gets it. He doesn't pry or try to get me to call my parents. He leaves me alone—he knows me and still loves me in the only way that I can be loved. He sits next to me and puts his head on my shoulder. "I guess Thanksgiving at the St Jameses is off the table."

"For me it is, but you should go. I'm sorry if this makes things awkward for you."

"Are you sure you don't mind? I won't, if you need me. I'm here for you, Nora. I can sit here in silence with you and sulk for a good few hours, days even, if it helps."

"I appreciate that, but I don't want you to change your plans with Austin for me. He's your boyfriend. You should be with him."

"You're my soul sister. That trumps everything."

"Thank you, but it's okay."

"All right. Imani will stay with you. She didn't really want to go in the first place."

I nod. "Mimi pushed too hard, Jay. Way too fucking hard."

"I'm sorry."

"I'm not cut out for this. For a relationship. But I'm really happy things are working out for you and Austin. Who would have thought? Juan Diaz head over heels in love with a respectable man."

"Not me, sister. Not me." He gives my knee a squeeze. "But I am."

I expel a sigh.

"On a scale of one to Juan, how much does it hurt?" Juan's always plus-ten in our world.

"Too fucking much." Because I did let her get close. I let Mimi in. Some part of me must have really wanted her very badly, but I'm still me. No matter how wonderful Mimi might be, I'm still better off alone. Because this pain will diminish over time, and in a few months, weeks even, I will have forgotten all about her. At least that's what I like to make myself believe.

CHAPTER 32
MIMI

I've already told the kids about my break-up with Nora, so I wouldn't have to announce it to them today of all days—on Thanksgiving. But, fuck. I have to blink away a tear when Austin and Juan arrive.

"Oh, Mom." Austin pulls me into a very tight hug. "I'm so sorry."

"Hey, Mama." Juan's hug is even tighter. "You and I are going to have a little chat later, okay?" He finds my ear. "I happen to be the number one expert on all things Nora Levine."

What does he mean? I wish I could have that little chat right now, because I've tried calling Nora a couple of times, before I gave up, but it's like she has blocked my number which, come to think of it, is such a Nora move. But, right now, everyone's arriving, my ex-husband and his wife included.

"How are you holding up?" Jennifer puts a few dishes she has supposedly prepared—more likely bought from the deli around the corner of her house—into the fridge. The kids have been nothing but sweet and caring. I raised them well enough for them not to throw a tantrum at their mother breaking up with their teenage idol.

"I'm fine, darling," I lie, because it has hit me much harder than I'm letting on. Even more so because when I left Nora's on Monday, I meant what I said. That this didn't have to be the end. Nora clearly thinks differently about that.

But I'm surrounded by my family, by the people I love most in the world. And I have a meal to assemble. Drinks to prepare. The kids offer to help much more than they usually would, but I need to keep busy. I need to do things. Because I don't know if whatever I had with Nora can be salvaged. Either way, when shooting of *Unbreak My Heart* resumes next week, I'll be paying a visit to the set. Even if there's nothing left to salvage, I need more closure than what Nora has given me so far.

As I check the turkey, the question that's been haunting me since Monday comes at me again: do I even still want to be with her? Despite Nora claiming it's impossible, I do love her. But that's all I know.

Because their father's here, I've asked the kids not to mention my all-too-brief fling with Nora. Eric and I are still good friends, forever tied together by our children, but I don't want any questions about Nora. Not today, on this day of celebration and giving thanks. And I have a lot to be thankful for as I look around the table. Still, I wish Nora was sitting next to me today. I was over the moon when she agreed to come, because I hadn't really expected it. Maybe asking her to celebrate Thanksgiving with my family was my first mistake.

After dinner, Juan whisks me away from the kitchen and takes me up to Austin's old room. "Talk to me, Mimi. What happened?"

"You don't know?"

"All I know is you pushed her too hard one way or another, but that could mean anything with Nora. I know what she's like."

"Apparently, I made the unforgivable mistake of asking her to call her parents for Thanksgiving."

Juan's jaw slackens. "Oh, fuck." He shakes his head slowly. "That'll do it."

"Yeah. I noticed."

"Did she not tell you anything about her family?" he asks.

"She gave me some vague information about how they never really talk and are supposedly so bad at communication, whatever that may mean."

"Even I don't know a whole lot more than that and I've known Nora for twenty years."

"Have you ever met her parents?" I ask.

"A couple of times. Years ago. When they still came to LA once in a while. But it's been a really long time." Juan clears his throat. "Nora may appear very cagey about the whole thing, but I don't think she means to be. She's very touchy about the subject, though, which is why we never discuss it. We have this unspoken rule between the three of us to never judge each other when it comes to our blood family. But it's much more obvious why my family hates me, and Imani's family hates her. In our cases, it's a clear emotion. It's much more complicated with Nora and I genuinely believe she doesn't have the skill to express how things are exactly. That it probably hurts her more than she lets on. But she's learned to live with it."

I'm not so naive to think every family is like mine, with kids who call their mother all the time, and where the love is so obvious, nothing ever needs to be questioned. It's all just there.

"It was just a simple question I asked her."

"To Nora, there's no such thing as a simple question about her family."

"That may be so, but she didn't have to fly off the handle. I told her beforehand, made it abundantly clear, that I was speaking from a place of love."

"Still, you must have made her feel judged and that the love you professed to have for her was somehow conditional." Juan holds up a finger. "I'm sure that wasn't your intention, but that's probably how Nora interpreted it."

I heave a deep sigh. "I don't really know what to do with that." I find his eyes. They're deep brown and kind. "Because, newsflash… Mama has feelings, too." Oh, fuck. Here we go. I've done a pretty good job of keeping my tears at bay, but here come the waterworks. "What Nora and I had was not nothing. It wasn't some meaningless fling. It was very precious to me." I wipe at my eyes.

"I know. I'm so sorry, Mimi." He holds out his arms and, fuck it, I don't care that I'm crying on my son's boyfriend's shoulder. "Maybe we can still fix this, though," he whispers as he pats my hair.

"How?" I say in between sobs. I try to square my shoulders, straighten my spine. I find a tissue in my pocket and dab at my moist cheeks.

"I don't know yet. This is new to me as well. Apart from a few brief dalliances decades ago, Nora really hasn't been with anyone. Literally, no one. So I'm not yet sure how to navigate this. She hates feeling manipulated more than anything." He taps his index finger against his chin. "I'll talk to Nora first."

"Did she give any indication that she, um, might want to patch things up?"

"Honestly…" He scrunches his lips into a tight pout. "No."

My stomach drops. Why are we even having this conversation? "I'm sixty-five, Juan. And yes, Nora got to me. I'm willing to give her another chance, if she wants it and she takes it. What I'm not willing to do is start over with someone who acts like a petulant teenager just because I ask her a question she doesn't like. I'm too old for that kind of bullshit."

"Got it." He nods slowly.

I hear a child shouting, then someone climbing the stairs. "We should get back."

"Yeah." Juan reaches for my hand and gives it a squeeze. "I'll try to work some of my special Diaz magic for you, Mama."

"Thanks," I say, but I'm not holding my breath.

It's late. I'm exhausted, physically as well as emotionally, and Jennifer's the only one left at the house.

"I think I'll stay over if that's all right?" she asks.

"Of course, darling." I'm more than happy with the company.

We sink into the couch together.

"When you came downstairs with Juan earlier, I could tell you'd been crying," she says.

"Yeah." I swallow another lump out of my throat.

"Do you love her?" Jennifer asks.

I nod and shrug at the same time. "I know you think the world of Nora, darling, but she can be infuriatingly complicated."

"I had to get used to the idea of you and Nora, because she's Nora Levine, you know? But I can't possibly imagine anyone not wanting to be with you. So I know it must be down to her."

"That's sweet of you to say, darling." I don't add that it's untrue. Cathy found plenty of reasons to dump me a few years ago. Although, I really don't believe this break-up with Nora is down to me. Although I keep mulling over what Juan said. That I somehow made Nora feel as though she wasn't good enough, even though that wasn't my intention. That my love for her depends on her behaving a certain way. There's not an ounce of truth in any of that, but if that's how Nora spins things in her head, what can I do about that? I can love her with all my heart, but I can't make her love herself enough so she doesn't have to twist my words into something they're not.

"At that party at her house a while back, she had a couple of drinks, and I had quite a long talk with her," Jennifer says. "Because I thought we were kindred spirits in being self-partnered." She arches up her eyebrows briefly. "Obviously, I didn't know there was something brewing between the two of you." She pauses. "From talking to her, it seemed her reasons for being single are the opposite of mine. Nora is not self-partnered. Not in the way that I am. She puts herself first, but it doesn't come from the same place that I do. She doesn't love herself like a partner would. I was quite shocked by her insecurity, to be honest."

"Yeah." My daughter might have just hit the nail on the head. Nora's not self-partnered because she finds all the love she needs within herself. She's single because she can't allow herself to be loved.

"It could be that she's just completely incapable of having a mature relationship, Mom. She has been single for a very long time."

"And I was a fool to think I could just swoop in and change that about her."

"You're not a fool for falling in love. That's just ridiculous."

Tell that to my foolish heart. "How about some mindless TV?" I'm done talking for the day. I'm done thinking about Nora.

"Sure." Jennifer switches on the television. Looking right back at us, is Emily Brooks in an inevitable *High Life* rerun. Jennifer quickly changes the channel. "We just can't escape her these days, can we?"

"We can from now on," I say, closing my eyes, trying not to think about Nora—again—and wondering what happened to that girl in her early twenties I just saw on my TV screen. What tricks life in Hollywood have played on her brain that she can only exist as a single recluse. I guess I'll never know.

CHAPTER 33
NORA

The Saturday after Thanksgiving Juan and Imani start ganging up on me.

"A woman like Mimi's not going to wait around for you to apologize forever," Juan says. "I hear her ex is sniffing around."

"Mimi's no longer interested in her ex," I bite back.

"Maybe she wasn't when things were unfolding with you, but you dumped her, so…"

"Jay." Imani shakes her head. "I'm not sure this is the way to go about things."

"I'm just telling it like it is. Mark my words, Cathy's going to make a move soon. She wants Mimi back."

"She's a little late for that," I say, but what do I know? Mimi dropped everything to pick her up from that bar. But it doesn't matter. It's not my business anymore. Juan's just trying to make me jealous. It's working, but only a little.

"Nora," Imani says. We're gathered around the table outside, as though we're having a meeting about something vitally important. "Are you a hundred percent sure that you're totally done with Mimi?"

"It's not a matter of being sure. It's just how it is."

Juan rolls his eyes. "Oh my god, Nora."

"What?" I know what he means. I'm sick of myself spouting bullshit like that as well.

"If you're waiting for an apology from Mimi, you will wait until the end of your days," Juan says. "She's not going to say she's sorry for what she said, because she's not. No matter how it made you feel."

"Fine, then." I know it's not exactly fair to expect Mimi to apologize.

"Nora." What Juan needs a few sentences for, Imani can convey just by saying my name. "I think you're making a big mistake."

"My life was fine before I met Mimi," I say. "Of course, I'm upset that it ended the way it did, because I really do—*did*—have feelings for her. You know that. But I'll be fine again soon enough."

"Argh," Juan groans. He taps his hand against his shoulder. "She was crying on my shoulder. It's not only your own feelings you have to take into account. You hurt her."

"I hurt *her*?" That's a good one.

"I think you know you did," Imani adds.

"I thought I didn't have to do this with you guys. That I didn't have to explain myself." This is a new one. Since when do my two best friends no longer unconditionally have my back?

"This isn't about us." Imani's gaze is kind on me. "You hurt another person. That's not okay."

"I didn't deliberately hurt her. I didn't mean to—she started it." I sound like a toddler bickering with a sibling I never had.

"I know what Mimi said," Juan says. "And I know it's a big no-no in your world, in this bubble you have created for yourself, but it really wasn't that bad. She was just trying to help."

"What the fuck?" Juan's breaking our pact. He's bringing family into it.

"Jay's right," Imani says.

My breath stalls in my throat. The raw sting of betrayal

burrows into my soul. It tastes foul in my mouth. What is this? An intervention?

"You have parents who pick up the phone when you call," Imani continues. Never in a million years had I expected such a low blow from her.

I can't believe they're doing this. This was never the deal. What the actual fuck is happening?

"I'm going upstairs." I push my chair away from the table. "When I come back in fifteen minutes, I want you both out of here."

"Nora." Juan stares daggers at me. What's he so angry about? "We're not going anywhere."

"We'll see about that." I'm too perplexed to move while I try to figure out the stunt they're pulling on me.

"You can't just kick everyone out of your house who disagrees with you about something," Imani says. "Unless you want to end up completely alone."

Being completely alone sounds like heaven on earth right now.

"Disagrees with me about *something*?" I cross my arms in front of my chest. "This isn't something. This is one of the things that connects us profoundly. That we've bonded over for years. And now you're throwing it back in my face? You're making it sound as though my feelings are not valid compared to yours and that's a pretty shitty thing to do to a friend."

"That is not what we're doing." Juan's demeanor is so stony calm, it's annoying.

"What if Austin told *you* to call *your* mother?" I ask. "How would you react then?"

"I would have an adult conversation with him," Juan replies. "I wouldn't kick him out of my house just because he means well."

"I tried to have a conversation with Mimi, but she had to keep on pushing, saying it hurt *her* that I supposedly 'shun my family', just because I'm not chomping at the bit to call my mom on Thanksgiving."

"Nora." Juan rises and walks over to me. "Why can't you just let it go? Why can't you make your life just a little easier on yourself?"

"But this is who I am. It's *how* I am. You know this. You've always known this. Why are you suddenly acting as though me simply being me isn't good enough for the two of you anymore either?"

Juan opens his arms to me. "It's not us you're not good enough for." His voice is hoarse. "It's yourself."

Again with this bullshit. I'd rather jump in the pool behind me with all my clothes on than step into his embrace.

"Fuck this." I storm inside. The dogs follow me upstairs. I throw myself onto my bed, but a tantrum isn't going to change anything. I text Juan and ask them to leave again. I'm not sure whether they will. Clearly, I can no longer predict their behavior toward me.

Time passes slowly and I can hear Juan and Imani downstairs, ignoring my wish to leave me alone. But I can wait them out. Surely, they will realize soon enough that they can say anything to me, except what they just said. I won't stand for it. What happened to their unconditional support, no questions asked?

There's a knock at the door. "Nora," Imani says. "Can I come in, please?"

I want to say yes and no at the same time. I can't give in to their emotional blackmail, but they are my two best friends in the world. The people that know me best. They can't just have turned on me completely. There must be another explanation.

"Yes," I say on a dramatic sigh.

"It's just me." Imani closes the door behind her. "Can we talk?"

Isn't that what we've been doing? "Depends. Do you understand why I feel betrayed?"

Imani gives me a look I can't decipher, while I can usually read her face like an open book. "Can I say something?"

I brace myself.

Imani sits in the armchair opposite my bed. "This thing with Mimi, the reason you broke up with her. I think we both know it's not about your family or specifically about what Mimi asked about them. That's what Jay and I meant earlier. You know we would never judge you when it comes to that. You do know that, right?"

"I thought I did."

"Come on, Nora."

"What you said about me having parents who pick up the phone when I call was totally out of line."

"Okay. I'm sorry. I shouldn't have said that. I was oversimplifying to make a point and I shouldn't have done that. Can we let that go now?"

"Just like that?" Is she serious?

"Yes, just like that, because focusing on that is an easy way to not have to focus on Mimi."

Easy? Sure. "Mimi was a mistake. A temporary lapse in judgment. She proved that to me very quickly, for which I should be grateful, really. Clearly, she doesn't want… me. She wants to change me, and I don't want to change."

"Maybe you should reconsider that."

"Excuse me?" Did she really just say that?

"I'm your friend, Nora. I love you. I want you to be happy."

"But I am happy." At least I was before Mimi St James came along.

"You think you can just brush this off? The fact that you fell in love with someone? That you let them into this place inside you where you haven't let anyone in for decades? You think you haven't changed already? Because you have and I'm telling you that it will be very hard for you to go back to how things were before you met Mimi."

"Not as hard as trying to be the person she wants me to be."

Imani shakes her head. "You only have to be yourself, Nora."

"Yeah, right." What's next? Call my mother every day?

"The self you are behind this huge wall you've put up."

Not Imani as well. Tears spring to my eyes because I've just lost my very last ally.

"You know when I'm truly myself?" I stare into her eyes. "When I don't have to perform for anyone. When I'm alone. That's what I'd like to be right now." I give her a terse nod so she gets the hint.

"Don't shut Jay and me out." Imani gets up and crouches next to the bed where I'm sitting. "We'll give you the space you need right now, but we're here for you whenever you need us."

As if she's picking up on what we're saying, Izzy whimpers next to me.

Imani rises, presses a soft kiss on the top of my head, and walks to the door. "You never have to perform for us. I hope you know that."

Apparently, I don't know anything. Apparently, I'm now no longer good enough for my best friends, either. And what's all this nonsense about me not loving myself enough and not being good enough for myself about? I like myself plenty. A little less when I'm with other people, but I've found ways to deal with that. I lie down and Izzy jumps into my lap immediately. That's why I have dogs. They love me a ridiculous amount from the moment they open their eyes in the morning until they go to sleep. I can't say the wrong thing to them. They don't care whether I'm close with my family or not.

But all of this has to be more than a misunderstanding. It must be more than me not adequately expressing myself. I do know that, but what I don't know is how on earth I'm supposed to do what everyone has suddenly decided to start telling me I should do: love myself more.

CHAPTER 34
MIMI

Despite myself, my heart skips a beat when the doorbell rings just past four on Sunday afternoon. Despite telling myself I need to forget about Nora. But it could be her. It's not entirely inconceivable that she has prepared a grand gesture.

I open the door and am greeted with a huge bunch of flowers. It wouldn't be the first time Nora has sent a lavish bouquet to apologize, either.

"I'm sorry." The voice from behind those flowers is not Nora's, but I know it all too well. My heart sinks. As well as trying to forget about Nora Levine, I now have to deal with my ex. Cathy moves the flowers away from her face and stands there smiling sheepishly at me. "I'm sorry for being such an asshole. For calling you out of the blue and saying those things. For calling Austin." She shakes her head. "That was a low blow." She holds out the flowers. "Even if you can't accept my apology, please accept the flowers."

On automatic pilot, I take them from her.

"Mid-life has me flailing a bit," Cathy says. "I'm such a cliché, but the last thing I should have done is involve you in any of it. I truly am sorry."

"Come in." I can't just let her stand out there. "Let's talk."

I usher her into the kitchen, where I put the flowers in a vase and make us some coffee.

"Ravi and I are back together. I almost screwed it up with her as well," she says.

At least, she hasn't come here to try and get me back again.

"You need to leave my kids alone, Cathy. Promise me."

"You have my word." She peers at me from over the rim of her mug. "Are you okay, Mimi? You don't look like your usual fabulous self. Are the kids all right?"

"Everyone's fine. We had a good Thanksgiving." Under the circumstances. "You?"

"At least I don't have to spend Thanksgiving with your ex-husband any longer." She snickers. "I'm good. I've come back to my senses."

We make small talk for a while about work and the kids.

"I know it's not my business, but why do you look like you're carrying the entire weight of the world on your shoulders?" Cathy asks.

I gaze at the flowers she brought. They make me think of the bouquet Nora sent me after she tried to kiss me right where I'm sitting now.

"Bad break-up."

"I'm so sorry, Mimi. Their loss, I'm sure—and I should know." She clears her throat. "I might have been obnoxiously drunk at the time, and totally out of line, but those things I said about you, I meant them." Her eyes are kind when she smiles. "Was it a mutual decision? This break-up?"

It wasn't even a decision. It was an argument that spiraled out of control, followed by Nora making herself unreachable to me. Juan said he'd talk to her, but I haven't heard from him, so I can only assume the worst.

"It wasn't even really a thing yet." As I say it, I know it's a big lie. I only told Nora I loved her—maybe that was another mistake.

"Anyone I know?"

Oh, yes. Everyone knows Nora—or they think they do. I shake my head. "You haven't met them." At least that's true.

"You seem pretty cut up about it."

Tears prick behind my eyes, but I'm not going to cry in front of my ex. I try to think happy thoughts. Wyatt saying something inappropriate. Lucas deploying his boyish charms when he wants a piece of candy. My granddaughter sleeping in my arms. Those are the things that matter. Nora may not care about her family, but I love mine to absolute pieces. Argh. Fucking Nora.

"I'll be fine. It's just still very fresh and raw."

"I'm sorry things didn't work out," Cathy says. "That sucks."

"It'll take some time, but I'll be fine." If only I could fast-forward a few weeks. Whereas a few days ago I was still adamant I'd confront Nora on set to at least get a tiny amount of closure from her, I'm not so sure anymore now. It's been almost a full week without a sign from her. Add to that what Juan told me about Nora not wanting to give things another chance, and I pretty much know where I stand. Why drag it out? Why put myself through another painful conversation full of miscommunication and Nora misunderstanding my words, anyway?

I've been non-stop mulling over all the things Juan said since Thursday and I still can't fully wrap my head around them. Nora has me questioning myself. My heart might have been in the right place when I broached the subject of her parents, but maybe I should have held back. I shake off the feeling. Unlike Nora, I have no problem with being myself and with the choices I make in the moment.

The bell rings again and my heart leaps into my throat again. It can't be any of the kids—they come in through the back door.

"My cue to leave." Cathy looks at me. "Unless you need me to stay." She slides off her stool. "You've just gone pale as a ghost, Mimi. Are you sure you're okay?"

I take a breath and nod. One thing I've learned from all of

this is that falling in love is destabilizing at any age. I'm not better equipped to deal with any of this because I have a few more years on me since last time I gave my heart to someone. How funny that someone is standing in front of me right now.

"I'd better get that." My heart hammers against my chest as I walk to the front door. It could be anyone but, against my better judgment, every single fiber of my being wants it to be Nora. I open the door. Juan and Imani stand in front of me. No sign of Nora.

Cathy says a quick goodbye, and then I'm sitting in my kitchen with Nora's best friends.

"We're going to need a good bottle of wine for this," Juan says.

"Is Nora okay?" I ask, because them showing up like this looks a little ominous.

"Physically, she's fine. Fit as an Olympic gold medalist." Juan obviously has some venting of his own to do. "Mentally." He huffs out a mouthful of air. "Complete and utter chaos."

I take a bottle of white wine from the fridge and pour them drinks.

"She's done a number on herself again," Imani says. "I'm sorry she hurt you, Mimi."

"Clearly, I hurt her, too."

"Nora's very good at hurting herself," Juan says. "She's trying to punish us as well now, but after two decades by her side, we're pretty immune to her drama."

"Still," Imani says. "It's different this time around. She's different because… Nora doesn't just fall in love like that. She doesn't let herself. But she let herself fall in love with you, Mimi, and that's not something we can ignore."

"It's as if she wants to punish herself extra hard because she considers herself extremely foolish and stupid for letting herself surrender like that," Juan says.

"Poor Nora," I say without thinking.

"No, Mimi. Our pity is the last thing Nora needs," Juan is quick to say.

"What does she need, then?" Why are they here? They must want something from me.

"Look." Imani shuffles in her seat. "What we're about to ask you is not fair or reasonable. It's pretty crazy, actually."

I arch up my eyebrows.

"By the time Nora's ready to apologize, to see how impossibly Nora she's being about this, you'll have moved on, Mimi, because it's going to take for fucking ever," Juan says. "It's not that she's not capable of it, but she's slow. Well, she's clueless, most of all. Despite having the best counsel possible from her best friends." He clicks his tongue. "She's being impossible, and we know it's way too much to ask of you, but we're here to beg for your help."

"My help?" I scoff. "It's like I've suddenly stopped existing as far as Nora's concerned."

"We know," Imani says. "What we're about to ask of you is selfish and foolish. A bit like how Nora can be, really. But that's not all Nora is. We have been friends with her, much more than friends, for so long for a reason. Nora has a huge heart. She has done so much for so many people, myself and Jay included, and no one will ever know about it. She has her heart in the right place, Mimi. She absolutely does, but when it comes to intimate relationships, she's completely oblivious."

"What do you want me to do?" Nora may have the biggest charitable heart on the planet, that doesn't give her the right to break mine again.

"Go to her," Juan says. "Because she can't come to you."

"Can't or won't?" I ask.

"Can't," Imani says decidedly. "Even though it looks like she doesn't want to. But she's definitely in love with you, and that tells me all I need to know."

"Guys, come on." I throw up my hands in despair. "What would I even say to her?"

"Unfortunately, we can't tell you that." Juan smiles apologetically. "But Imani and I think if we can get you and Nora in the same room, it will spark something in her. She'll see reason, or be more inclined to, at least."

"What does that mean in Nora's case? Seeing reason?" I don't want to do this. Not that I think it's imperative Nora comes to me, or that I think it undignified for me to go her. It's not about that. It's whether Nora even wants to see me again. I have boundaries, too. I'm not looking to get the door slammed in my face again.

"She's in crisis mode right now. She can't think straight to save her life, even though she's probably convinced she's making the only possible decision there is: shut you out and pretend you and her never happened," Imani says. "Jay and I can't get through to her, but we think you might. Just to snap her out of this downward spiral." Imani smirks. "But I get that it's probably too much to ask of you."

"Why would I consider doing this? She kicked me out and it's not the first time she tried to. I'm not into that kind of fickleness." I remember what Jennifer said to me on Thanksgiving about Nora being single because she can't allow herself to be loved.

"Because..." Juan extends his hand to me. "Sometimes, in life, you have to go the extra mile for someone, even if they've treated you like shit."

Way to tug at my heartstrings. I glance at his open hand. I have nothing to lose by putting mine in his.

"Like you're doing for Nora now." I give Juan's hand a squeeze.

"Nora's our girl. We'd walk through fire for her."

"We're not asking you to do the same," Imani says. "But we are asking you to look beyond what you can see right now. To trust us that Nora is someone you can love, and who can love you, even though she's doing everything in her power to make you believe the opposite." Imani puts her hand on top of mine.

"One of the reasons I love Nora so much is because I feel deeply connected to her. We're very different, with different backgrounds and life stories, yet, on some level, we're also exactly the same." Imani swallows. "I haven't always fitted in seamlessly everywhere. Feeling like a fish out of water was my natural state of being for a long time. Regardless of her reasons, that's how Nora feels a lot of the time—and I understand that feeling like no other. It eats away at you. It corrodes your soul."

She pauses. "Jay and I are not innocent in this. We've let her get away with too much. We've allowed her to retreat deeper and deeper inside herself. But to see her fall in love with you was like witnessing a miracle, Mimi. You have no idea how exceptional this is. Which is why we're here. There are no guarantees, but we can't give up because we want this for her so much. We're begging you to give Nora one last chance. Please."

"Nora doesn't know the half of how lucky she is." I glance at my hand that's sandwiched between theirs. "To have friends like you."

"She knows," Juan says and looks me straight in the eye.

"I'll do it," I say. "I'll go to her."

CHAPTER 35
NORA

Someone knocks on the door of my trailer. My muscles tense. I can only throw my weight around so much. Demanding the head of our production company be banned from set is not an option. So there's a chance it's Mimi.

"Yes." My voice is all unwelcoming tightness.

"Only me." Stella pops her head in. "Here you go." She comes in and hands me a Tupperware. "I know you won't eat it, but my mom insisted I give you some leftover pecan pie. That's my daughterly duty done."

"Thank Mary profusely for me."

Stella sits down. "How was your Thanksgiving?"

"Just, um, normal," I mumble. "Yours?"

"Kev and Bridget came home with all the kids. It was a loud, chaotic, utterly gorgeous Flack family feast." She sighs contentedly.

Ironically, Mimi should be proud of me, because I called my mother on Thanksgiving—I didn't have much else to do.

"Did you celebrate with Juan and Imani?" Stella asks.

"Just Imani. Juan has basically been adopted by his future in-laws already."

"By Mimi and her family?" Stella nods, then chuckles. "About Mimi… is there something I should know?"

"What do you mean?" My heart shrinks in my chest, like it wants to physically shy away from the question.

"I'm not blind and I don't hide in my trailer between takes like you do most of the time. I notice things."

"Yeah, well, whatever you might have noticed is no more."

"Oh." Stella scrunches up her lips. "I'm sorry. Did something happen?"

"I need to prepare, Stella. I don't want to talk about this. There's also nothing to talk about."

"If you say so."

"Sorry. It was nothing," I lie. "Between Mimi and me. It fizzled out before it could turn into anything." I should get an Emmy for saying that line alone—but acting's the opposite of lying.

"Are you going to be okay?" Stella sounds genuinely worried.

"Of course."

"If you need cheering up, you're always welcome at our house."

"Thanks, Stella."

"Don't worry, I won't invite Mom." She grins at me. "I *will* tell her you loved the hell out of that piece of pie, though."

Stella and her perfect mother. The kind of mother who accepts her daughter falling in love with her son's wife. The kind of mother who heads a family that can get through that and have everyone over for Thanksgiving without them being at each other's throat. We may not get to pick our family in life, but we damn well can choose who to spend our time with—and thank goodness for that.

"I think your mom is absolutely wonderful, Stella," I say. "Be sure to tell her that I love every minute in her company."

"Not a chance in hell," Stella says. "That would make you her favorite daughter, and you're not even related."

I've spent too much time contemplating my own family since Mimi so bluntly made me. But I can think about them all I want, it doesn't change anything. When I spoke to my mother on Thanksgiving, the call went exactly as expected. Polite, distant, and with that sad, uncomfortable undertone of all we lack between us. The feeling that there should be more than there is because we're family, but there just isn't.

Stella and I are being called, and as I exit my trailer, I glance warily around me, terrified to run into Mimi.

Juan texted me earlier to say that, even though it's a Monday, he would be coming over, and no further protests could stop him. He took a page right out of Mimi's playbook there, by trying to preempt my arguments before I can make them. But I don't want to live at odds with him, nor Imani, for too long. It will give us a chance to hash things out now that we've all calmed down. To get back to our true selves and just be friends again, no questions asked, no expectations to live up to.

Juan usually lets himself in, but for some reason he's ringing the doorbell today. Before I can ask what his deal is, I stand face-to-face with Mimi.

"As you can see, I'm not alone," Juan says. "I am going to leave you alone, though."

"Hi, Nora." It's probably a coincidence, but Mimi's wearing the same stark, white suit she wore when I first met her. I've always remembered—maybe because she irritated me so much that day. "Can I come in?"

Juan ambushed me. Smart move, I have to hand it to him. But I don't have time to consider Juan's tactics. I have a decision to make.

"Please, Nora." Juan presses his palms together. "Say yes."

"Okay." I take a step back to let Mimi in. "Yes." I can't

believe she has come to my house after everything I said to her. She must really be a sucker for punishment.

"Thank you." Mimi walks past me.

"Call me if you need me." Juan gives me the slightest of nods before heading back to his car.

"You have very persuasive friends," Mimi says when we're in the living room.

"They are—yeah." Juan could have given me a heads-up so I could have prepared for this. But who am I kidding? He had to spring this on me so I couldn't say no.

I look at Mimi and now she's here, all the things I haven't allowed myself to feel since last week come flooding back. It's not only regret that I feel. There's a hefty dose of raw, acute desire at the sight of her mixed in as well.

How annoying.

Because for a minute there, Mimi made me feel safe. Secure. Until she didn't. Until she pulled the rug out from under me, and I didn't see it coming because I let my guard down too much.

Instead of chasing her away again, despite everything—who I am and the rules I choose to live by—I very much want to kiss her. Although we'll need to have a conversation first. Things always need to be said, words that can never convey what truly goes on inside us need to be spoken.

"Can I get you anything?" I ask.

"Nora." Mimi steps closer. "It wasn't an easy decision for me to come here, because—well, for many reasons, but that's what I want to make clear. Maybe, for now, we shouldn't care about reasons and why we do and say certain things. Why we had that argument and all the things we could say about it."

"T-thank you for coming," I stammer.

"I didn't come here to have another frustrating conversation with you," Mimi says. "Frankly, I don't see the point in that at all."

"Okay." Why is she here then? She probably needs me to say

I'm sorry. It's probably my best bet if I want her to stay a while longer—and I do, because that desire for her isn't going anywhere. "I'm sorry for how things end—" I start.

"No. Nora." Mimi holds up her hand. "You don't have to say you're sorry and neither do I. At least not right now. I think what we need to do, what we need to practice, is just letting things be and then..." She takes another step closer. "See what happens."

I can't say I understand any of this, not on a present, conscious level, but my body seems to get it loud and clear. My skin reacts to her closeness. My pulse quickens. My heart's all over the place.

"Do you think you can do that?" Mimi's voice has lowered to a whisper.

"Fuck, yeah." I may not fully grasp what she's getting at, yet every word she says is music to my ears. Because I don't want to go down the deep end of a draining conversation again. Most days, I'm perfectly happy not talking at all. Maybe Mimi's about to give me the best gift of my life in not forcing me to express the unsayable.

"Can I kiss you?" Her lips are so close to mine, she may as well already be kissing me.

A long-held tension in my stomach uncoils as I nod. And I let her kiss me. We'll see what comes after.

I open my lips to Mimi. I let her in. Her tongue is even softer than I remember, but her hands on my back are full of intention. She pulls me close and to stand pressed against her body like this is so unexpected, yet it feels so right. It makes me forget why I asked her to leave that day in the first place. It makes me forget where I am altogether. It makes me forget myself and my head full of reasons to not do things.

Maybe, sometimes, a kiss is all you need to reset, to start again. To gauge what's really there between you and another person. Mimi's not just any person, because she's here. I was going to apologize, but she doesn't need me to.

We break from the kiss, and she looks at me. "Come here." She curls her arms tightly around me. "It's going to be okay, Nora."

Ninety-nine percent of the time, when someone speaks those words, they're just saying something, because no one can predict the future. Yet, I believe Mimi when she says it. Because I want to. Because I want her and I'm ready to disappear into her embrace.

"If you want to talk, we can talk," Mimi whispers in my ear. "But we don't have to."

"Do you want to go upstairs?" I whisper back.

Her chin bumps against my shoulder as she nods. Yet we don't move. We stay tangled together in my living room for a good while longer, the heat of her body against mine melting the coldness in my soul.

CHAPTER 36
MIMI

On the way to Nora's house, doubts nearly got the better of me. But as soon as I saw her standing in the doorway, I knew I'd made the right decision. I knew I had to stay, and I knew what to do. I knew what Nora needed, and it wasn't more dialogue.

I've always taught my kids that communication is important, and it is, but there's more than one way to communicate. The number of hugs I've dispensed when my kids were too furious about something to talk, or too sad to express themselves in words, or too tearful to squeeze a coherent sentence out of their mouths, have taught me that. I've learned as much from my kids as they have from me.

I can tell Nora I love her all I want, but maybe I should just show her instead. While doing so, we can assess if what we had before is still there. Whether our feelings for each other are strong enough to withstand what life has made us.

We're in Nora's bedroom and the vibe is quickly shifting from serious to something more playful. I can see it in Nora's eyes. I can't read her to save my life, but I can see that much.

"You're quite something," Nora says. "To show up like that and just have your way with me."

"You're quite something," I reply. "Because as it turns out, that's exactly what you want from me."

Nora reaches for me. "Thank you for coming."

"I haven't yet," I joke.

Nora smiles, and the whole room lights up. "Okay." She sinks her teeth into her bottom lip. "Let's make that happen, then."

I rake my gaze over Nora. As usual, she's in jeans and a tank top and her shoulder line looks even more impressive than I remember. Her biceps curve deliciously. Her skin is so smooth, it glows. I can't wait to hoist up that tank top, to reveal the six-pack that hides underneath. But I'm not here for Nora's body—I've seen what it costs her. Or no, I shouldn't think like that. I've seen what it would cost me, or any other mere mortal, to have a body like that. Two hours every day with No-Mercy Marcy.

Nora makes her own choices and it's her choice to look like this and do what she needs to in order to do so. It's her choice to eat the food she chooses and she should be able to do it without me judging her for it, no matter what her reasons might be, or what I might guess them to be—or how I feel about that.

Nora gets to be whoever she wants to be, and she can do whatever she likes. If she didn't, she wouldn't be Nora Levine. I'm not talking about the Nora my kids adore, that hybrid of how Nora looks and her *High Life* character's chirpy personality. I'm talking about the real Nora. The one who danced so freely with my kids, but also the one who's so scared of something real, something that touches all that she's been hiding deep inside herself for so long, that she had to kick me out of her house for fear of where it might lead.

I'm here for all the parts that make up Nora, for all that she has already revealed to me and the many aspects of her that are still hidden. For the force for good she is in the life of people who need help, for the joy she has brought to millions by being irresistible to a camera, but most of all, for the impossibility of her letting me in. Of her wanting to try. Of her being responsive to the gut instinct I had when I laid eyes on her again. For her letting me kiss her lips and knowing, in her soul, that this might be the way through for us.

I might not be here for her body, but that doesn't mean I'm not insanely attracted to it. It's a great perk of being with Nora Levine. Because I love running my fingertips over her rock-hard abs—I'm not above shallowness like that. I love seeing her tank top ride up and slowly revealing her perfectly sculpted belly. My clit pulses when I hoist her top over her head. My breath stalls when I free her breasts and her nipples perk up. Heat thunders through my flesh when I kiss her collarbone. When my lips trace up her neck. When she opens her mouth to me. My knees buckle when our tongues dance.

By the time we tumble onto the bed, I'm wild with lust. Maybe this is a time to take things slowly, to run my hands over her body deliberately and thoughtfully, but I can't. Because my body's reacting, too, and it's telling me, loud and clear, that I made the right choice coming here.

Before I do what I'm about to do, what I so desperately need, I have to check in with her. I have to make sure she's right there with me.

When I look into Nora's eyes, all I see reflecting back at me is the same lust that's rolling through my veins, the same heat that's coursing through my blood. Maybe this is how Nora does her best communicating. Maybe this isn't just the only conversation we can have, but also the one we need to have.

Her fingernails scrape over my skin. Her lips latch onto my nipple, but I want them somewhere else.

"Nora, please," I beg. "Touch me."

She lets my nipple drop from her mouth and grins up at me. Then she does something wholly unpredictable again, but in the best possible way. She cups my ass cheeks and pulls me to her. My knees shuffle along the sheet as I straddle her. I maneuver until she has me right where she wants me—and where I relish being. The anticipation is almost too much. I swear I could come right there and then, with myself on offer to Nora like that, my legs wide in front of her face. My clit pulses as I hold on to the headboard of the bed. I have a feeling I'm going to need the support. I glance down at Nora and most of her face is obscured by my thighs, but that grin she must have plastered across her lips has reached her eyes. They beam back at me with devilish delight.

Whatever she has failed to say with words, she can tell me now. I brace for the contact of her tongue on my clit. She licks along my center first, tasting, teasing me. When her tongue finally touches down on my raging clit, it's restrained more than intentional, as though she wants to drag this out a good long while.

I push myself toward her. In response, Nora digs her fingertips deeper into my ass cheeks. I might have dreamed of this in an unguarded moment, might have wished it to happen in a few split seconds of foolishness, but I could never have dreamed up this scenario—that I would find myself clasped to Nora's lips like this—because I was ready to walk away. I was steeling myself to accept her one-sided decision of kicking me to the curb. To let her fear seal our fate.

I'm thrilled that things turned out differently. That her friends came to her—to our—rescue because they wanted this for Nora. Maybe not specifically what Nora's doing right now, though—she's teasing me with the tip of her tongue, licking me as though she has all the time in the world. But I don't. I need to come. I need to release this tension. I need it expelled from my body, cleansed from my muscles, so we can start again at the other side of this.

"Fuck," I groan, hoping it's enough. Hoping that she gets it, although this is, for once, not a matter of Nora not getting it. She knows exactly what she's doing. Driving me utterly insane. Taking me to the edge and not letting me fall. Maybe she doesn't want this to end because she's afraid of what might happen after. But no, in this bed, in this room, there's no space for fear. It's not welcome here.

My body doesn't wait for Nora. My arousal needs a way out and is finding it against her tongue, no matter how softly she swirls it around my clit. She can try to drive me insane all she wants, I won't let her.

Once the first tremor thunders through me, Nora catches up. She latches on to me, flicks her tongue with the purpose I wanted from her all along, and she lets me come. I shudder against her, my muscles releasing everything I've been holding onto the past week. I steady myself against the headboard, gasping for air.

"Fuck," I sigh. I roll my head back and take a breath, fill my lungs with some much-needed air, before I clamber off her.

"Again," Nora says, a smug grin on her face, "thanks for coming."

It feels so good to laugh with her, to just let it all go, to let our bodies do the talking.

"Just wait until I catch my breath."

Nora shakes her head, then slides on top of me. "I've waited long enough," she says.

CHAPTER 37
NORA

"I'm all over your face," Mimi says, but kisses me regardless.

"Right where I want you," I whisper in her ear. Because we can't stop now. I won't stop. Not because I'm chasing a climax—though I am pretty desperate for some release—but because I don't want this to end. Here, in my bed, is where Mimi made me feel the safest I've ever felt, and I want to hold onto that feeling. I'm trying not to think about what might happen after we leave this room, when the sun comes up tomorrow and we face each other in the light of day. I want to stay wrapped up in her, under the cover of darkness, forever.

If only I could feel like this all the time. If only I could, for once and for all, shake the unease that lives under my skin, ready to swamp me whenever it pleases, whenever I'm not careful enough. That's what Mimi does for me: she takes it away. She makes me dream of a life without it. Without the constant second-guessing and the self-doubt and the always there feeling that the real Nora Levine isn't good enough for the outside world.

Here, with Mimi, there's none of that. There's only one version of me. There's only me and her, what we have between us, and this love we make. This love that makes everything else go away. This love that replaces a million apologies and a thousand sorries that she doesn't need me to say—because I don't need to apologize for being who I am. For this person I've become, this random sum of my genetic material and the odd, extraordinary life I've lived so far. This person who is the consequence of the choices she made, good and bad. Wise or unwise. At least I had the wisdom to allow her in. To not let the urgency of my desire be hijacked by some negative thought spiral again. To just let it go. To just be—be with her. Because if this isn't heaven on earth, I don't know what is.

Until now, I believed it was lounging in my couch with my dogs sprawled across my body, and it can be that—but it's not only that. Because it's also this. It's also letting this gorgeous, phenomenal, accomplished woman into my life and letting her shake my foundations. Giving her the key to the overly complicated lock around my heart. This doesn't have to be so difficult. It can be as simple as Mimi and me in this bed. At least it is for now.

Mimi topples me off her and glues her body to my side. Her fingertips roam across my belly.

"Your body really is a work of art," she whispers. I make a mental note to remind her of those words when my alarm goes off at five tomorrow morning. Then there's no space left in my brain to make mental notes at all. Mimi circles a finger around my nipple. More than anything, it's her gentleness that floors me again. As though she can somehow read my body and knows this is what I like. Or maybe I showed her earlier, when she was straddled across my face and I made her wait for it—but I didn't test her patience for that reason. I just wanted to keep her there, in that intimate position, for as long as possible.

Mimi shifts upward and sucks my nipple into her mouth. A jolt of electricity courses through me. Something inside of me must have sensed this when I tried to kiss her that very first time. When, unbidden and unexpectedly, I tried to get my first taste of her.

She touches the part of my brain that my conscious mind can't reach. The instinct that lurks in my body that only reacts to certain people. No wonder I went crazy for Mimi. My subconscious recognized something I'm always on the lookout for. An older woman because, as Juan likes to put it, I'm a walking mommy issue on very shapely legs. Mimi is an amazing mother with a flock of children who adore the living daylights out of her. That will always touch a nerve inside of me. But Mimi is much more than that.

She exudes the kind of energy that's irresistible to me, a sort of command over the world around her that excites me. Her constant control of everything speaks to the incorrigible control freak in me. It could even be that what irked me about her so much when we first met, that need to show us who was in charge when she waltzed into the room, is what excites me the most now.

She flicks her tongue against my nipple one last time before making her way down. Her hand follows the path her lips are taking. My skin is on fire and there's only one way to put this fire out.

She kisses my lower belly while her hand dips between my legs.

A smug smile graces her face as she looks up at me. "No lube required tonight," she says. It turns me on even more. It makes me even wetter for her.

She leans over my thigh and her lips touch down. She sucks my clit into her mouth as she did with my nipple earlier, and I all but lose my mind. Her fingers bide their time, but her tongue doesn't. There's something about the way she does this—soft and warm and slow—as though she's gauging my body's tiniest reaction, that gets to me. Because it's an extension of how she is outside of the bedroom. Beneath her glitzy TV executive exterior, Mimi's all nurturing warmth, and I can't get enough of that. The combination of the two makes the last of my defenses crumble once and for all.

She pushes herself up and replaces her tongue with a fingertip. She draws slow circles around my clit while she finds my eyes with hers. Mimi looks at me, her gaze as gentle and kind as her tongue was on me earlier. Her finger slides down and she pushes inside me.

I keep my eyes open because I need to see her face. I couldn't look away if I wanted to. Mimi adds another finger. Her thumb edges along my clit as she pushes high inside of me.

I pull her to me and kiss her hungrily. She has given me the best gift ever. Not this orgasm that's about to roll through me, but the kind of trust that when expressed in mere words could never be enough. The kind of trust you need to feel in your bones, that goes beyond words—beyond my flawed communication skills.

But I feel something else hum in my bones and quake in my muscles. Our kiss deepens before it stalls. I look into her eyes as I come at her fingers, clamping around her, and giving myself to her. My body surrenders, and I know, as the buzz in my clit intensifies, that I'm more than enough.

"I want to say something." I can't imagine a safer place than where I am right now, cradled in Mimi's arms.

"You don't have to," Mimi says.

"I know, but I want to."

"Of course." Mimi's spooning me, one arm curled tightly around my belly, pulling me into the endless warmth of her skin. "Do you want to stay like this? Is that easier?"

I roll over in her embrace. I want to say this when I'm looking at her, just as I wanted to experience the joy of that climax with her gaze on me earlier.

"Hi." Mimi's expression softens when she lays eyes on me. She leans in and kisses me lightly on the tip of my nose.

"This is not something I talk about, not even with Juan and Imani, so I'm not sure exactly how it's going to come out."

Mimi nods and smiles.

"I want to explain something to you. Well, try to, at least." That delicious relaxation in my muscles is turning into tension again, but that's okay. I've been teaching myself to live with the tension, to just let it be and accept it without reacting—especially overreacting. Most of the time, it doesn't work. But tonight, with Mimi's arm draped around me, and the residual afterglow of making love, I can try, even though it's definitely going to be uncomfortable.

"Okay." Mimi gently strokes my back.

"I don't hate my parents, nor do I actively 'shun' them, as you put it." I pause. How to even express this? But some issues do require words. Some feelings need to be spoken out loud so they can't grow into something unmanageable inside of me. "I love them, even though I know it's not a given that children and parents automatically love each other. I've seen enough of that to not believe in that fairy tale. But..." I take a breath. "Seeing you with your kids and how you are with each other... To grow up in a house like that, with a family like that, is my ultimate fantasy. It wasn't like that for me. It wasn't horrible, and my parents did the best they could with what they had, but emotionally—I mean, they're like me."

I chuckle nervously. "Can you imagine two people like myself raising a child? With a short fuse like that? And no way to express their feelings? But I can't blame them for who they are, nor can I blame myself for who I am. I am their daughter. I'm so much like them, and it fucking kills me sometimes, because I want to be... different. I want to be better." I focus on a tiny freckle Mimi has on the left side of her chin. "I know that, even though they can't say it, they love me and they want me to be happy more than anything. They may even be proud of me, who knows, but if they are, your guess is as good as mine, because they've certainly never told me. They wouldn't dream of it." I swallow something out of my throat. "I sometimes dream of it, even though it would be the most awkward conversation if they were ever to say something like that out loud. But I know exactly what it's like, to be like that. To feel something profoundly but, for the life of you, not be able to share that feeling."

Mimi's fingertips are still gliding gently over the skin of my back.

"I understand them, I really do. But that doesn't make me want to spend more time with them—on the contrary. Maybe that's cruel, and that makes me a bad daughter, but I am me and I can only act accordingly. When I do visit them, the tension between us, the negative energy because everything is pent-up and unspoken, is unbearable to me. So I decided a while ago to minimize visits because they frustrate me more than anything. I should probably work on mending this thing that is wrong between us, but it's too hard. And that's the decision I made for myself. That I don't have to spend more time with them just because they're my parents. I know that's selfish, because it might be hurtful and disrespectful to them. They would never say if it was. They would never demand anything of me. I get the feeling that they may prefer things the way they are as well. But I don't really know." I let the tears that well in my eyes tumble freely. There's no use trying to hide them now.

Mimi brings her thumb to my cheek and tries to catch them.

"I'm sorry for pushing you, Nora. I shouldn't have done that. I shouldn't have assumed I know better."

Mimi's apologizing to me now? It only makes me cry harder.

"It's not on you to make things better." Mimi cups my cheek. "I say that as a mother—and as a damn good one at that."

I bury my face in her hair. I let Mimi take me in her arms. In the space of the past five minutes, just by being able to tell her this, I've done more healing than I've done in a lifetime.

"I too have some things to say," Mimi whispers in my ear.

"But I'm not going to say them now. You're too vulnerable. But I really appreciate you sharing this with me. This must be so difficult." She kisses the side of my head. "I only love you more for it."

Because I grew up emotionally repressed, I'm quite allergic to this kind of emotional exhibitionism. It always seems so unnecessary, almost vulgar to me. But not right now—and not ever, really. And especially not when sharing this part of myself with Mimi. This aspect of my personality I've buried under layers of shame and guilt. While telling Mimi doesn't change anything about the reality of the situation, it's life-changing for me nonetheless.

CHAPTER 38
MIMI

I expected to wake up to the excruciating blare of Nora's alarm at an ungodly hour, but to my surprise, it's fully light out, and Nora's naked body is still huddled against mine under the covers.

As far as I know, Marcy didn't barge into our room at five a.m. demanding Nora join her in the gym either.

"Hm." Nora slides her leg over mine as she wakes up.

"Excuse me?" I say. "Who are you? Are you Nora Levine's doppelgänger, because if you are this is highly inappropriate."

In response, Nora takes my hand and puts it on her belly. "Would my doppelgänger have abs like this?"

"Speaking of abs, why aren't you working on them right now?"

"Oh, sorry, Ms. St James." Nora pushes herself up and looks at me. "Is that what you demand of the lead actors in your company's flagship show? How terribly last century of you." She smiles down at me.

"Morning." My lips curve into the biggest grin. "I'm just surprised." I nuzzle my nose against her neck. My skin reacts to her body heat immediately.

"I texted Marcy after you fell asleep." Nora moves her hand

into my hair. "Let's be honest, at your age, you need your beauty sleep." Nora bursts into laughter.

"You're damn right I do." I fall back onto the pillow. "I could get used to this."

"Marcy's not happy, by the way. Nor is she stupid. You will totally get the blame for this so you might not want to be here when she comes over tomorrow."

"I'll happily stay in bed until she's long gone."

"I'll figure out a way to get out of bed without having to wake you as well." Nora nods. "I've never had to take another person in my bed into account before."

"Did you sleep okay?" I have no idea how I'm actually going to get out of Nora's heavenly bed this particular morning. Waking up with her like this is divine.

"Out like a light. I was exhausted. You?"

"Yes. Thank you again for sharing with me. It means a lot to me, Nora." I push a strand of hair away from her cheek.

"It was good to share." She's no longer that vulnerable woman who cried in my arms last night.

"I don't want you to do anything you don't want to or are not ready for, but I would like to continue the conversation. I'd like to share a few things of my own, if that's okay."

"Sure." She looks at her watch. "We can talk over breakfast. Ricky must be so confused right now, wondering where I am. And where Marcy is."

Every time Nora says Marcy's name, a twinge of tension travels through my muscles. "Are you close with her outside the gym?"

"With Marcy? Hm." Nora ponders my question. "We spend a lot of time together and that does create a certain amount of closeness, but we don't have heart-to-hearts or anything like that. She's definitely not the kind of personal trainer who dispenses life advice while torturing my body." Nora shakes her head. "Marcy's a real hard-ass, but I like that about her."

"Do you know anything about her personal life?"

"Not much." Nora brings her hand to her mouth. "Is that bad?" She shrugs. "When I train with Marcy, there's not an inch of space left in my brain to even consider asking a personal question. There are no easy days with Marcy. She doesn't believe in them." Nora throws the duvet off her body. "This is the result."

"I'm not complaining." It's hard to tear my gaze away.

"I'd like that in writing next time I get up early for Marcy."

"Do work on that alarm clock solution. A smart woman like yourself should have that figured out in no time." I can't help but pull her to me, nor can I help feeling like a bit of a hypocrite for admiring Nora's impossible body—for what she puts herself through to maintain it at her age. But I can accept this ambivalence easily, because it's not my body, and I don't have to work out with Marcy at the crack of dawn.

"We should get up," Nora says, but instead of hopping out of bed, she kisses me full on the lips. "That was a really amazing thing you did last night. Coming here like that. No one's ever done something like that for me before. No one's ever given me the benefit of the doubt like that."

"Your friends do." If you can take the measure of a person by who their best friends are, Nora is one of the most wonderful people on the planet. "They love you so much, Nora. It's a beautiful thing."

"They told me some things I definitely didn't want to hear."

"That's also what friends are for." If my son's going to be with an older man, then let it be a charming, heart-in-exactly-the-right-place older man like Juan.

"What did Jay and Imani say to you?" Nora props herself up onto an elbow. "That made you come over here and have your wicked way with me?" Her grin is gleeful.

"They asked me to look beyond your overly dramatic antics."

"Oh, really?" The fact that Nora takes the joke easily, makes me believe we've turned an important corner already—and that I won't have to do much looking beyond anymore.

"I don't want to pretend that I know better," I say, then realize that's a horrible thing to say. "Sorry. That came out wrong."

"I get it." Nora sips from her coffee. "I'm the world champion in that particular discipline."

"I'm a mother and once you are a mother, there's no switching off the Mom perspective. It's not possible. So I will always look at everything from the Mom angle as well."

"Sure."

"I don't know your parents." I'd sure love to meet them, but I will not make the mistake of ever pushing that family meeting. "But, Nora, there's no way that they're not proud of you. And sure, you can argue all you like that I can't know that, not for certain. And you would be right, but I would still argue my case. It's not because you can't express an emotion that it's not there. On the contrary."

"I know." Nora pushes her plate away. She ate barely half of what Ricky made for her—probably because Marcy didn't give her the workout from hell. But this, too, I need to let go. It dawns on me I might have just as many things to let go of as Nora if I want this thing between us to work. "I'm feeling a lot of emotions right now that I can't express." By the tone of her voice, I can tell she's joking. It's probably her way of dealing with stuff she doesn't want to deal with—if it's no longer possible to avoid it, then make a joke of it.

"Like what?" I'm happy to play along. I'm not Nora's therapist. I'm her… lover, for now, I guess.

"Just wondering if we should warn Ricky not to come outside for the next fifteen minutes." She catches my ankle between her feet.

"You're doing a fine job of expressing your emotions, by the way."

"Who knew I had it in me?" Nora flashes me another grin.

"I did," I say. "Remember when you tried to kiss me in my kitchen?" I lean to her and put my hands on her knees. "That was the first of your suppressed emotions trying to find a way out."

Nora chuckles. "Maybe." She slants her head toward me, coming in for a kiss.

I hold her off, pull my face away from her a little. "Please know that you are very loved. There's nothing Juan and Imani wouldn't do for you. They literally begged me to give you another chance."

She gives a tiny nod.

"I love you," I say. "I'm here. I came back and I was pretty easy to convince. No arm twisting was required, because I've seen you, Nora. I've seen glimpses of who you really are, and I can't wait to see all of you. Your big, big heart that hides under all that needless insecurity. I want all of it. I have zero interest in Emily Brooks. I only want Nora Levine." I rest my forehead against hers. "You are more than enough for me and there are no conditions attached to my feelings for you, to my love for you." I dig my fingertips into her thigh. "Your family loves you, Nora." Even though I have no authority to say this, no knowledge to back this up, I need to say it. I need her to hear it. "I bet even Marcy loves you a little bit."

"I think I might actually love Marcy a little bit," Nora says, and I'm not sure if she's deflecting again or is being serious. "Don't get me wrong. For two hours every morning, I absolutely hate Marcy's guts for what she pushes me to do, but the way she makes me move and use my body, helps me process so much." Nora nuzzles her nose against mine. "Like you did last night. I know you didn't just do that because you find my Marcy-made body irresistible."

"Then you know the most important thing." I let Nora kiss

me now. I kiss her back greedily, until we're disturbed by Ricky clearing his throat behind us.

"I'm sorry, Nora." Ricky sounds a lot more gleeful than sorry. "But your car's here."

"What?" Nora shoots up. "I've lost track of time." Her gaze shoots around helplessly. "Fuck. I never lose track of time." Her eyes land on me. "You." She points at me. "You made me lose track of time."

"Happy to be of service." I wink at her.

"Thanks, Ricky." Nora holds out her hand to me. "Can I drop you somewhere or do you want to come to the studio with me?"

I take her hand and let her pull me up. "I need some clean clothes before I go to work."

"I'm surprised you didn't bring an overnight bag, what with how you so brazenly seduced me last night." Nora slips her fingers between mine. She tugs me to her. "I love you too," she whispers in my ear.

CHAPTER 39
NORA

"Guess who called me yesterday?" I ask Mimi, who's lounging with me in the couch, the dogs sprawled between us.

"With the small number of people who have a direct line to you, this game should be easy." She pushes herself up. "You wouldn't make a fuss about Juan or Imani calling you." Mimi arches up her eyebrows. "Your mom?"

"No." I'm not going there again. Not today. Christmas is just around the corner and the guilt for all the things I'm not as a daughter is starting to set in, as it always does this time of year. "It's work-related."

"Okay. Hm. One of the *High Life* producers for a reunion?"

"Promise me here and now, if that offer ever comes, you will help me to say no."

"Really? You wouldn't do it?" Mimi sits all the way up.

"Not for all the money in the world, although I could put it to good use." This is how doubt always creeps in. If some Hollywood bigwigs want to throw a bunch of money at me to reprise the role of Emily Brooks, shouldn't I just do it to fund my charities?

"Even if it would make millions of people ecstatic?" Mimi asks.

"You mean your kids?"

"My kids have direct access to Nora Levine these days. I'd like to think they cherish that more than seeing Emily Brooks or *High Life* again."

"I wouldn't be so sure of that."

"What's going on?" Mimi fixes her gaze on me. "Who called you?" Izzy jumps into her lap.

"Elisa. They're doing an *Underground* movie and she wants me to be in it."

"Elisa Fox?" Mimi fans herself with her hand.

I prod her gently with my toe.

"That sounds a whole lot better than a *High Life* reunion to me," Mimi says.

"They're sending over the script later, but I'm not sure I should even read it. I'm not sure I should do it."

"Why not?"

"When I'm doing a TV show, I like to keep a low profile during the hiatus. I'm not like Stella who goes off to shoot two movies back-to-back. I like to just do nothing so I can replenish my energy for the next season. If there is one."

"There will be," Mimi says, and she should know.

Izzy's trying to turn on her back in Mimi's lap. She fails, but produces some hilarious slapstick comedy in the process. Mimi and I fawn over her for a few moments—which is what she wanted all along.

"How long has it been since you've done a movie?" Mimi asks.

"Years." Long before *Unbreak My Heart* came along.

"There are a couple of other things you haven't done in years that you've vigorously taken up again recently." Mimi grins at me.

"A movie is very different than a TV show. Doing *Unbreak My Heart* is right in the sweet spot of my comfort zone. I mostly get to work with the same people again every season, with Stella and Jo and most of the crew that I know, while doing what I love the most."

"You know Elisa."

"I know her, but we're not that close."

Mimi plasters a huge grin on her face. "Sorry. I was already picturing you in that movie with Elisa Fox. I'm not sure I can erase that image from my mind."

"Are you dreaming of another woman while I'm sitting next to you?" I grin right back at her. "Or are you having a senior moment and forgot who I was for a second?"

"Ouch." Mimi pretends to be very offended. "You have no respect for your elders."

That couldn't be less true, and she knows it. Being with Mimi, who has such a relaxed view on aging and all it entails, has been enlightening. Since we got together, I haven't made any appointments to add filler to my lips or Botox to my forehead. Not because she tells me I don't need it, but because she shows me, every single day, what aging gracefully can look like. That it can be natural and joyful, instead of resorting to chemicals and stressing out about how that wrinkle's going to look on camera.

"My kids claim that sixty-five is the new fifty," Mimi says. "I trust them completely." She lifts Izzy from her lap and cradles her in her arms. "But back to that movie. How about you wait for the script? We can read it together and see what it feels like. If it's so good you can't ignore it, we'll talk more then. No need to worry about it too much now."

"Okay." I keep my gaze on her.

"What?" Mimi tilts her head as she returns my gaze.

"I've been thinking about something else. About you."

"Do you hear that, Iz? Your mommy's been thinking about me." Mimi waggles her eyebrows.

"Maybe… you should direct an episode of *Unbreak My Heart* one day. Not this season, but maybe the next one."

"Me?" Her eyes go wide. "But I'm not a director."

"That doesn't mean you can't still be one. You just said sixty-five is the new fifty."

"This isn't about my age. I don't have any experience. I don't have the first clue about directing a TV show."

"Of course you do, Mimi. Especially with the amount of time you like to spend on set." I nudge her with my toe. "Or did you have other reasons for getting hands-on with our show?"

"I plead guilty to that." She sinks her teeth into her lip. "But directing is not something you pick up by osmosis. I don't have the technical knowhow, for starters."

"Yet," I say. "But you can learn. If you want to. You'd have to check with the CEO first, obviously. Ask her if the assistant director could use a mature intern."

"A *mature* intern?" Mimi shrugs and it's hard to say whether she's taking me seriously or not. Either way, it's just a suggestion—but maybe one she wouldn't necessarily think of herself.
"That's very sweet of you." She puts Izzy on the couch and leans over. "That you remember I told you about wanting to become a director. But that was a long time ago, Nora." Her face is close to mine, but I can still make out her smile. "I've pretty much become everything I've wanted to be."

"Or maybe you just can't face the prospect of being an intern again. You might not have that kind of humility in you." Mimi's been plenty humble with me, but I'm just teasing her.

"How about I think about it, just like you will think about doing that movie." Her lips move against my cheek as she speak.

"Deal," I say, before I pull her in for a kiss.

"Between action and cut, those magical minutes when I play a character, when I'm someone else but also still me, that's what it's all about," I say. I might have made a couch potato out of

Mimi in the past few weeks. I didn't think it would be possible, but she fits right into it, and I fit right into her arms when she's lying here with me. "It doesn't matter which character I'm playing, as long as I get to embody someone else." I'm pretty sure I'm not explaining it right—story of my life. "I'm addicted to that feeling."

"Of embodying someone else?" Mimi strokes the side of my arm.

"Yeah. To be someone more..." I have to be careful what I say, not just because I'm talking to Mimi, but because I'm talking about myself, and I'm trying to get the hang of saying much nicer things about myself than I previously would have. "To be the kind of person I've secretly always wanted to be, but never could be when the camera's not rolling."

"But the women—the *characters*—you play don't exist. They're made up. Entirely fictional," Mimi says.

"I know that, but..." Maybe some things can't be explained. Maybe I've run out of ways to explain the gap between who I am and who other people think I am. Or, just maybe, Mimi's right. Maybe the person I've always believed I needed to be, simply doesn't exist in real life.

"You wouldn't be the first person to hold themself to an impossible standard," Mimi says. "Not by a long shot." Her chest heaves below me as she sighs. "We all do it, but most of us haven't had paparazzi cameras aimed at our every move for the better part of our lives."

My chin bumps against Mimi's shoulder as I nod. Even though I'm trying to express something difficult, something that has seeped into my bones so deeply, it has become an elemental part of me, the only tension I feel in my body comes from her stroking my skin—from the effect she has on me that way.

Because Mimi gets it. I don't have to explain myself to her over and over. I don't have to spell out why I've made my life small and slow, and why the kind of life I've chosen for myself makes me happy. That, for me, it's a good life—my best life—

because when nothing is ever straightforward, when there's always some kind of alarm going off in the back of your brain, small and slow makes things manageable.

Although my life has felt a lot less small since I've let Mimi in with her big heart—and her big family.

"Are you ready to have those cameras aimed at you?" I ask, because it's only a matter of time. We've been careful and stealthy, but sooner rather than later, someone's going to clock that the executive I'm spending so much time with isn't just the CEO of our show's production company.

Mimi sighs again. "I can just picture the headlines already." Her chest puffs up beneath my cheek as she inhales. "Nora Levine Likes Them Older." She chuckles and I can't tell whether it's a real laugh or more of a nervous one. "My age in between brackets after every mention of my name, of course, because it's just so damn important."

"I'm fifty-one." I hardly think Mimi's age will be the headline. "It's really not that big a deal." I curl my arm around her a little tighter. "And I love that you're older than me."

"I gathered." With the way her chest bounces below me, this particular laugh can only be very real.

I wish it wouldn't be news that I'm in a relationship. Millions of people start new relationships every single day. But through a couple of twists of fate, I have become that elusive one-in-a-million person that the world can't stop caring about. I should be flattered the mere mention of my name is enough to sell a few extra magazines, yet I don't wish it on anyone—especially not on the woman I love.

Mimi's body stills. "Whatever comes next, we'll face it together," she says. "And it's going to be okay because of that. Because we have each other."

Lying in her arms like this, safely ensconced in her warm embrace, I'm very much inclined to believe every word she says.

CHAPTER 40
MIMI

"Where's Nora?" Jennifer asks on Sunday morning.

"She had a thing." I can't hold it against my kids that Nora's whereabouts always seem so important to them. Even though it's been a few weeks now, they're still processing that their mother and Nora Levine are dating. They're a few more weeks, perhaps months, removed from being able to see Nora as just Nora, as just another human. Witnessing their continued reaction to her helps me understand Nora better. It's easy enough to judge, but when you haven't lived someone's life, if you haven't experienced all their ups and downs, it's impossible to know what it's really like.

"Mom!" Austin bursts through the back door. "You're on the front page of TMZ."

My muscles tense, because just as my kids aren't used to their mother dating Nora Levine, I'm not used to seeing my face on the cover of a magazine—or on the front page of a gossip website.

Austin shows me his phone. Nora and I haven't officially stepped out together, but we aren't locked away in our houses either. We are working women with places to go and people to see. Some sneaky paparazzo has managed to snap a blurry picture of us after we exited a restaurant together.

"Oh well." Despite my initial worry, it's fairly easy to shake off. Although Austin tends to get worked up about these things. He has set a Google alert for my name in combination with Nora's. "Is it just you, darling?" I change the subject.

"Juan's at the Center."

"Nora is coming over for Christmas, right?" Jennifer asks, helping me change the topic. "Or are we all invited to her house?" Her voice goes up in pitch.

"Forget it," Austin says. "Every Christmas Day, Nora throws a big party at the LGBT Center for everyone who has no family to celebrate with."

"Oh." I guess Jennifer can't argue with that.

"Nora's coming over on Christmas Eve." I was planning on having this conversation later, over a meal, but I might as well announce this break with tradition now.

"Christmas Eve?" Jennifer scrunches her lips.

"I was thinking we'd do things a little differently this year." I send my daughter a consolatory smile. "How about we go to Nora's party at the LGBT Center on Christmas Day instead?"

"I'm up for that," Austin says—that was probably his plan already.

"We can have our family dinner on Christmas Eve, with Nora, Juan, and Imani." Juan and Imani might as well be family now—they and Nora come as a package, just like I do with mine. "Then go to Nora's party at the LGBT Center on Christmas Day."

"Sure." Jennifer shrugs. "Lauren and Heather aren't here, anyway." She perks up. "And I get to spend Christmas with Nora Levine." Her eyes light up. "Do any of the other *High Life* cast members go to this party?"

"It's not a glitzy celebrity affair," Austin says, sounding earnest. "It's a party, yes, but most of the people there have been rejected by their families. Christmas is triggering for them. Nora just wants to make them feel a little better."

"All right. I get it." Jennifer looks at me. "What about Nora's family? Are they visiting?"

"Nora's family is complicated, darling." I've learned to let Nora set the pace of the conversations we have about her family, because they are *her* family, not mine. "As far as I know, they won't be coming over."

"Did you know," Austin says, "that Juan and Imani are lifelong beneficiaries of a trust set up by Nora, no strings attached whatsoever?"

I didn't know that. I also don't know why Austin is suddenly enlightening us with this nugget of information—nor do I know why Nora hasn't told me, although getting to know her better, it makes sense that she hasn't.

"Well, duh," Jennifer says. "They don't exactly have regular jobs."

"They volunteer at the LGBT Center all the time." Austin glares at his sister. "Not everyone's as privileged as you, you know?"

"Me?" Jennifer returns his glare with an annoyed stare. "What about you?"

"I'm just saying that not everyone has a mom like Mom." Austin's the first to back down. He turns to me and sends me a wink that melts my maternal heart. "The stories I've heard from Juan." He shakes his head. "It makes me extremely aware of my privilege."

"In that case, it will be my privilege to spend Christmas Day at the LGBT Center," Jennifer says. "With Nora," she adds, under her breath.

A few moments later, Heather and Lauren arrive with their husbands and kids. It's the last time we're all together before they head off to spend the holidays with their respective families-in-law. We'll have a big St James dinner at their father's house when they're back. I'm not sure yet if Nora will be up for that, although I sure would like to have her there with me. But even if she decides not to come, Nora opening herself up to me again after the Thanksgiving disaster, is the best Christmas present I could ever hope for.

CHAPTER 41
NORA

For someone who dislikes parties so much, I'm in my element today. I feel more at home here at the LGBT Center, between the misfits and the outcasts, than at a Hollywood premiere party. Not because I feel I'm better than anyone here—on the contrary. Being here makes me feel connected to other humans in a way that rarely happens.

Everyone wants a piece of me this afternoon, but I knew it was going to be like this, and I have plenty of time to recover after—and, this year, Mimi's here. When I catch her glance from across the room, a delicious blend of heat and comfort shoots through me.

Marcy's making her way over to Mimi. I wish I could hear the conversation they're about to have, but I'm being accosted by Austin and Jennifer.

"We would really like to volunteer here as well," Austin says. Of all the St James kids, he's most at ease with me, which makes sense because we've spent more time together because of Juan. "If the Center will have us."

"I'm sure you'll be welcomed with open arms." I point at Imani who is discussing something with the chairperson of the board. "Imani's the woman to talk to about volunteering."

"I'll go do that right now." Austin saunters off, leaving me with Jennifer. I would understand Mimi's kids being a bit wary of me being with their mother after I didn't show up for Thanksgiving. Mimi's not one to keep secrets from her kids. She told me that she couldn't hide her pain from them, because they're her family and they love her.

I glance over at Mimi again, who's gesticulating wildly as she explains something to Marcy. I'm dying to find out what the topic of their lively conversation is—maybe Marcy's trying to convince Mimi to hit the gym with me and Mimi is summing up all the reasons why that's an insane proposition. I can't help but crack a little smile.

Now that we have this rare moment alone, part of me expects Jennifer to grill me about my intentions toward her mother, but she just smiles at me, and says, "This is so wonderful, Nora. As if I could adore you any more."

Although I seem to have endless credit with all the St James kids, I wasn't expecting that. Nor was I expecting to fall for Mimi.

The chairperson taps a microphone. She thanks everyone for coming, then beckons me over. Time for my speech.

"Don't worry, we'll sit to eat *very* shortly," I say. "But before we do, I'd like to say a few words." Public speaking is a far cry from acting, from playing a character in the hyper-controlled environment of a set, but I've been speaking here for so many years, it doesn't make me nervous any longer.

I find Mimi's gaze. Marcy's still standing next to her. Mimi sends me a quick wink. Never in a million years had I expected to bring a significant other to this party, let alone two of her kids. I cast my gaze over the people looking at me. Most likely, none of them ever expected to spend Christmas at a place like this, away from their blood families. If me being here can light up this difficult day for them even for a few minutes, it's worth it. If serving them a restaurant-quality meal will add an ounce of joy to their lives, it's worth it. If all of us being here together, in the glowing warmth this gathering creates, adds a tiny extra shred of dignity to their lives, it's everything.

"You," I say. "All of you, are *my* family. Obviously, I'm nowhere near old enough for this to actually be the case, but today, you're all my godchildren, and I'm here to take care of you. To assure you that, today of all days, you needn't worry about anything else but having a good time. Even if you can only put your worries to rest for five minutes, take those five minutes away from the stress of your day-to-day life. I wish I could give you more than those five minutes, or this afternoon. I wish I could give you everything you deserve every single day." When I was preparing this speech, which is a variation on what I say every year, I couldn't help but think about my own family. Try as I might, I think about my parents much more than I would like. About how, in our case, time seems to have done the opposite of healing. About how the scar tissue on our relationship has grown out of control, because we've let it. Maybe next year, as I stand here to deliver the same kind of speech, things will be different, or they will be exactly the same. It's not for me to know, because if I've learned one thing since last Christmas, it's that no matter how much you try to control life, it will always remain utterly unpredictable. I only have to look over at Mimi to be reminded of that.

CHAPTER 42
MIMI
EPILOGUE

"I've been sitting on this for a while." I smooth the wrapping paper of the present I'm holding. "Waiting for the best moment to give it to you." Tomorrow is the table read for the *Underground* movie that Nora, eventually, said yes to. The fact that Nora was so reluctant, and that Elisa Fox had to come by the house a few times to convince her was an unexpected perk.

"You got me a present?" For someone so universally adored, and who has every material whim taken care of, Nora can still be knocked completely sideways when someone does her a small kindness. It touches the part of her she has shielded for decades. "No way." She clasps her hands in front of her mouth.

"You already have a copy of this, but this one's rather special." I didn't have to move heaven and earth to procure this special gift. Dropping Nora's name opens many doors. I hand her the gift.

"Thank you so much." Nora looks me in the eye. She's a bit on edge because she's stressed about tomorrow, about meeting a bunch of new people and how to react to them and fit in at a new place of work. She tears at the wrapping paper and reveals what's inside.

She grins at me. "I do already have a well-worn copy of

this." She gazes at Isabel Adler's face on the cover of her biography. "Which can only mean one thing." She opens the book.

To witness Nora read a message written especially for her by someone she adores is so precious.

"Oh, my god." Nora brings two fingers to her lips. "No way." Her eyes are fixed on the page.

I stand next to her and put my hand on her shoulder. I read the message Isabel Adler wrote especially for Nora.

Dear Nora,
Sometimes how we see ourselves is not how we are at all—I should know.
Lots of Love,
Izzy xo

Behind the next page, there's a card. Nora takes it out. I read along over her shoulder.

Nora,
Leila and I would love to meet you. We are huge fans. We love Unbreak My Heart *even more than we love* High Life, *and we're beside ourselves that you're going to be in the* Underground *movie. We can't wait to see it because we already know you're going to crush it.*
Izzy A. & Leila Z.

"What the hell?" Nora looks at me. "I don't want to meet Isabel Adler," is the first thing she says—of course, it is.

"We'll see." There's no need to push her now, just to plant that first seed. Over the past few months, I've been studying Nora Levine's complex owner's manual and I'm getting better at being with her by the day. I've learned when to leave something alone, when's the right time to put out a feeler, and when it's opportune to nudge her a little.

"I can't thank you enough for this." She runs a finger over

Isabel's words in the book, then looks at me. "How did you swing this? You must have spoken to Isabel for her to write something so personal?" Her eyes narrow. "What did you tell her about me?"

"Nothing she doesn't completely understand herself." I smile at Nora. "Something tells me that you and Isabel Adler would make great friends. I'm not just saying that. I mean it. It makes perfect sense when you think about it."

"Pff." Nora puffs out some air. "As if Isabel Adler would ever be friends with me."

I take Isabel's card from the book and hold it in front of Nora's face. "Exhibit number one," I say.

"I can't believe any of this." Nora's wise not to object further. "You're amazing."

"I must be, if I get to be Nora Levine's girlfriend." It's not even a joke.

Nora clasps the book against her chest. "Best present ever. For real. Thank you."

"You're very welcome." I take the book from her because I very much want to take its place against Nora's chest.

"I'm serious." Nora's eyes are a little moist. She reaches for my hands. "I'm a handful, I know that, and you… you keep showing up, you keep being your kind, understanding self. You get me in ways that no one else does."

In ways that you've never let anyone else get you, I think, but it doesn't matter.

"You accept me and all my silly quirks, although…" Her solemn expression transforms into a smirk. "I'm surprised you wanted me to do this movie so badly, because it means more weeks of early wake-up calls for workouts with Marcy."

Any time she has to get up before seven, Nora's smartwatch wakes her up by discreetly buzzing against her wrist. While it's infinitely better than the obnoxious blare of an alarm clock, half the time, I wake too. I don't mind because I'm perfecting the art of falling asleep again after I've run a hand over her gorgeous body—Nora's not ready to say goodbye to her abs just yet, and who am I to tell her otherwise?

"Anything to see you in that movie, just like Leila and Izzy."

"You're calling her Izzy already, are you?" Nora strokes my hand with her thumb.

I nod. "I think the four of us are going to hit it off like a house on fire. We should plan a trip to New York as soon as you finish this movie."

Nora heaves a deep sigh, but I know she's only pretending. "My life used to be quiet and simple. Now you have me doing movies when I'm not making TV, and are taking me to New York to meet Isabel Adler."

"Isn't life funny that way?" I gaze into Nora's bright blue eyes. They're still a little wet, but mostly, they sparkle with joy and light—and endless amounts of love.

I pull her to me. "I love you, Nora Levine," I say. "I love all of you."

GET THREE E-BOOKS FOR FREE

Building a relationship with my readers is the very best thing about writing. I occasionally send newsletters with details on new releases, special offers and giveaways.

And if you sign up to my mailing list I'll send you all this free stuff:

1. An e-book of *Few Hearts Survive,* a Pink Bean Series novella that is ONLY available to my mailing list subscribers.
2. A free e-book of *Hired Help,* my very first (and therefore very special to me) lesbian erotic romance story.
3. A free e-book of my first 'longer' work, my highly romantic novella *Summer's End,* set on an exotic beach in Thailand.

You can get *Few Hearts Survive* (a Pink Bean Series novella), *Hired Help* (a spicy F/F novelette) and *Summer's End* (a deeply romantic lesfic novella) **for free** by signing up at www.harperbliss.com/freebook/ or scanning the QR code below

GET THREE E-BOOKS FOR FREE

ABOUT THE AUTHOR

Harper Bliss is a best-selling lesbian romance author. Among her most-loved books are the highly dramatic French Kissing and the often thought-provoking Pink Bean series.

Harper lived in Hong Kong for seven years, travelled the world for a bit, and has now settled in the Belgian countryside with her wife, Caroline, and her photogenic cat, Dolly Purrton.

Harper loves hearing from readers and you can reach her at the email address below.

www.harperbliss.com
harper@harperbliss.com

Printed in Great Britain
by Amazon